MW01273098

I SEE YOU

I SEE YOU (ORACLE 2)

Copyright © 2015 Meghan Ciana Doidge

Published by Old Man in the CrossWalk Productions 2015

Salt Spring Island, BC, Canada

www.oldmaninthecrosswalk.com

All rights reserved under International and Pan-American
Copyright Conventions. No part of this book may be produced
in any form or by any electronic or mechanical means, including
information storage and retrieval systems, without permission
in writing from the author, except by reviewer, who may quote
brief passages in a review.

This is a work of fiction. All names, characters, places, objects,
and incidents herein are the products of the author's imagination
or are used fictitiously. Any resemblance to actual things, events,
locales, or persons living or dead is entirely coincidental.

Library and Archives Canada

Doidge, Meghan Ciana, 1973 —

I See You/Meghan Ciana Doidge — PAPERBACK EDITION

Cover art by Irene Langholm

Cover design by Elizabeth Mackey

Stock: Oliver Sved/Shutterstock

ISBN 978-1-927850-34-3

ORACLE SERIES  BOOK 2

I SEE YOU

MEGHAN CIANA DOIDGE

Published by Old Man in the CrossWalk Productions
Salt Spring Island, BC, Canada

www.oldmaninthecrosswalk.com
www.madebymeghan.ca

For Michael
without you there is no me

Author's Note:

I See You is the second book in the Oracle series, which is set in the same universe as the Dowser series.

While it's not necessary to read both series, the ideal reading order is as follows:

- Cupcakes, Trinkets, and Other Deadly Magic (Dowser 1)
- Trinkets, Treasures, and Other Bloody Magic (Dowser 2)
- Treasures, Demons, and Other Black Magic (Dowser 3)
- I See Me (Oracle 1)*
- Shadows, Maps, and Other Ancient Magic (Dowser 4)
- Maps, Artifacts, and Other Arcane Magic (Dowser 5)
- I See You (Oracle 2)

Other books in both the Oracle and Dowser series to follow.

I See Me (Oracle 1) contains spoilers for Dowser 1, 2, and 3.

IF MAGIC WAS REAL, then what? Was it simply a form of energy? The energy I felt when I touched Beau, Chi Wen, and Blackwell? Energy from where? From some divine providence? From the very earth?

If magic came from somewhere godly, then why come to me? Why communicate through me? What purpose did the visions have?

Could I actually change the future? And if yes, would I change it for better or for worse?

Over a year and a half had passed since Jade Godfrey — aka the dowser — fixed my mother's necklace. Since I'd thwarted the vision of the death of love. Since I'd made a deal with a devil and acquired a demigod for a mentor.

I still didn't understand or control my power, my magic, but it had been a great year. A year of rest. A year of love and light.

But now the reprieve was over.

Now it was time to see.

Magic willed it so.

CHAPTER ONE

"THERE ARE ZOMBIES IN FLORIDA."

I looked up from ironing butterfly patches onto my well-worn blue jeans just as Lina, the owner of the laundromat, plugged another quarter into one of the dryers in the bank she'd commandeered for the day. She was crazily talented at reading off her iPad and doing laundry at the same time.

We called it "the laundromat" because it didn't appear to go by any other name. It was situated in the middle of Yachats, Oregon, though the coastal town was so tiny that there really wasn't much of a middle to it at all. The underutilized laundromat got my business every Friday. I'd been going there weekly since Beau and I got into town. Today, I'd rented an old iron and an ironing board for an extra two dollars.

"Did you hear me, Sid?" Lina called out to her husband, who was doing some sort of paperwork behind the cash counter to my right. "Zombies in Florida?"

"That's drugs," he replied. "Weird drugs making people eat other people's faces." Normally Sid suffered from selective hearing, but apparently zombie-related topics were interesting enough to pull him away from his bowl of cheese puffs.

I dropped my gaze to the butterfly patches I was applying to the tear in the left thigh of my jeans. I'd already loosely darned and interfaced the rip from the inside. Beau had bought me the fuchsia, electric blue, and deep purple butterfly patches from Etsy because they were reminiscent of the butterfly tattoo on my left inner wrist. Also, money was tight, so patching jeans was way cheaper than buying a new pair right now. Not that I minded. I wasn't big on the accumulation of clothing — or anything else, really. I was going to hand stitch the patches after I ironed them on, just to be extra careful. I didn't want them peeling off.

"Drugs," Lina scoffed as she crossed behind me and around the peeling laminate counter that held the squat cash register and not much else. She stole a handful of cheese puffs and settled back into her folding beach chair. "Who'd want to take something that makes them want to eat people?"

Zombies, huh? I knew that shapeshifters, were-wolves, sorcerers, witches — and whatever Jade Godfrey was — existed. So why not zombies? Except, of course, it would be difficult for the Adept community — aka magical peeps — to keep flesh-eating zombies on the down-low. Yeah, I had figured out pretty quickly the Adept were big on secrets. Which made sense, since they were massively outnumbered by nonmagical people and all their pitchforks.

Sid didn't answer. I could never figure out what he was working on all day. Yachats boasted a full-time population of six hundred and ninety people, all of whom probably owned their own washers and dryers. Even with the seasonal influx of tourists, the laundromat certainly didn't do so much business that Sid needed to pore over the receipts with such attention.

I doubted, however, that he was the local pot dealer or anything. First, he just wasn't the type — meticulous records or not. And second, weed was now legal in Oregon.

The purple butterfly was hovering — suspended in the air — about an inch above the gray, heat-resistant liner of the ironing board. I'd been about to press it into place, and now … this.

No, wait. I could see the butterfly patches — all three of them — still placed carefully over the darned tear in my faded jeans. It was my butterfly … my butterfly tattoo …

What the hell?

The translucent black butterfly tattoo flicked its wings as I slowly flipped my left palm up, confirming that the spot on my wrist was now blank. Yeah, my wrist was now tattoo free.

My stomach twisted, fear shooting through my chest and limbs in a cold wash, though the mid-July day was lovely and warm.

I carefully set the iron down. The butterfly flitted upward until it hovered a few inches from my nose.

Then, inexplicably, it … it … kissed my cheek … as if it were playing with me.

Oh, damn. Now I was hallucinating playful butterflies.

No.

Not hallucinating.

Seeing.

I saw.

Usually visions of the future. Though not my future. And not for the last year and a half. Not even a blip, not even a hint of white mist or a headache. Not since Portland and Blackwell. Not since meeting Jade Godfrey and Chi Wen.

I was an oracle. Well, usually.

Apparently, I now also saw my tattoos coming to life. That wasn't disconcerting at all.

I wrapped my fingers around the raw diamond necklace that hung over my black tank top, between and just below my breasts. The magic of the stone and the large-linked chain of rose gold from which it hung tickled my fingertips with tingles of static electricity. The necklace had belonged to my mother, who'd died twenty-and-a-half years ago — at the moment of my birth — from injuries sustained in a car crash just outside of Vancouver, British Columbia, Canada.

Jade Godfrey had repaired the chain of the necklace and somehow tuned its magic to my oracle magic, which helped me control the visions. I told anyone who asked that the massive fifty-thousand-dollar diamond was just a crystal — but very few people talked to me voluntarily, let alone asked me personal questions. Yeah, I was a bit off-putting. I didn't mind. I wasn't a big fan of people anyway. Well, I liked certain people. A lot.

My demigod mentor, Chi Wen, was the far seer of the guardian dragons. He said I should be able to 'pull forward' the 'focus' of the necklace to help me 'navigate' the visions. Yeah, I had no idea what the hell that meant.

I narrowed my eyes at the manifestation. The butterfly was impervious to my glare, though, so I considered whether I should try it without my tinted, white-framed, bug-eyed glasses. Everyone else seemed put off by my weird pale gray eyes. Though I seriously doubted the butterfly cared about appearances.

I glanced over at the cash counter. Sid and Lina were still wrapped up in their electronic devices. The laundromat was otherwise empty.

I looked back. The butterfly was gone.

No. It had flitted away to dance over top of the grubby glass entrance.

"Ah, geez." Sid spoke from behind me.

My stomach bottomed out as I turned to look back at the counter. Could Sid see the butterfly? How the hell was I going to explain my tattoo flitting around the storefront windows?

"That old guy is back," he said.

"What guy?" Lina didn't look up from her iPad.

"The Chinese guy who just wanted to watch the dryers last week and kept asking for Oreos."

I snapped my head back to the front door, actually hurting my neck with the sudden movement.

An ancient-looking Asian man was grinning at me from the sidewalk beyond the door of the laundromat.

Chi Wen, the far seer of the guardian dragons and my old-as-ass mentor, had apparently decided that his typical gold-embroidered white robes and sandals would stand out too much in Yachats. So he was now clothed in a baby blue, oversized short-sleeved T-shirt emblazoned with a fuchsia pink *Cake in a Cup — Taste the Magic* logo. The shirt hung almost to his knees, his cargo pants ended at his lower calves, and he was wearing black combat boots to complete the ensemble.

"Don't call him Chinese like that," Lina snapped as she stood to cross back to the dryers she was manning. "You don't like people calling us Indian."

"He's homeless."

"How does that make any difference?"

Chi Wen opened the glass door, triggering the bell as well as allowing a warm gust of the sunny day inside.

The chime of the bell mystified him, and he paused — still grinning madly — as he looked around for the source of the sound. Instead, he saw my butterfly tattoo fluttering over his head. He lifted his hand and the butterfly landed in his palm.

"No, no!" Sid called out from behind the counter. "No sit here. No watch. Go. Go!" For some reason, his previously perfectly-articulate-though-accented English broke down as he confronted one of the nine most powerful beings in the world.

"Wait," I said. "That's my ... grandfather."

Sid eyed me distrustfully. He was wearing a canary-yellow turban today. I was fairly certain it had been tangerine orange last week. I wondered if there was a religious significance to the color. I'd been coming to the laundromat for a few weeks now, and Sid and Lina accepted my business but didn't particularly like me. It might have been my full arm-sleeve tattoos, or the weird white streak that wouldn't take the jet-black dye with which I colored my hair, or maybe they didn't trust anyone under twenty-five. Which was cool, because remove 'under twenty-five' from that misgiving and neither did I.

Apparently, being my grandfather rather than the 'homeless Chinese guy' didn't elevate Chi Wen by much in Sid's estimation.

"Fledgling," Chi Wen said as he shuffled over to me, carrying the butterfly. "Is this your drying?" His English was heavily accented. He pronounced the word 'drying' as if he'd just learned it. He was pointing at my final dryer load.

"Yes," I answered. I always answered when Chi Wen questioned me. I always listened when he answered a question of mine — especially on the rare occasions he did so straightforwardly. He didn't understand sarcasm and sass, or maybe he just didn't have time for such things, and he had a habit of not showing up for months between our training sessions.

So yeah, going against every defensive mechanism I'd carefully employed to get this far through life relatively unscathed, I attempted to transform myself into a receptive sponge around my mentor.

Settling down on the gray-painted bench that spanned the area between the rows of washers and dryers, Chi Wen began to observe the laundry in my dryer as if it were one of the Seven Wonders of the World.

Sid grumbled something to his wife. She grumbled back and settled into her folding chair with her well-used iPad. Hundred to one it was streaked with cheese-puff dust.

I turned off the iron, ignoring that my stomach was now churning like the dryers before me. The laundromat was a peaceful place, full of comforting, homey noises and fresh scents. A visit from the far seer was the exact opposite. Not that he smelled. Just that I was now waiting for the 'epic' thing I was sure he had to tell me.

I'd been waiting for this anticipated revelation for over a year and a half now. Which also happened to be the exact amount of time since I'd had my last vision. A vision of Beau dead at the sorcerer Blackwell's feet. A vision I thought I'd thwarted, but was never one hundred percent sure that it wouldn't come to pass some other day, or month, or year.

"Two pairs of pants, ten T-shirts, and twenty-five socks," Chi Wen said.

"Twenty-five? Really? Damn." I settled down on the bench next to the far seer, near enough to not be rude but far enough away that we wouldn't accidentally touch. Even this close, I could feel the magic that constantly emanated from him like a field of electricity, buzzy hum and all.

Chi Wen, his eyes still locked to the dryer in front of him, shifted his hand until it hovered over my lap. He was still cupping my fugitive butterfly tattoo.

I'd been resting my left arm on my thigh, but for some reason, I now turned it palm up as if to accept the offering of the butterfly.

No.

The tattoo was on my wrist again.

The far seer closed his empty hand with a satisfied sigh. "Time to see, fledgling."

"What do you mean?"

He didn't answer.

I waited, a thousand questions on my mind. Questions about the butterfly, about my oracle magic, and about 'seeing.' But I waited. Not to put the old guy up on a pedestal, but every second with him was precious. In a completely different way from how every second with Beau was precious.

Chi Wen was like me. Well, like me with a thousand years of experience being me. He saw. I was fairly certain he was way stronger than the old-man visage he wore like a comfortable hoodie. I was also fairly certain he could read my thoughts, and maybe even make me think or do things … not that I'd caught myself doing anything weird.

"What do you mean?" I finally asked again. The question was a tense whisper that I wanted to temper the moment I let it loose. "Time to see? Have I been not seeing for a reason?"

"For a rest."

I squeezed my eyes shut as the ramifications of his simple words hit me. "You took the visions? Stopped them?"

"No," Chi Wen said. "Magic moves where it wills. I simply pushed it into a different direction."

"The tattoos," I muttered. I'd been sketching a crazy amount of tattoos lately, and not even ones I wanted to get. Thankfully, they had sold well in my Etsy shop

— Rochelle's Recollections — because I was running out of vision drawings to sell. Though I felt I had to charge way less for a simple smudged image.

"The drawings, yes. But now you must once again see more fully."

"Why?" I cried, then immediately swallowed the rest of the anticipated pain that had attempted to bleed into my protest. "Never mind. I know there is no why."

"There is always the question."

"But it isn't for me to ask."

"It's for you to know."

Right. The oracle sees all, but doesn't judge … I was a conduit and an interpreter. "Jade Godfrey," I whispered. "Jade needs me to see?"

"Soon," Chi Wen said. "Events are accumulating."

"And the tattoos? The butterfly?"

"You are an oracle by birth. Perhaps rechanneling the oracle power has opened up other possibilities."

"What possibilities?" I snapped. I hated being scared. Every second word coming out of Chi Wen's mouth was piling one fear onto another.

The old man grinned. "The drying has completed."

The dryer pinged, then slowed.

"Show-off," I muttered.

Chi Wen chuckled. I stood to pull the clean clothing out of the machine, ignoring my shaky legs. Moving and doing were always good distractions.

"You will survive," Chi Wen said, his tone casual as if we were still discussing the drying and not my possibly impending death.

"Yeah," I said, attempting to match his tone and failing. "And Beau?"

He didn't answer.

I shoved the laundry into my already half-full basket, then locked my gaze to the far seer's. "And Beau?" I growled.

His grin widened. "The boy, too. For now."

"We all die, right?"

"We do. But I was concerned ... for a moment." He stood up and started shuffling toward the door of the laundromat without another word.

"So you did what?" I called after him. I darted back to grab my jeans and butterfly patches off the ironing board, then returned the still-cooling iron to the counter.

Ah, hell. Despite the old-man pretense, he was already gone.

"I'll be right back!" I yelled at Sid and Lina, grabbing my satchel out from underneath the bench and sprinting after my cryptic mentor. I never assumed he did it deliberately — the infuriating, all-over-the-place conversations and weird segues. He just had too much in his head. I knew what that felt like, and I wasn't the far seer of the guardians. Guardians who supposedly watched over the entire world and all the magic in it.

I couldn't have been more than an insignificant speck in the universe of magic that constantly flooded the far seer's brain. Yet he had shown up in Yachats, Oregon, to chat with me in a laundromat.

Well, he had shown up, then disappeared.

The far seer wasn't on the sidewalk, not in either direction. He also wasn't wandering down the middle of the street, but I wouldn't have put it past him to be doing so. Yachats might be a tiny town built around two miles of Interstate 101, which was carved along the edge of the

West Coast of the United States. But it was tourist season, so getting mowed over by a massive RV was always a possibility.

Chi Wen usually said goodbye if a conversation was over. I hated leaving my things behind unprotected, but I hazarded a guess and darted down Fourth Street toward Ocean View Drive and the Seaside Walk.

Yachats was pretty. Quaint, even, but in a real-life-real-people sort of way. Tourism might be the area's biggest industry, but the town itself wasn't overtly picturesque. A few dozen single-level homes on large lots, a couple of pretty white-painted churches, a small library, and a few restaurants made up the bulk of the town. What made the area truly beautiful was the raging ocean with its gray-sand beach a block to the west.

And that was where I was guessing the far seer of the guardians would head.

I'd taken only a few steps off the road and up the dry grass that bordered the dune blocking my sight of the sandy beach, when a tall, dark-haired teen wearing a green printed T-shirt and black leather pants fell into step beside me.

"Hi," he said. "Rochelle."

My sneakered feet slipped in the sand underneath the dry grass, but I managed to stop myself from following through with a face plant. A few more completely ungraceful steps brought me to the top of the dune. The cool wind blowing from the savage ocean pounding the beach twenty-five feet away hit me, actually buffeting my clothing.

Somewhat anchored on this sandy perch, I turned to look at the teen. His face was lifted to the wind, squinting into the sun. His dark hair was long enough to be wild in the breeze. He was tall and broad shouldered, though not as tall as Beau. He was also some-part Asian, as I was.

Magic rolled off him, prickling the exposed skin of my right arm, neck, and face. This power came with a different tenor than that of Beau's or the far seer's, but it was no less intense.

"Don't know you, man," I said.

He turned to look down at me, an easy smile spreading across his handsome face. "I'm Drake. The far seer's apprentice."

He held out his hand as if to shake. I hesitated to take it. I shifted my glasses up until they sat on my head and I snared his brown-eyed gaze. He didn't flinch at my eyes — but then, he was the far seer's apprentice, so I doubted that he would. I always liked to try to rattle intimidatingly powerful people, though.

Drake's smile widened. He leaned into me with his hand still extended between us. "What do you see, tiny oracle?"

"You're the apprentice. You tell me." I dropped my glasses back down over my eyes. The sun was way too bright to bother with any further attempt to discomfort Drake. Plus, I got the idea pretty quickly that he wasn't easy to shake up.

Drake threw his head back and laughed. I swore the sand underneath my feet shifted with the magic that now rumbled off him. I glowered at this display, but the expression didn't have any effect on the teen.

"So you're a dragon?" I asked.

"I am."

"And you're here why?"

"The far seer wished us to meet."

"Why now? Are you new?"

Drake chuckled. "No. Are you going to shake my hand? I understand it's a polite gesture between humans."

"That matters to you?"

"It does."

"I thought Adepts didn't touch."

Drake's constant grin widened again. "I suppose that Adepts who fear their power or the magic of others might not touch."

Taking his words as a challenge, I firmly wrapped my hand around his. Our pale skin was almost the same tone. Magic shifted between us, but he didn't let go.

"Are we related somehow?" I asked.

He tilted his head, considering the question. "I don't think so."

I loosened my hold and he let my hand drop. I turned back to survey the beach.

Chi Wen had appeared from who-knows-where and was now standing a couple of dozen feet away at the edge of the surf. He'd lost his boots somewhere and appeared to be curling his bare toes in the wet sand.

"The far seer rarely walks the earth these days. Except for visiting you, Rochelle Hawthorne." Drake's use of my birth name felt deliberate and pointed. Though only because it was odd to think of myself as anything other than Rochelle Saintpaul. I hadn't even known my mother's last name until Blackwell had informed me of my parentage over a year ago.

"And why am I so important?"

"I thought you might tell me."

I turned to look up at the young dragon. He was watching the far seer. "Do you see?" I asked.

Drake rolled his shoulders. "Not yet. But I will."

"Soon?"

"Hopefully not in your lifetime."

"That's nasty."

He laughed. "I'm not wishing you ill. But even if your magic makes you long-lived, I hope to not assume the mantle of the far seer for a hundred years or so. That would be a long life even for a sorcerer-bred oracle."

"Oh." My mind reeled at the chunk of info he'd just delivered in a few dozen words. I was standing beside the next far seer. "So ... Chi Wen isn't immortal?"

"No."

"Is Jade Godfrey going to 'assume a mantle' as well?"

Drake turned to look at me. "No."

"Because she isn't a full dragon?"

"Not all dragons become guardians."

"What makes you so special?"

"You tell me. You're the oracle." He laughed as he half-stepped, half-surfed down the other side of the dune and crossed toward the far seer.

"I'm not playing games!" I yelled as I scrambled after him.

"Neither am I," he called back, raising his voice over the wind.

Chi Wen stepped back from the water's edge and turned to us as we crossed to him — me still trailing after Drake. I couldn't see the far seer's boots anywhere nearby. In fact, the beach was empty, which was strange for the middle of July. It felt like I was walking toward the edge of the world, pressing into the wind and finding my footing more easily on the hard-packed wet sand.

Drake bowed formally before the far seer, which gave me pause. I hadn't really known I was supposed to do that sort of thing in the presence of the guardian.

They exchanged some words that I thought at first I couldn't hear properly because of the wind. But then as their voices filtered through my brain, I realized they weren't speaking English. Cantonese, maybe.

Drake turned back to me, bowing swiftly and more shallowly than he had to the far seer. "We are well met, Rochelle Hawthorne, Oracle of the Brave."

I narrowed my eyes at the young dragon, not at all amused by whatever joke he was making at my expense. Then I realized he was referencing the 1975 Brave Winnebago I called my home, combining that with my magic to give me a formal title of sorts. Feeling like an idiot, I bowed back and mimicked his formal address. "We are well met, Drake, apprentice to Chi Wen, the far seer of the guardian nine."

"I'm at your disposal. A call to Jade Godfrey will bring me to your side."

"I don't exactly have the dowser on speed dial."

"You will," Drake said.

My stomach bottomed out at this assertion. Jade equaled chaos and mayhem. I preferred to keep her out of my head and my phone for as long as possible.

Drake smiled as if he might be picking up on what I was feeling. Then he nodded toward the far seer and stepped past me the way we'd come. I turned to watch him walk away.

"Your apprentice, eh?" I asked Chi Wen.

The old man didn't answer. He'd turned back to the raging surf.

"Why did you want us to meet?" I raised my voice against the wind, spitting a hank of hair out of my mouth. "Why now?"

The far seer took so long to answer that I thought he might not have heard me. Then he said, "I didn't care for the meeting I saw."

"Sorry? You saw us meeting and you decided to change it? You told me the future was immutable. You told me it was dangerous to try to manipulate it?"

"Destiny is immutable. The future is fluid."

I snorted. "For you, you mean. And the dangerous part?"

Chi Wen turned to look at me. His Buddha smile was firmly in place. "What is dangerous for some isn't dangerous for others."

"Drake, you mean. He's powerful, strong. I could feel his magic."

"And now you will see him."

"Because you think my oracle powers pick up on the strongest magical signatures I come into contact with?"

"Or those most relevant to you. May I look at your sketchbook?"

"Here?"

"If you please."

Grumbling, I pulled my sketchbook out of my hand-painted satchel. How he was going to look at it in all this wind, I didn't know. But our conversations got way too convoluted if I questioned him too much.

I handed the almost-full book to the far seer, barely keeping its pages closed within my grip. But as soon as he touched the sketchbook, those pages stilled as if the wind didn't exist.

I grumbled some more as Chi Wen flipped through my latest tattoo ideas. I didn't really get how magic worked at all. You'd think there'd be some sort of manual for newbies, though I got the impression that oracles were pretty rare and usually trained by a family member. Since I didn't have any family — other than Beau — that wasn't an option for me. And Beau was enough anyway. I could pick up all the other stuff I needed to know slowly, steadily. If I even really needed to know it.

"Will you commit any of these to your skin?" Chi Wen asked.

I shrugged. "Nah, I'm not all over any of them."

The far seer ran his fingers across the sketchbook's spiral spine and loosened a few flecks of paper trapped within the wire. The torn paper tabs were left over from a sketch Chi Wen had requested I rip out of the book a few months back. A charcoal of a centipede, which I had actually considered tangling within the barbed wire tattoo twined around my left arm.

I opened my mouth to ask the far seer what had become of that sketch, then just as quickly shut it. I already knew he'd given it to Jade Godfrey, and I really didn't want to know the particulars. I was actually glad I hadn't seen whatever transpired over the last year and a half. I had the sense that Jade couldn't stay out of trouble if she tried. Based on Chi Wen's devotion to my training and the gist of his questions, rare as they were, I was certain the guardian had plans for the dowser.

Static electricity danced across my left forearm, just below the elbow. I glanced down to where the far seer had turned his attention from the sketchbook to the tattoo of the skeleton key on my left arm. The barbed-wire tattoo passed cleanly through the intricate series of Celtic-looking knots at one end of the key.

"This will come in handy."

"What do you mean?"

"Do you know how sorcerer magic works?"

"No." And apparently massive segues were the theme of the day.

"Your father was a sorcerer."

"Was, eh? So he's definitely dead?"

That was the wrong thing to ask the far seer … as were any questions touching on time. He fell into his staring-into-the-distance thing … or maybe he was counting the grains of sand roiling within each five-foot wave as it crashed onto the beach before us. I never knew with him.

Staying quiet was usually the best course of action as he sorted through whatever was going on in his head.

"I must go," he said, so abruptly that I flinched. "The warrior calls."

My blood ran cold. I'd pieced together enough background info to know that the warrior was Jade's dad. Not that he scared me. I didn't know him. But what I'd seen of his daughter freaked me out daily for the year or so that I'd had her in my head and thought she was a hallucination.

"Things are not clear between us," I said. That was as carefully as I could phrase my frustration with the entire meeting, including the brief handshake with Drake.

"You will soon see, oracle." Chi Wen brushed his fingers across my skeleton key tattoo again. "Trust the magic. Move where it wills, where it leads, but don't try to alter the path."

"I know," I grumbled. "Interpret, don't act."

"You will survive."

"Helpful," I groused, only to look up to find the beach empty.

According to Beau, the old man simply moved too quickly for the human eye to track. Either way, the far seer had disappeared.

A wave rolled across the sand and lapped against the toes of my black-and-white Converse sneakers. As the water receded, it removed any evidence that the far seer had ever walked the beach.

CHAPTER TWO

"Fifty should cover it."

I paused on the weatherworn sidewalk at the sound of Beau's voice. He was talking to a customer in the two-car garage he rented from our landlady, Old Ms. McNally, from whom we also rented the concrete pad behind the garage for the Brave. I shifted my full laundry basket to my other hip as I listened to the customer laugh and clap Beau on the shoulder.

Yachats didn't have a full-time garage or mechanic — or the population to support one — though there was a mobile guy who came through a couple of times a week. The mobile guy occasionally sent clients Beau's way if he was too busy to get to them, and word travelled fast that Beau was good with cars. So he had a steady cash business within a couple of weeks of renting the garage.

The garage didn't have a lift, but Beau's shifter strength paired with a winch — behind closed doors, of course — took care of that if necessary.

The adjacent house lots were closely spaced, but not crammed together. The neighbors to the west were overly protective of their meticulous landscaping. But everyone else — kids, dogs, and the occasional morning jogger — were fairly friendly. To Beau anyway.

As the customer exited the garage to jog over to his car where it was parked up the street, I stepped off the sidewalk onto the long, brown grass that ran along the edge of the garage so I didn't bump into him. I'd poke my head in through the back door on my way to the Brave, which was parked between the garage and our landlady's overgrown backyard. Not that I could ever sneak up on Beau, but I liked to savor the moment before I laid eyes on him. It was a silly game, but I liked being prepared. Sometimes when I looked up and caught sight of him without realizing he was nearby, I would just stare at him like a blithering idiot. Yes, even after a year and a half, I had no defense against Beau's beauty — and no idea what he was still doing with me.

A vision hit me halfway to the back door.

The white mist that flooded my mind left me sightless and breathless between one step and the next. I dropped the laundry basket onto the dead grass, belatedly hoping it hadn't dumped over and strewn clean clothing everywhere. I pressed myself back against the rough, aged cedar siding of the garage, then slid down into a crouch as my legs gave out.

The vision didn't hurt, but it was startling. Any weakness came from my own reaction, not the magic flooding through my mind. I hadn't had to deal with this for long enough that it triggered all the old pain and fear I'd carried with me.

Fear of being different, of being damaged … broken.

I wrapped my hand around the raw diamond resting against my lower rib cage and tried to calm my breathing.

I had to accept the magic. I had to welcome it.

"Show me what you want me to see," I whispered. Even though I had no idea if I could communicate with the energy that brought the visions, uttering the words calmed me.

The white mist shifted in my mind. I could still smell the neighbors' recently clipped grass, which they'd kept green despite the summer watering restrictions. I could feel the heat of the afternoon sun on my face and the rough boards against my back. But I couldn't see anything but the mist that always preceded the oracle visions.

The mist thinned but didn't recede. A shadowed shape appeared before me, then resolved until I found myself crouched before a young woman with blond hair. I forced myself to lean forward into the vision rather than throw myself backward at the sight. Moving wouldn't change what I was seeing, but attempting to be steady and rational would get me through it.

My immediate thought — based on the blond hair — was that I was looking at Jade lying before me. But I wasn't. This woman's hair was straight, and judging by the shadow of darker roots at her crown, it had been dyed blond. Her mud-brown eyes were open, staring blankly over my shoulder. Her head was canted to one side. She had a gold stud in the shape of a magnolia flower underneath her lower lip, but otherwise she was vanilla through and through.

As I watched, a pool of blood began to form at the back of her head, spreading across the dark asphalt on which she'd died.

"Dead girl," I whispered.

I had no idea who she was.

The white mist reformed, taking away my glimpse of the bottle blond before I could look around for any further understanding or evidence of what I was seeing. Or why.

Beau was crouched before me. I couldn't see him, but I knew he was there. I could practically feel the energy that constantly rolled off him. His magic, his presence, was a lower frequency than Chi Wen's or Drake's. It was a comforting hum that was uniquely Beau.

"Hey," I said.

"Vision?" he asked. His tone was deep and intimate. His lyrical Southern accent thickened with concern.

I nodded as I reached for him. He gathered me up in his arms, lifting me effortlessly off the ground to carry me into the garage.

I still couldn't see, but it was cooler out of the sun. I felt the breeze of the standing fan Beau always placed at the open back door as we passed through it.

"I left the laundry outside."

Beau grunted like he didn't give a shit about laundry.

"It's practically everything we own," I added.

He huffed out a sigh, then sat me down somewhere that felt high off the ground. The hood of a pickup truck — or so I assumed as I placed my feet on the bumper. "Stay put."

"Well, I can't exactly wander off blind while perched up here."

"Exactly."

I felt him move away from me, taking his energy with him as he stepped back outside to retrieve the laundry basket. The breeze from the oscillating fan brushed me again, and I closed my still-unseeing eyes against its cool gust.

Beau was back before I'd exhaled a second time.

"You smell like magic. Your magic," he murmured as he set the basket down and closed the space between us. His voice was husky in that way that let me know, even without being able to see him, that he was turned on.

Ignoring that the slowly fading white mist still filled my mind's eye, I reached for him, tracing my fingers up his neck, across his jaw and cheeks. I knew his face intimately. I didn't have to see it.

He licked the tips of my fingers as they found his lips, and a familiar, comfortable desire rolled through my lower belly.

"Is the door closed?" I whispered against the sweaty skin of his neck.

He stepped away, pulling the overhead garage door closed and locking it with a click. Then he had his hands up underneath my tank top before I'd registered that he'd moved at all.

I laughed as he tugged off my top, but my amusement immediately dissolved into a gasp, then a groan as he applied all his attention to my nipples.

Beau's focus was epic, and he never played favorites.

The mist of the vision had cleared the next time I opened my eyes, but my head was now swimming with desire.

Making quick work of my sneakers, Beau started tugging off my jeans. I yanked his sky-blue T-shirt over his head, revealing miles of smooth, tightly muscled, mocha-colored skin as he lowered his head between my now-bare legs. As his tongue made contact with my very center, I cried out and arched backward, momentarily worried that I was going to slip off the hood of the truck.

The afternoon light in the garage was muted to whatever could seep through the imperfectly sealed doors, but Beau and I didn't need to see each other to do our dance.

I brushed my fingers against the back of his neck, enjoying his ministrations but impatient for more. With a grunt, he tugged me forward until I was half-hanging off the slightly sloped front of the truck and he was buried deep inside me.

"Whose truck is this?" I asked with a breathy gasp.

Beau laughed. Obligingly, he lifted me off the hood and hobbled over to a metal stool near the grease-spattered workbench. His pants were down around his ankles, but they didn't seem to hamper his movements. He settled down on the stool with me in his lap and our bodies still entwined.

"Better?"

"I wasn't interested in leaving an ass print on the hood."

Beau laughed huskily, settling his hands over my hips to lift and lower me at a languid pace.

I didn't have much leverage in this position, with my arms around his shoulders and legs around his waist, but I knew Beau pretty well now. I knew he always liked to be face to face. I knew he liked to be kissing me when I orgasmed. And that he liked it when I talked to him while we were connected on this level.

My lips brushed his ear as I whispered, "Do I taste as good as I smell?"

His reaction was instantaneous. A fierce groan rumbled through his chest. His grip on my hips tightened and his rhythm became erratic for a few beats, then picked up.

I cried out, arching my head, neck, and chest away from him, even as he corrected the angle of my hips to maintain perfect contact.

Pleasure lapped up over me, first as delightful shivers, then as almost-painful convulsions as I orgasmed.

At least I managed not to scream.

I wrapped myself back around Beau as he groaned into my neck and came. I lightly scratched my nonexistent nails up his spine and the back of his neck as he shuddered with the final pulses of pleasure.

"You do," he whispered. "You taste even better than you smell."

"But not in a weird, woman-eating way, right?"

Beau threw his head back and laughed. "You know the pack frowns on man-eaters."

"Well, that's one of their more reasonable rules." I tugged his head down so I could reach his lips, then pressed a light kiss against them. "Thank you."

"Thank you. Bathroom?"

"Yes, please."

Beau obligingly carried me to the tiny bathroom at the back of the garage. I cleaned this about once a week, because otherwise it got so disgusting I couldn't set foot in it. He left me there to wash up in the sink and went back to retrieve our clothing.

The cold water — there was no hot option — was shocking against my sex-warmed skin. For a moment, a glimpse of the vision took my eyesight again.

I shook away the mist-shrouded image of blood seeping across dark asphalt and the life fading from murky brown eyes. I shouldn't know what life fading from someone's eyes looked like, but apparently I did.

Beau appeared in the doorway of the bathroom, passing me my discarded clothing. The mere sight of him was always a welcome distraction. If only I could fill my mind's eye with pictures of him as he looked now, leaning against a paint-challenged doorframe and looking terribly satisfied with himself. That would be bliss. His work pants were still undone and his discarded T-shirt dangled from his long, very talented fingers. He was the most beautiful person I'd ever seen — again and always. All I could do in the face of his utter beauty was to return his grin.

"What did you see?" he asked, referring to the vision that had preceded our lovemaking session.

"A girl. Woman, really. Blond, murky brown eyes. Dead … I think."

Beau grunted. "The dowser?" His tone was light, even as his grip tightened on his T-shirt.

"No."

"Okay. Why now? What triggered it?"

"The far seer dropped by the laundromat."

"And?"

"He said it was time to see."

"Like he'd been blocking the visions?"

"I'm not sure."

Beau tilted his head, waiting for me to explain further. I hesitated, then pushed through my fear-based reticence.

"Also ..."

"Yeah?"

"I met his apprentice, Drake."

"Okay," Beau said, then smiled sweetly. "Now tell me what's really worrying you."

He wasn't going to judge me. He wasn't going to think I was crazy. "My butterfly tattoo did this thing."

Beau tensed his shoulders, though his smile held steady. "Thing?"

"I'm not sure. It left my arm. Flew around. The far seer wasn't really helpful."

"Typical."

"He said something about sorcerer magic that might have been connected. Or he was talking about something else without, you know, actually communicating anything I could really follow."

Beau nodded but didn't answer. He gazed at the scuffed vinyl floor between us, thinking. If there were any questions about sorcery that needed to be asked ... well, we knew only one sorcerer, and Beau really wasn't a fan of Blackwell.

"Okay," he said. "Weird."

"Yeah."

And just like that — despite the morbid topic, the sudden resurgence of my oracle magic, and the tattoo oddness — we were grinning at each other like idiots again. Morons, really. Even with the impending doom that always loomed behind the mist of a vision, we were okay as long as we were together. That had to be one of the first signs of insanity, but it didn't stop me from continuing to grin as I tugged on my jeans, pulled on my tank top, and laced my sneakers.

Beau didn't take his eyes off me while I dressed. I didn't bother to pretend he wasn't looking. Maybe I didn't know why he liked to look at me like that. Maybe some part of my damaged brain still insisted that none of this was real. But I was beyond caring, beyond listening to that stupid voice.

I brushed by Beau to pick up the laundry basket and sauntered over to the back door. He followed, reaching around to unlock and open the door for me like a gentleman.

"It's like that, huh?" he asked teasingly. "Use me and leave me?"

"Yep," I said. "We have dinner with Gary and Tess in an hour. Don't be late."

Beau chuckled to himself. I walked off without looking back. The stupid grin was still plastered all over my face.

"I'll be there in thirty minutes," he called after me.

"Promises, promises," I called without looking back. Then, as his warm laugh followed me, I turned around the back of the garage to cross to where the Brave was hooked up.

Even though Beau and I had been living out of the 1975 Brave Winnebago for over a year and a half, the RV didn't look much different than it had when I first bought it from Gary in Richmond. My intention then had been to flee the nonlife I'd been surviving as an orphan in foster care for nineteen years.

We were currently hooked up to water and electricity at the back of the garage Beau rented, because living out of RV sites full time was way too expensive, and dry-docking in a remote location made it difficult to earn any money. No cellphone or Wi-Fi signal meant no updating my Etsy store. No other vehicles around meant Beau didn't have any work, either.

I had to place the laundry basket down to unlock the side door of the Brave. The lock was fiddly ever since Beau had replaced it. He'd also installed a crazy heavy-duty bolting system on the inside of the door, but only locked that down at night. I never mentioned to him that most of the predators we knew could just claw through the side of the RV if they intended us harm. I also didn't mention that I doubted locks would stop many witches or sorcerers either. If Beau wanted to be protective, I wasn't going to hinder him. The lock meant he cared for me, and fiddling with it every time I needed to get into the Brave only served to remind me of that.

The garish orange, green, and brown interior of the RV was definitely fading around the edges from constant use and sun exposure. But the assault of color was, as always, a calming influence on me.

I lugged the laundry through the tiny galley kitchen and dinette to the tall shelves next to the bed at the very back of the twenty-one foot RV. Other than the few items that had obviously tumbled out of the basket when the vision had taken my eyesight, I'd already folded all the clean clothing and just needed to put it away.

Yeah, something about living in a tiny space made me a neat freak. I was constantly cleaning. Of course, this was the most space I'd ever had before, so to me it was all a luxury. I could count on one hand how many times I'd had a room of my own, and I wouldn't need my thumb or forefinger.

The basket collapsed all funky-like, then was stored next to my portfolio between the shelving unit and the bed. Beau had bought the basket for me. He'd been upset when he'd seen me using a garbage bag for laundry.

I ran my finger along the edge of my zippered portfolio. My very empty portfolio ... though I suspected it wouldn't be empty for long. I wondered if I should try to draw the girl with the dying eyes, but I didn't feel the urge to do so yet. Something about that nagged at me. More was coming. But there wasn't any point in dwelling on it. It would come and we would deal with it.

Yeah, I was a 'we.'

Grinning again like a moronic baboon, I crossed to the fridge and started pulling out fixings for the salad I was contributing to dinner tonight. The constantly full fridge and well-stocked dry goods cupboard was the only really new thing in the Brave, even after a year and a half.

Tess didn't exactly like me bringing food when she and Gary were hosting, but I knew it was the proper thing to do. And for some reason, that kind of thing was starting to matter to me. Like seeing Drake bow to Chi Wen, and the language he'd used when saying goodbye to me. There were rules in place. Rituals that helped ... well, that smoothed life. And the smoother things were, the easier they would be to deal with when everything fell apart.

Yeah, I was waiting — and not waiting — for that to occur. Though I didn't know what 'that' was. Just that it would show up or simply happen, like a train wreck or a heart attack. It always did.

Beau slipped silently into the Brave while I was shredding the carrots. At least he tried to slip in silently, but the entire RV dipped as his weight landed on the outside steps, then righted itself as he came inside. Winnebagos hadn't come with stabilizers for long-term parking in 1975.

"Nice try, Mr. Stealthy," I said, not looking up from the cutting board that fit perfectly over the tiny stainless steel sink. "We don't have time for a training session."

Beau huffed out a laugh as he shut the door. Then, stepping to the side, he pressed a kiss to my neck. "I still can't figure that out," he mused.

"What?"

"The weight distribution thing."

I shrugged. "You're big. Heavy."

"Hmmm, yeah." Beau tossed a package on the lime-green laminate dinette table behind me and started stripping.

I kept my eyes on the salad fixings. Beau and I had an embarrassing habit of being late. For everything. Watching him undress was a surefire way to miss dinner.

"Is that what you and Audrey have been working on? Weight distribution?" I asked. The beta of the West Coast North American Pack took her duties annoyingly seriously, checking in about once a month.

Beau turned toward the front of the Brave and reached into the tiny bathroom to turn on the shower. "She thinks I should be able to take half-form."

"Half-human, half-tiger?"

"Yeah, warrior form. All the strength and abilities of the tiger. But, you know, upright with opposable thumbs."

I glanced over, catching a glimpse of broad, muscular shoulders as Beau stepped into the shower. I didn't like the sound of this 'warrior form' thing. I didn't like the training Beau did with Audrey at all. The only reason he was this bound to the West Coast North American Pack was because of me. And the only reason people needed warriors was to fight their battles for them.

Beau wasn't a fighter. Or rather, he shouldn't have to be.

I eyed the package on the table. The narrow cardboard box could have held anything, but the Amazon shipper's address wasn't particularly illuminating. Beau wasn't buying tools, or books, or video games from Amazon when we were low on funds. So I knew the package contained something for our tactical training or end-of-the-world prep.

Beau might not be inherently aggressive, like the pack werewolves, but he was a prepper. Or he'd become one for my sake.

My magic didn't come with enhanced strength or healing like Beau's shapeshifting ability did. So now we had escape scenarios, emergency routes, and contingency plans worked out for every situation he could think of. Each plan was tweaked and adapted for every town we moved to.

"Open it. It's for you." Beau wandered out of the bathroom, still toweling himself off. I hadn't heard the shower shut off, and my brain was momentarily scrambled by the sight of the naked size of him. All his breadth and width filled the space before me — and then around me as he brushed by to pull clean clothing off his shelf.

"Closing the blinds might have been an idea. Old Ms. McNally will be getting an eyeful from her bedroom window."

Beau grinned at me, then buried his face in a clean T-shirt and inhaled deeply. My stomach flipped at this sight, and suddenly blurry-eyed, I turned back to tossing the salad in a sealable Tupperware container before I started weeping like a mooning idiot. Yeah, tears of joy over the simplicity of Beau appreciating clean laundry. Over him appreciating the fact that I washed and folded his clothing for him. It was the absolute least I could do in exchange for all he did for me.

I reached for the package on the dinette while Beau pulled on shorts and black Tevas. I sliced through the packing tape that sealed the box with the paring knife I'd been using to chop cucumber.

I dug through the bubble wrap and pulled out a pen. At least it looked like a pen. But a weird, heavy, black metal pen with an oddly scalloped grip. I looked at Beau questioningly.

"It's a tactical pen, military and police issue. Smith & Wesson."

"Well, that's illuminating."

"Using a pen in a self-defense situation should be a last resort. It's a weapon of opportunity."

"Okay. It's … ah … heavy."

Beau nodded, deadly serious as he stepped closer to switch my grip on the pen. "It's constructed out of aircraft aluminum, and when used correctly, it can inflict some serious damage to an attacker's eyes or throat. But you have to understand the pros and cons of using such a weapon. Because the drawback is you need to be very close to use it against someone who's trying to hurt you. And we don't want you to be close, right?"

"Right."

"Because when I say run, what do you do?"

"Beau ..."

"Rochelle."

"When you say run, I run."

"No questions. No hesitation."

"I hear you. I'm listening. If I can't run right away, I aim for the soft parts. Then I run."

Beau nodded. He brushed his thumb across my knuckles where they were gripped around the thick grooves that made up the body of the pen. "We're going to be late. We'll work the pen into our training tonight on the beach."

"Ah, the beach?"

"Good footwork practice."

I pressed the pen into Beau's hand and shifted over to the clean clothes, quickly swapping out my jeans for a black jersey skirt and putting on a clean tank top. "Sure. Gary and Tess will get a real kick out of me trying to stab you with a pen."

Beau wagged his eyebrows as he leaned against the dinette. He took his turn to ogle me while he flipped the pen in the air and caught it without looking.

I laughed, shoved my feet into some black flip-flops, and crossed back to grab my satchel from the dinette bench seat. Yeah, this was my version of dressing up.

Beau blocked me playfully with his body, reaching over the dinette to retrieve my hand-painted satchel from the bench beside and behind him. He pressed a kiss to my forehead as he looped the strap of the reclaimed army duffle bag over my head and across my shoulders.

Then he held the pen out to me, completely serious. "Put it in your bag, please. Have you got your sketchbook?"

"Always." I took the pen.

Satisfied, Beau grabbed the salad and headed for the door. "I'm sure Gary and Tess will be overjoyed watching you attempt to stab me."

I looked down at the pen in my hand. It didn't seem like much of a weapon. But then, since it had taken eighteen months of training with Beau for him to not be afraid I'd accidentally stab myself, I seriously doubted whether I should be wielding anything deadlier.

"It writes, too," Beau said.

"Well, that's useful at least." I tucked the pen in my bag and followed him out of the RV.

I trailed Beau around the back and side of the garage. We usually walked the two blocks to the interstate, then hitchhiked to Gary and Tess's campsite. My skirt-and-tank-top combo was definitely a cooler outfit for this time of year, but I hated the way the dry grass and pebbles got caught up in my flip-flops. I stopped to shake my left foot free of annoying debris and got buzzed by some insect.

No, not some insect.

A black butterfly flitted through my peripheral vision.

My stomach churned even as I raised my head to follow the butterfly's flight path. It danced along the eaves of the garage, then up over Beau's shoulder. He didn't seem to notice as it stopped to kiss his ear.

In fact, he was standing awfully still, staring at something ahead. Or maybe across the road. I couldn't see beyond his broad shoulders.

I glanced down at my left wrist. Yep, it was bare. Now tattoo free.

I stepped forward just until I could see the huge black SUV with dark-tinted windows parked across the street. Beau was gripping the salad Tupperware so tightly that I was fairly sure he was going to permanently dent the plastic.

The butterfly flitted across the road as someone turned off the idling SUV and the driver's door opened.

Beau was holding his breath.

A slight, tautly muscled woman in green capris and a goldenrod printed T-shirt stepped out from the vehicle. The butterfly danced about three inches over her green-dyed, shag-cut hair. She lifted her face as if tracking its movements.

No, she was sniffing the air. And possibly smelling the magic of the butterfly?

Kandy, Jade Godfrey's werewolf bodyguard, was in Yachats, Oregon.

That couldn't be good.

"Real or not real?" I asked Beau. My voice was a tense whisper. My eyesight wasn't obscured by the mist that normally accompanied my visions. But the butterfly tattoo thing was new, and I wasn't sure anyone but me and the far seer could sense it. So Kandy might be a different sort of visual manifestation as well.

"Real," Beau said. His single-word answer was filled with a completely different kind of tension. A possessive fierceness that instantly muted the anxiety building in my belly.

Kandy slammed the SUV door behind her, then leaned against it. She crossed her arms and grinned in our direction. The smile wasn't a greeting. With her chin dipped against her chest and the green of her shapeshifter magic rolling across her eyes, she appeared deceptively relaxed.

Beau passed the salad to me as the butterfly tattoo returned to my wrist. That was the second time it had shown me the arrival of an Adept. Also, I didn't often see magic in color, which instantly reminded me that Kandy was a particularly powerful werewolf.

Beau stepped off the sidewalk.

"Wait," I whispered. "We go to her?" I'd been trying to sort through all the formalities that the pack insisted on.

"Yeah. Our territory."

I trailed behind Beau, glancing around at the empty street. It was nearing dinnertime. I could smell our neighbors barbecuing and could hear kids playing, but I couldn't see anyone.

Beau stopped a few feet away from Kandy. She eyed him but didn't change her stance. She turned to look at me, dropped her folded arms, and nodded. "Oracle."

I swallowed. "Kandy."

Her goldenrod T-shirt was printed with a picture of a chicken and the question 'Guess What?' in green lettering. A red arrow was pointed to the chicken's back end. Someone had used a black fabric marker to add a second arrow that pointed to an additional squiggle of black just behind the chicken.

Kandy also wore three-inch-wide gold cuffs on either wrist. These were inscribed with symbols and edged with hundreds of what looked like tiny diamonds. They were like something that belonged in ancient Greece, not on the skinny, muscled arms of a werewolf.

"I don't get it," I said, with a nod toward her T-shirt.

Kandy's grin widened. "The shirt was a gift from the dowser, but it needed a little something."

"Chicken butt," Beau said. "Guess what, chicken butt?" His arms were loose at his sides, but he'd widened his stance as if he was expecting to be attacked.

"Guess what, chicken shit?" Kandy added. Her answer was full of laughter that was more threatening than joyful.

I tilted my head to look at her. She was actually only a few inches taller than me, but she came off as much larger. Intimidating and fierce.

Kandy lost her smile under my observation. Tension gathered in her shoulders. Though I only noticed it because Beau stifled a growl in response.

"Not interested in what you see, oracle," the green-haired werewolf said. "Ground rules, you know. I'm here as requested, but not interested in what you see if it pertains to me."

"The far seer sent you."

"He did?" Beau asked.

"Audrey can't stand me hanging around the place," Kandy said. "So when the old man suggested I check in on you a few months ago, I decided I'd come the next time she asked. So here I am."

"And the dowser?"

"In Vancouver, last I checked."

I couldn't help releasing a sigh of relief at that news.

Kandy curled her lip in a sneer and folded her arms, bringing my attention to the cuffs on her wrists again. "You'd be so blessed to have Jade at your side. I'm second best."

"Chi Wen mentioned …" I hesitated, then pushed through. Beau and I didn't keep secrets from each other, but I probably should have mentioned this before Kandy showed up. I always unwittingly erred on the side of us not having quite enough time to talk through everything, before the crunch of whatever crisis was about to befall us actually befell us. Well, this was the second time at least. So maybe I was making a big deal out of nothing. Or maybe I was stalling while being stared at by a scary-ass werewolf. "He mentioned being concerned about … Beau. But that he'd done something about it. I guess you're the something?"

As anticipated, Beau hissed under his breath. He really didn't like the idea of having the far seer's concern focused on him. Who would?

Kandy barked out a laugh. "So I'm here to save your ass, hey kitten?"

Beau shifted his shoulders but didn't answer.

"Don't worry about it too much. I was bored out of my mind anyway." The werewolf eyed the salad in my hands. "We going somewhere for dinner?"

Right.

Apparently we were.

CHAPTER THREE

"DID THE FAR SEER SAY WHY he asked you to come here?" I asked as I buckled into the back seat of the SUV behind Kandy. Beau had opened the door for me, then crossed around to climb into the front passenger seat. I gathered he deemed it less likely that Kandy could throttle me while she was driving if I sat behind her. Except I'd seen the werewolf in action — in my head, at least — and knew she was capable of anything she decided to do. So the seating arrangements probably didn't matter in the least.

"Yeah, you know." Kandy started the pristinely clean and completely conspicuous SUV, then executed a U-turn back toward the highway. "He laid it out in exquisite detail. Time, place, players, and ultimate outcome. Completely coherently. Like always. Then I bought him Oreos."

"Right," Beau said. "So no."

The too-cold air conditioning blasted against my bare legs from the back vents, causing me to shiver. The vehicle was immense. I could practically stretch out my legs and not touch the back of the front seat. I attempted to ignore the leather interior, but my skirt was short enough that I could feel it underneath my thighs. I wasn't a fan of slaughtering animals, not for food or furniture.

"Dinner?" Kandy asked as we rolled up to the stop sign at the edge of Interstate 101.

Beau glanced back at me over his left shoulder. I nodded. He stretched out his arm and pointed south without taking his eyes off me.

Kandy gunned the SUV onto the single-lane highway, slipping between two high-end RVs, then flooring it over the yellow line to pass the one in front. "Ah, you guys are so cute."

I didn't have to see her face to hear her heavy, mocking sneer, but that was fine. I didn't give a shit what anyone thought about Beau and me. Though tension was rippling along my jaw as I attempted to ignore her manic driving and focus on getting us through the next few hours. "Our hosts are human."

"Well, I doubted you'd be dining with demons."

"She means that Tess and Gary aren't Adept," Beau said.

"They're ... I bought the Brave from them, back in Vancouver. Richmond, actually." I stumbled over the explanation, weirdly awkward about why I'd formed a friendship with a couple old enough to be my parents.

Kandy's silence didn't particularly help. I'd figured out that werewolves were isolationists. Well, they preferred to be. Though Kandy was friends with Jade Godfrey, who wasn't a shapeshifter, so maybe I shouldn't assume. "We've kept in touch. They like to cook for Beau and me."

"They're parked at the Sea Perch RV Resort. About seven miles south," Beau said.

I looked out the window and stopped talking. Forest stretched away from the interstate on either side of the winding road. A ton of hiking trails spread out for miles to the east, but the ocean was just on the other side of the bank of trees to the west. Gary and Tess had been parked at Sea Perch for about a week. The pad rental was crazy high, but the RVs there were parked along the edge of a sandy beach with the surf only fifteen or twenty feet away at high tide. So you got what you paid for.

This was the third time we'd seen them this year. I'd decided that Gary just liked checking up on the Brave, though they both really seemed to adore Beau. Tess fed him constantly, and Gary always had some project for him to look at.

Kandy was pulling off into the resort before any of us bothered to speak again.

"There's visitor parking just behind the check-in," Beau murmured, but Kandy was already turning that way, following the signs. "I'll register the plates."

Beau stepped out from the SUV before it had fully rolled to a stop. I waited to unbuckle until Kandy had shut off the engine, watching the werewolf as she watched Beau saunter into the tiny, gray-shingled admin building. A band of trees stretched between us and the ocean, though I could dimly hear the crashing surf even through the closed windows.

"Do you know why I'm here?" Kandy finally asked without turning around to look at me.

"No."

She nodded, then lifted her eyes to the rearview mirror. I removed my sunglasses and met her gaze.

"Were you the third werewolf?" I asked, not really knowing where the question came from. "In the barbershop parking lot?"

"You mean, after the dowser helped you sneak out to meet with Blackwell?"

I was slightly surprised that Kandy knew the fine details of my getaway from Desmond's house in Portland.

But then, Jade did like to be pissy with the alpha, so maybe she'd deliberately told him she'd helped me.

"Yeah."

"No. That was Christian, some flunky Audrey's training."

"Like she's training Beau?"

"No."

"No?"

Kandy looked back to the admin office, but Beau hadn't reappeared. "Beau won't be an enforcer, even if he decides to become a full member of the pack. Cats don't fight in packs, and they aren't as skilled as wolves are for tracking. Cats are single-focus stalkers. Precision killers."

A chill ran through me that had nothing to do with the cool air trapped in the SUV. "He doesn't want to be pack."

"I know." Kandy opened her door as Beau reappeared and stopped a few feet away to wait for us. "We all do things we don't want to do for the people we love."

"Is that why you're here?" I stepped out of the SUV after her. "For Jade?"

"I have no idea." Kandy slammed her door shut to saunter over to Beau. "I hope meat is on the menu, kitten. You need it. You're easily twenty-five pounds underweight."

Beau snorted. "Look who's talking."

"Yet I could outdo you on the bench press, even without the cuffs."

Beau glanced over Kandy's head as she brushed by him. His dark aquamarine eyes were bright in the dappled late-afternoon sunlight coming through the trees. I closed the space between us, curling my fingers around his.

Kandy whistled from around the corner of the building. "Nice rigs," she said. "Wow, nice view."

"See? Even werewolves can be impressed," I whispered to Beau.

He offered me a grin, but I could see the tension that still simmered underneath it. Kandy showing up obviously bothered him. "Blond hair, brown eyes?" he asked. "In the vision?"

"Yeah. No one I know."

"But someone important enough for the far seer to send Kandy?"

"I don't know. I don't think she's here about the vision. Chi Wen isn't exactly clear about these things."

"But he thinks something is going to happen."

"He knows that something is going to happen."

Beau nodded, then dropped the questioning to tug me after Kandy. "We better give the werewolf some directions. Otherwise, she'll start randomly pillaging people's barbecues."

Gary was already heating his grill when we wandered up to the site. He always looked exactly the same as when we'd first met. Gray buzz cut, big gnarled hands, and modest beer belly. He and Tess had rented one of the primo spots, right on the edge of the Pacific Ocean. Gary had placed their large gas grill between himself and the surf so the wind didn't constantly blow across it. But based on the conversation he'd had with Beau last week, this method of cooking was a work in progress. I thought the grilled vegetables were great, but I gathered that nailing the temperature on the steaks was more difficult.

The screen door of a mammoth, forty-foot RV slammed open as Tess cried out, "Rochelle! Beau!" She climbed down into the seating area they'd set up with brand-new-looking wicker furniture underneath their side awning.

"Tess," Beau said, reaching out to shake her hand and accepting a hug instead. Tess was only a few inches taller than me. Around Kandy's height, actually. Her curly hair was short cropped and streaked with various shades of blond. She was slim and favored white and beige tailored clothing. At about seven or so years younger than her husband, she was maybe fifty-two or fifty-three.

Tess turned to take in Kandy with a welcoming smile. She didn't hug me by mutual agreement.

"This is our ... friend," Beau said. "Kandy ..."

"Tate," Kandy said. She held out her hand for Tess to shake. "Sorry to drop by without warning. I wanted to surprise Rochelle and Beau. I shouldn't have assumed they'd have the evening free on a Friday."

My mouth dropped, then hung open. That was the most civil I'd ever heard any werewolf be.

Tess shook Kandy's hand. "We're glad to have you. Gary always puts on extra when he knows Beau is dining with us. Oh, that is if you eat meat?"

Kandy laughed, then looked back at me over her shoulder. "Yeah, I wouldn't get far on vegetables alone."

"Perfect. Come, come meet Gary." Tess directed Kandy over toward the nose of the RV, where Gary was fiddling with the still-empty grill. "Gary. The kids brought a friend."

Kandy tagged after Tess, but only after wagging her eyebrows back at me. "You're going to catch flies, oracle."

I snapped my mouth shut and looked at Beau, who was watching Kandy with narrowed eyes.

"I don't trust her as far as I can throw her," he muttered.

"You could throw her pretty far."

"Exactly." He stuffed his hands in his pockets, following after Kandy and Tess. I carried the salad up into the RV to get it out of the heat before dinner.

Gary and Tess had popped for their insanely expensive RV when he'd taken early retirement. Tess still took contract work with one of the colleges in Vancouver. She taught first- and second-year sociology, not that I had any idea what that actually entailed. The study of people, maybe. Anyway, the RV was plush. Like a high-end apartment. Lots of fabric and wood and full-sized appliances. Beau thought it cost easily a hundred and twenty grand. They also towed a practically brand-new Jeep behind it, which Gary had tried to pay Beau to 'tune up' more than once in a thinly veiled attempt to put some extra cash in our pockets.

I tucked the salad in the fridge, which was crazy full of food. Fruit, veggies, and at least a dozen types of cheese. I didn't look too closely at the marinating steaks. I usually stood upwind of the grill when Beau and Gary were cooking.

I was pouring myself a glass of water when the vision mist took my eyesight. Thankfully, the glass didn't break as it dropped into the sink. I managed to turn off the water, then just gripped the edge of the counter as I waited for the mist to clear or resolve into something more.

"Rochelle?" Tess whispered. I hadn't heard her return to the RV. "Are you okay?"

"Yes." I got the word out politely enough, but I couldn't pretend to be completely okay. I didn't know the RV well enough to wander around it as if I wasn't blind. I was glad I was still wearing my sunglasses, not that I was sure Tess would be able to see anything weirder than my eyes normally were.

"I was just grabbing beers for Kandy and Beau," Tess said. Her tone was completely normal, as if I wasn't standing there staring straight ahead like a moron and holding myself upright. The mist rolled around in my mind's eye but didn't resolve into anything. I loosened my left hand and fished my necklace out of my tank top.

Tess stepped up next to me, brushing her shoulder lightly against mine as she retrieved the glass I dropped, then turned on the water.

I gripped the raw diamond of my necklace so tightly in my palm that it hurt. Then I just tried to relax into whatever my magic was attempting to manifest. Chi Wen had said I could use the diamond as a focal point, but I wasn't exactly sure how to accomplish that feat. Thankfully, the mist started lessening rather than increasing.

Tess touched the top of my right hand, loosening my grip on the counter and passing me the full glass of water. "Drink," she murmured. Then she stepped away to open the fridge.

I lifted the cool water to my mouth. My hand was steady as I drank. The mist clouding my sight cleared further, until I could see the interior of the RV again. The kitchen window faced the neighbor's RV pad. They had three kids, close in age, and a golden retriever.

"I'm okay," I finally said, though without looking away from the comforting reality before me. "It's just the edge of a migraine."

"I know," Tess said. "Drink another glass, then join us. Gary and Beau are building a fire on the beach. We'll have s'mores for dessert."

"Okay."

Tess left with the beers. I poured another glass of water, noting that Tess had dried off the glass before she'd filled it for me. My hand started to shake. I hadn't had to cover for the visions for over a year. I was out of practice. But Tess hadn't cared. I pressed the glass onto the counter to still my shaking hand.

I'd been completely weird and Tess hadn't cared. I would have heard it in her voice. She was the kind of person who was open like that.

I drank the second glass of water, poured a third, and then wandered outside to watch Beau and Gary joke around while they barbecued our dinner. I wasn't the only one who Tess and Gary had accepted, no questions asked. I wasn't the only one who secretly wanted to be accepted like that.

That was why we came for dinner whenever we were invited. Or answered emails and text messages, even if Gary was just sharing RVing articles or Tess was sending vegan recipes I was never going to try to cook.

I didn't spend a lot of time trying to figure out what Gary and Tess wanted from us long term. It was pretty obvious with them being childless and all. What was weird was that Beau and I had just accepted the older couple in our lives without question as well.

So even I had to admit that making s'mores by a bonfire as the sun set over a crashing surf only steps away was pretty fun. And Tess had bought vegan marshmallows for me. Yeah, she was extremely cool like that.

During dinner, Gary happily tossed two more steaks on the grill when Beau and Kandy attempted to eat their combined weight in red meat. Tess split a bottle of red wine with Kandy — some fancy Pinot Noir she and Gary had picked up from a winery on their way down to the coast. Then they discussed the bouquet and taste profile of the wine as the sun dipped in the horizon.

All and all it was a pretty weird dinner, almost … homey, and a seriously stark contrast to my vision of the dead girl.

While I sat by the fire, Kandy and Beau wandered away down the beach to train and Gary puttered around cleaning the barbecue. Next to me, Tess was knitting a sock with double-pointed knitting needles that looked deadly enough to take someone's eye out.

I dug my toes into the sand and burned my final few marshmallows layer by layer. I would peel off a layer after it bubbled, eat it, then return the skinless, skewered marshmallow to the fire to repeat the process.

Kandy flipped Beau over her head. He landed on his back in the sand, laughing.

Worried about this display of strength, I glanced over at Tess.

She smiled at me and kept knitting. "They've known each other for a while?"

"Friends of friends, I guess."

"What kind of martial arts is that?"

"Mixed."

"I keep asking Gary to take tai chi with me."

"But Gary thinks he'll just fall asleep upright," Gary said with a chuckle. He sidled up behind us to dangle a half-full glass of wine over Tess's head. "Going once …"

Tess sighed as if she was terribly put upon, but she set her knitting aside to take the wine. She twirled the ruby liquid in the glass until it looked molten in the fire-light … like molten blood …

The vision hit without warning or mist. One second I was watching Tess's glass of wine and burning the roof of my mouth on a too-hot marshmallow. The next, I was watching dark crimson blood spread out from underneath a young woman's head.

I cried out before I could stop myself. I clamped my mouth shut, turned my head away from Tess, and started frantically digging around for my sunglasses in the pockets of the sweater I'd borrowed from her.

"What is it, Rochelle?" Tess asked, her voice barely a whisper.

I shook my head, unable to focus on answering her as the vision reset. Or maybe it was restarting from a beginning I hadn't yet seen.

In my mind, the back of the blond girl's head smashed onto the asphalt, somehow denting it. Then her head lolled to the side, her murky brown eyes staring out at nothing. Blood seeped slowly out from underneath her hair to form a pool on the ground.

And repeat.

I moaned, squeezing my eyes shut and abandoning my search for my sunglasses.

"What is it?" Gary murmured, moving closer behind Tess.

"Will you get Rochelle a glass of water?" Tess asked. "Oh! And her satchel from the chair there. Do you want Beau? Should I call for Beau?"

I managed to shake my head as the vision repeated a third time. Becoming numb to the sudden violence, I saw more detail. Or perhaps I was just starting to understand what I was seeing.

The blond falling ... her head and shoulders hitting the ground at the same time. The angle suggested she was falling from a height, rather than just tripping or being knocked down.

The asphalt denting underneath her head indicated that it was hot where she was dying, or going to die. Hot enough to soften the blacktop. I'd seen that only once, on an August day when I was seven or eight in a newly paved area of East Vancouver. It rarely got that hot on the West Coast, but I assumed the phenomenon wasn't that unusual.

Yeah, whatever magic wanted me to see, I saw. Now, following Chi Wen's guidance, I just tried to not let it overwhelm me.

"Beau said you might need your sketchbook." Tess was pressing my satchel into my hands. Or she was trying to, at least. I released my hold on my necklace to take the bag from her.

The vision stopped repeating, leaving me staring down at the dead blond as if I were crouched beside her. Except I wouldn't be crouched there, not when this actually happened, because the visions were never about me.

"Thank you," I managed to mumble to Tess, even as I was wondering what exactly Beau had told her about my need for a sketchbook.

"Gary has water as well. Will you drink?"

"No, thank you."

Firelight kissed the paling-with-death cheeks of the dead woman, and for a moment, I thought the vision was expanding. Instead, it dissolved until I was once again staring at the bonfire before me. "Thank you," I muttered again, already digging in my satchel for charcoal.

Tess brushed her fingers across my shoulder, then stood and started tidying up the dinner with Gary. How they weren't hounding me with questions or staring at me as if I was insane, I had no idea. And I didn't have any time to dwell on it, because my left hand was itching like mad. Itching to draw what I'd seen, to capture the image on the page and hold it there.

Why? I had no idea.

I just did what it told me to do.

I started with the woman's eyes. Hunched over my lap, I found a fresh page and pressed the charcoal to form the arch of her eyebrow and the curve beneath her eyelid. I'd feather and smudge the lines later. Now, I simply sketched out the skeleton of her face.

I wasn't sure how much time I'd spent drawing, but it wasn't terribly long before Beau threw himself down beside me in the still-warm sand. He was winded. Kandy circled around behind us and chatted with Gary, but I couldn't hear their words.

"Vision?" Beau asked. His tone was hushed and confused. "You should have called me."

"It's okay." I didn't lift my head from my task. Beau brushed his fingers against my bare foot, just lightly enough for me to feel it.

"You're too cold." He rolled to his feet and padded away.

Again, I could hear conversation behind me, but I was more concerned with the blond's face. I just couldn't capture the look in her eyes ... the nothingness of her eyes. I was on my third attempt, and frustratingly, the vision was fading. As if by committing it to the page, I was erasing it from my mind.

Beau dropped a fleece blanket over my shoulders. Then he stilled, looking over my head.

"Should you be touching her?" Kandy asked quietly. I hadn't heard her approach.

"Doesn't seem to affect the magic," Beau murmured. "That's the blond woman, Rochelle? The dead girl?"

Kandy glanced back over her shoulder warily, but I was fairly certain Gary and Tess had gone inside their RV.

"It's not finished," I said stubbornly, hunching my body farther over the sketch to block it from his sight.

"You know her?" Kandy asked.

Beau didn't answer, but his hands tensed on my shoulders.

Kandy swore, loosing a vicious string of words under her breath.

Adrenaline flushed through my system as I turned to look up at Beau. His eyes were the green of his shape-shifter magic as he gazed down at me.

"You know her, Beau?" I asked.

He nodded, looking away from the sketch and out across the fire toward the dark ocean. "I bought her the lip stud for her seventeenth birthday. Two days before I left," he said.

I wanted to jump to my feet suddenly. I wanted to race across the darkening beach, to flee the truth spilling from Beau's lips. The truth brought forth by the vision. A vision of death. A vision I was suddenly and irrationally sure was going to tear us apart.

But I didn't. I reached up and touched my cold fingers to the back of Beau's warm hand on my shoulder.

He shook his head as if clearing it. "She's my sister. My half-sister. Ettie."

"Ah, shit," Kandy said. Then she stomped off.

Beau crouched down next to me. I closed the sketchbook and lifted my charcoal-covered hand to touch his face.

"She's dead, then?" he asked.

"Or going to die." My voice caught in my throat, but I couldn't lie to him or soften the blow in any way.

He nodded. "Okay."

I dropped my hand, placing it on the closed sketchbook balanced on my bent knees. "Okay?"

"Yeah. Not our problem."

"But if I'm seeing it ..."

He shrugged and looked back out at the dark ocean. "The far seer said you'd pick up things from the Adepts you spend the most time with."

I abruptly felt as if I couldn't really see him, though he was fully lit by the fire before us. I couldn't really hear him with the surf roaring in my ears. It was as if a dark, thick veil had dropped between us. I wanted to reach up and rip this barrier away, but I didn't know how to do so.

"You could call," I said, instead of confronting the slow dread that was hunkering down in my belly for the long haul.

"Yeah, I could." Beau straightened, reaching his hands down for me. "Let's say goodnight and go to bed."

I tucked my sketchbook in my satchel, then let him lift me to my feet. Beau's family wasn't my business. He never even spoke of them. But something about his reaction scared me, as if a yawning pit of silence and secrets had opened between us. A pit that might swallow us up …

I brushed away the silly thought as Beau laid his arm across my shoulders and tugged me closer.

"Kandy's not bunking with us, is she?"

Beau laughed. "Overleaf Lodge."

A flash of murky brown eyes tugged my attention back to the vision. I opened my mouth to ask Beau about his sister, but then Tess poked her head out of the RV.

"Heading home?" she asked, smiling.

"Thank you for dinner. It was great as always." Beau stepped forward and hugged Tess. Their heights perfectly matched while she was standing on the middle step of the RV. She laughed.

A splash of green caught my eye. I glanced toward the back of the RV to see Kandy shoving her cellphone back in her pocket as she crossed toward us. Her unfocused gaze slid across me, as if she didn't want to look too closely. She plastered on a smile as she stepped up to shake Tess's hand.

I was still surprised that the werewolf had joined us for dinner, and even more so that she had managed to chat amicably throughout the evening with nonmagical people. Maybe I was the judgemental one.

"Thanks for the marshmallows," I said to Tess as Beau stepped aside. I glanced behind her to see Gary washing dishes deeper within the brightly lit RV.

"We're here for another week, Rochelle." Tess's gaze was fixed over my head as she watched Beau and Kandy saunter back toward the visitors' parking. "If you need us."

"Okay." I scuffled my feet on the mix of sand and dried fir needles that salted the ground everywhere in Yachats, then stopped. It was odd for Beau to wander off without me. And I wasn't sure why I was just hanging out there in the comforting glow from the RV's lights with Tess standing on the steps, almost looming over me.

"You'll text me?" she asked.

"Sure."

"Oh, wait." Tess stepped back into the RV and retrieved the Tupperware I'd brought the salad in. She stepped all the way down the steps to pass it to me. It was heavier than it had been when it was full of salad. Suspicious, I peered through the side and saw what appeared to be cookie-like shapes inside.

I looked up at Tess to protest.

She grinned, cutting me off before I could speak. "If I don't send them home with you, Gary will just eat them all. And we both know he doesn't need more cookies."

"I heard that, Tess," Gary mock-grumbled. His hands were deep in soap suds.

I laughed, an involuntary sound that made it out of my mouth before I could edit it.

Tess chuckled and managed to squeeze a brief hug around my shoulders while my hands were occupied with the Tupperware. I didn't twist away from the embrace.

"Goodnight, Gary," I called over Tess's shoulder.

"See you two next Friday?" he asked.

"Sure." I stepped back from Tess and she let her arms fall to her sides. "Goodnight, Tess."

"Sleep well," she murmured. Then she turned back to climb the steps of the RV.

I walked into the darkness between the RV-occupied concrete pads, clutching the cookies to my stomach and feeling utterly unsettled. Torn between two moments, two lives. It was as if I'd built up an unaccustomed sense of security, and with the return of the visions, it was slipping away.

Beau had found me, saved me from myself, and showed me who I really was. But then, the visions had ceased and life had been … idyllic.

And now I was seeing his sister dead or dying.

What if trying to save Ettie meant losing Beau?

Again, I shook the idiotic thought off. I simply wasn't accustomed to being content. I was sabotaging myself, based on nothing but a fleeting hint of reticence I'd picked up from Beau the moment after he figured out the dead girl was his sister. Who wouldn't be thrown by that revelation?

Anyone. Everyone.

A werewolf and a shapeshifter were waiting for me in the deep of the night, my visions had returned with a vengeance, and I was going to do what I was supposed to do … try to trust the magic and go where it led.

CHAPTER FOUR

"IF YOU'RE NERVOUS and your hands are sweaty, then expect your grip to be compromised. Your strike will be less effective due to the pen slipping." Beau folded my fingers around the tactical pen to demonstrate the grip, then stepped back and lifted his arms like he was going to grab me again.

I tucked the pen back in my satchel, from which I was supposed to grab it when attacked. I adjusted the satchel strap across my chest as I glanced up to see a curtain twitch in Old Ms. McNally's back bedroom window. At least I assumed it was a bedroom, if the antique-white lace curtains were reliable evidence. It also had the best view of the backyard where Beau and I were doing our usual morning training session. She usually ignored us, except when Beau paid her rent every Sunday. Though I was currently trying to stab him with an odd-looking pen, so maybe that was intriguing.

"My hands don't sweat," I sneered, laying on the bravado.

Beau grinned, then wagged his fingers at me to attack.

I lunged forward, pulling the pen out of my bag in the same motion. He grabbed for me.

I tried to feint but tripped in the dead grass instead. I went down, managing to roll over onto my back in line with Beau's right sneaker. Then, as if I'd meant to fall, I halfheartedly jabbed him in the thigh with the pen.

He collapsed beside me in a fit of laughter.

I twirled the pen in my hand with a flourish, as if it were a magic wand. Beau laughed harder and I giggled.

"You know," he said, still laughing, "you should get a good three or four inches of penetration with that pen. A regular plastic ballpoint would break off at around an inch and just end up pissing off your attacker."

"Even deeper if I manage to stab someone in the throat or the eye," I said, as serious as I could be while posing the idea that I could manage to stab anyone anywhere at all.

Beau started laughing again.

Grinning, I enjoyed his contagious mirth as I watched the slow drift of wispy white clouds in the azure morning sky. The clouds would burn off in the next hour or so. It was going to be hot. Beau and I both had the day off. I was thinking that maybe we would go swimming later.

Beau's laughter slowly subsided, enough that I thought he might have fallen asleep. I'd woken in the early morning to find him gone, then slept fitfully myself before he'd returned at dawn. I hadn't asked him what he'd been doing. I could tell by the magic still sparking off him as he pressed his body against mine and we made love — still half-asleep and without whispered questions or worries — that he'd been running in his tiger form.

I'd never lain in the grass just watching the sky like this before. Not alone, and not with anyone I loved as fiercely and painfully as I loved Beau.

That sky was about to fall. And even if I tried, even if I pushed Beau to seek out his sister, I wasn't sure I could do anything about it. Maybe pushing him was what made it worse. Maybe us contacting Ettie would turn out to be what caused her death. All I could do was breathe in this moment, so that was what I did.

"When I say run …" Beau murmured sleepily.

"I run," I answered by rote.

"When I say run," Beau repeated.

"I run, Beau. I know I run."

"No questions, no hesitation."

"You say run, I run."

Beau rolled over onto his side, facing me with his head cradled in his arm. "Are you going to sketch more?"

I mimicked his movement, only a foot of flattened, dead grass between us now. "Probably."

"Do you have an idea of place or time?" He was asking about the vision of his dead sister. I'd been waiting for his questions, even though I didn't think I had any concrete answers.

"Hot weather, because the pavement is soft, but no hint of the location … yet."

Silence fell between us. Not as comfortable as before, but I still waited. Beau never pushed me to talk about anything. I wasn't going to push him.

"You think we can stop it," Beau said. His eyes were closed now, as if he were sleeping.

"If it hasn't already happened. I think we should find out. I think we should try. I think I have to try. I have to … take control …" I tamped down the well of emotion that pinched my chest. I wasn't that girl anymore. I wasn't lost.

"You're not helpless," Beau murmured, picking up on my thoughts. "You're not crazy."

"I know."

"Didn't the far seer tell you to not try to change the future?"

"Pretty much. Of course, he's the one who sent Kandy. I don't think she's here for grilled steaks and s'mores."

Beau sighed. "I don't want you anywhere near them."

"I'm not helpless."

He huffed out a laugh, but he wasn't remotely joyful. "You really think I should call."

He was so torn, so out of sorts about it all that I almost didn't answer. I almost lied before I remembered Beau would be able to smell the falsehood on me. Before I remembered that wasn't who we were. I just didn't want to drive a wedge between us — or push deeper the wedge I was fairly certain the vision had already created but hadn't cemented yet.

"It's the right thing to do," I whispered. "This is your family."

"No, you're my family," he said, his tone unyielding but not nasty. "They're just people who couldn't give a shit about me."

Annoyed at myself for still feeling vulnerable and insecure about being rejected because of the visions, I reached out to smooth my fingertips over Beau's eyebrow. He instantly captured my hand and pressed a kiss to my palm.

"We could at least … warn them somehow."

He growled, resigned. Rolling over on his back, he laid my hand over his heart while he dug his cellphone out of his pocket.

He paged through the phone. He hadn't carried one before, not until Audrey insisted. I was surprised he'd bothered to program any numbers into it. I lightly scratched his chest with my nonexistent nails, hearing him grunt contentedly as he selected a number and held the phone to his ear.

After a breath, I heard the operator. Or, rather, a recorded message of some sort. Beau hit end and tried a second number. Same result.

"Out of order?"

"Yeah. They aren't so great with paying bills." Beau continued to stare up at the sky. "Cy probably has some burner phone, or could possibly be in jail. But there's no way I'm bothering with tracking down the son of a bitch."

"Ettie's dad?" My information about Beau's family was sketchy at best. He'd never even called his stepfather by name and had always referred to his sister as Claudette. "It's been, what? At least three years since you've seen them? You think he's still in the picture?"

"More like four. But yeah, Cy Harris is like a cancer. He ain't going nowhere." Beau tucked his phone away in his pocket. "We're paid up for the week," he said. "I've bought tools."

"Ms. McNally isn't going to rent to anyone else. She likes you. You take the garbage out, lift heavy things."

Beau grunted but didn't continue the conversation.

So I pushed. I knew I shouldn't do it. I knew that Beau had more than just issues with his family. I knew he carried scars. I knew this would reopen those scars. But I didn't have anyone — no one blood-related, anyway — who called me sister, daughter, family …

"We could make a trip of it."

"You won't like it. It's hot and shitty."

"I'll be with you."

"I like it here."

"So do I."

Beau rolled over to look at me again. This time, he was the one to reach out and trace my eyebrow. "If we're going there. If you're meeting them … I should tell you … everything."

"We have a lifetime to share, don't we?" I smiled even as the pool of dread that had taken up residence in my stomach roiled.

"I don't want you to see me with them," he whispered. "What I'm like when I'm with them."

"I see you, Beau. I only see you."

He nodded. "I'm who I want to be when I'm with you."

"So am I."

He leaned toward me, lightly brushing his lips across mine. I wanted to throw my leg over his hip, to climb on top of him and claim him ... show him ... love him. But I didn't. Sex was easy between us. Words and feelings about our pasts were way, way harder. But without the words, I was worried that the sex wasn't enough to keep away the dark veil I'd felt fall between us last night.

He pulled away as if sensing my thoughts. "I could try some more phone numbers. Maybe find an email address?"

"Do you have more people to call or email?"

"No."

"Why do you think Kandy is here?"

Beau sighed, the sound of which hurt my heart. "Well, I was kind of hoping she was here to teach me how to achieve half-form. But now I'm guessing not. There weren't any claw marks on Ettie, were there?"

"Not that I saw. Geez, you don't think ..."

"No." Beau's voice was flat. "No shifter is going to kill my sister. Her own father is responsible for her death. I'm one hundred fucking percent sure."

"Does he ... hurt Ettie?"

"No. Not when I was there to take the beatings, at least. I'd just bet that the asshole has gotten himself in some deep shit. Probably having to do with stolen cars, drugs, or aggravated assault. Maybe all of the above."

I waited, but Beau didn't expand his theory about Cy. I wasn't sure that the visions would center on anything as mundane as domestic violence or drug trafficking, but I wasn't going to say anything hurtful like that to Beau right now. Or ever. The visions usually centered on magic — Adepts or magical confrontations. Large-scale magical events. Though maybe that was only when Jade or Blackwell were involved. And as far as I knew — based on Kandy's say-so and my infrequent text messages with the sorcerer — both of them were currently out of the country, where I hoped they'd be staying.

"Well, I guess we're going to Southaven, Mississippi," Beau said. "I never wanted to say those words to you. Ever. Home sweet fucking home."

Despite the fact that Ms. McNally was probably still spying on us from her upstairs window, I wrapped my hand around the back of Beau's neck, then pressed my lips against his. He instantly deepened the kiss, pulling me closer until I was sheltered along the long length of his body. The trepidation that had built up during the conversation faded, though not completely. I wasn't stupid enough to ignore that Beau was this wary about having me around his family, but I still thought it was the right thing to do.

Magic wanted it so, didn't it? Otherwise, why show me the vision?

Except I wasn't too sure magic was something to be trusted implicitly.

After exchanging a series of text messages with Beau, Kandy met us out front of the garage in almost the exact spot she'd parked the night before. Only for this trip, I'd be driving the Brave. Yeah, it might have been quicker to blast over to Mississippi in Kandy's SUV, but it would be way more comfortable in the RV. Plus, I wasn't sure I could leave it behind. It was literally my whole world.

Beau had finished the tune-up on the pickup truck he'd been working on, then had driven it back to its owner while I looked up routes to Mississippi. We'd left a note for Ms. McNally, estimating when we'd be back, and texted Tess that we'd probably miss dinner next Friday.

I rolled down the window of the Brave as I pulled even with Kandy, who was leaning against the SUV and squinting madly in the sun.

"You'll follow?" I asked.

Kandy shrugged. "Maybe."

"But you're coming?"

"I said I was."

I glanced over at Beau in the passenger seat beside me. He shrugged as well. I shook my head and looked back at Kandy.

"The far seer said we'd survive," I said.

"All of us?" Kandy asked. "Because he told me I really, really wouldn't like what was coming next."

"Great," Beau groused, though he was grinning.

Kandy returned the grin, her smile more maniacal than Beau's. Shapeshifters loved being in the shit. Werewolves most of all. Given his magical heritage, and after a year and a half of Audrey 'check-ins,' I was constantly surprised Beau was so even keeled.

"I'll follow," Kandy said as she turned to climb into the SUV. "But we're going to need to stop for lunch within the hour."

I opened my mouth to mention we had food, but Kandy cut me off.

"And not that veggie shit you keep feeding him. He needs real food. Beau's a predator, not a kitty cat."

I snapped my mouth shut, then started to roll up my window. I wasn't going to get bitchy. The best way to win an argument with a werewolf was to ignore her.

"My treat," Kandy yelled through the glass.

"I know you're not a kitty cat," I snapped to Beau. "You eat plenty of meat."

He snickered. "You know werewolves. The bigger you are, the stronger you can be."

"Well, you're plenty big."

"Oh, yeah?" Beau wagged his eyebrows at me.

I laughed. "We have the craziest conversations."

Beau instantly sobered. "We're just getting started."

He leaned across the orange-carpeted hump that divided our seats and clipped something onto my necklace. I glanced down to see a tiny red vial hanging off the gold link nearest to my diamond. No, not red. Clear glass with a stopper, with something red inside it.

I looked up at Beau.

"My blood. For tracking."

"I … I can't …"

"It's not for you to use. And you won't need to have anyone else use it unless … unless you think I'm in serious trouble. After you've run, like you promised."

I just stared at him.

"Like you promised, Rochelle," Beau repeated.

I nodded.

He reached over to take my hand, inhaling deeply as he pressed a kiss to my palm. "I'll be able to track you anywhere," he murmured, his magic tingling against my fingers. "I just thought you'd feel better with the same option."

My stomach did that weird flip it did when I wanted Beau. But since having a sexual reaction to him giving me a vial of blood was pretty creepy, I refrained from climbing into his lap like I wanted to.

Beau smirked. He knew exactly what I was thinking.

I laughed, then yelped when Kandy laid on her horn behind us.

Beau snorted, dropping my hand so I could focus on the road as I carefully pulled away from the curb and drove the two blocks to the stop sign before the interstate.

"You're not going to need it," Beau said. "I'd never leave your side voluntarily."

"Yeah? Me neither." Keeping my tone light, I wrapped my hand around the vial and the diamond as about a dozen other RVs rolled by on the highway in front of us. "Except you keep demanding that I make all these promises to the contrary."

"Options," Beau corrected. "I'm just making sure you have options."

I looked over at him, but he was looking away out the window at the oncoming traffic. "I don't need options, Beau."

"You might."

I was suddenly terrified that we were having a completely different conversation than the one we'd started. One that somehow involved me leaving him.

I gripped the steering wheel. "Not going to happen," I said, as fiercely as I could. Then I hit the gas and turned north onto the interstate. I'd drive us to Waldport, then connect to US-34E to head east.

Beau leaned forward and turned the radio on quietly, brushing his fingers against my knee as he withdrew his hand.

I glanced at him and he flashed me a sad smile.

"It's going to be okay," I said. "Our version of okay, at least."

"I know," he answered, though I could sense that he didn't believe himself any more than he believed me.

More than anything else he'd said or done so far, that alone told me that Beau's family might not be worth the trip. I seriously hoped I hadn't made a huge mistake pushing him to act on the vision.

But, as always, all I could control was myself and my reactions. And I knew — absolutely unequivocally — that I wasn't going to let anyone or anything come between Beau and me.

The trip to Southaven took us east through Oregon and into Idaho, Utah, Wyoming, Colorado, Kansas, Oklahoma, and Arkansas, then just across the border into Mississippi. And that was the short route, according to Google Maps. The drive was supposed to take thirty-six hours, but even shapeshifters needed some sleep.

We dry-docked at a rest stop in Utah the first night, where Kandy slept in the SUV. For the second and third nights, the werewolf insisted on a campsite and occupying the bed that the Brave's dinette converted into.

The vision hit me again after a late dinner somewhere in the middle of the sweltering heat of Kansas. Near Wichita, according to the interstate signage that had become a blur for me after driving for too long. Kandy and Beau had gone off to train in the nearby wooded area, which I thought might be a national park but didn't bother looking up. I was updating my Etsy shop while we had free — though frustratingly slow — Wi-Fi with our RV pad rental. The campsite had only one spot left when we pulled in, near the showers and the dumpsters, though that didn't bother us. We were only there to sleep — and to run, in Beau's and Kandy's case.

Even before the vision swamped my mind, my head was already pounding. Beau had been right about me not liking the heat. I was padding around the curtained RV in black panties and a black cotton tank top while wishing desperately we'd thought to bring the standing fan from the garage. I'd even gathered my hair into silly pigtails, because it was too short and thin to twist back into a bun without it continually falling down. Beau thought the combination of panties and pigtails was adorable. And I seriously hoped my headache would ease before he got back and wanted a cool shower.

The vision floored me. Literally. It flooded through my mind so quickly that I lost all sense of where I was in the Brave, and had to simply hunker down where I'd been standing.

In my mind, I was standing in a mist-shrouded alley … or maybe a passageway between two buildings. The mist was slowly dissolving, leaving behind a blisteringly hot day, a blazingly blue sky, and barely a hint of shadow anywhere. It must have been midday, then? With the sun directly overhead.

I was learning to gather and interpret clues in the visions as quickly as I spotted them. Yet I still felt like a newbie, constantly behind and struggling to catch up to the point of it all.

Glass shattered somewhere above my head. I threw my arms up across my face and pressed back against one building even as I reminded myself that I was watching a vision from the safe zone of the Brave. Nothing bad could happen to me.

Something thumped sickeningly to the ground before me. I forced myself to lower my arms. I forced myself to see.

Though nothing bad could happen to my physical self within a vision, my mind wasn't always so lucky.

Beau's sister Ettie was lying on the ground before me. Her head was canted to one side, her murky brown eyes staring sightlessly. She was wearing a white sundress with blue printed flowers on it. Forget-me-nots, I decided, even as the irony made me sick. She was tanned, though her skin was rapidly paling as blood seeped from the back of her head. For the first time, the expanded parameters of the vision let me see that she was bigger than me. Taller and heavier. Which made sense, because even though she and Beau were only half-siblings, he was tall enough that he might well have inherited that trait from both his mother and father.

I forced myself to relax into the vision, and to ease my grip on my necklace. I'd grabbed it instinctively. I needed to see. I needed to collect information — and to resist the urge to try to thwart the magic channeling into my mind.

But I knew I couldn't stop it even if I'd tried. Only acknowledging the moment, then immortalizing it in charcoal would make the vision stop haunting me. It might have been over a year since I'd suffered a full-blown episode, but I still knew that much.

I stepped forward, quickly glancing around the passageway in an attempt to absorb as much of the image as I could before the vision ceased. The newly constructed buildings had an industrial look from the sides. I couldn't see any traffic or people nearby, though the vision might not show me such things. In fact, I was fairly certain that my visions showed me only things that were magic in some way. As such, the area might be full of terrified nonmagicals and I wouldn't know it.

The shattered glass appeared to have come from a window on the second floor. I expected it to crunch underneath my feet, but it didn't because I wasn't actually there. Which was good, because I'd forgotten I was currently barefoot.

I couldn't see any street or business signs. Ettie didn't appear to have any marks on her or to be carrying anything, but it wasn't like I could look through her pockets.

Had she jumped? Or had she been thrown through the window?

I stepped around her, thinking I might be able to see more of the building. It was funny how quickly I could accustom myself to stepping around a dead body. I blamed TV for my insensitivity.

But as I stepped away, the mist of the oracle magic flooded my mind's eye, taking my sight with it once again.

I was back in the Brave. Not that I could see anything yet.

I was shaking, vibrating with energy that didn't feel like it belonged to me. I was still hunkered down. I stretched my legs out before me, just able to press my toes against the edge of the bench seat of the dinette and my upper back against the kitchen cabinets.

My trembling gradually eased in this position. Or, rather, it fled the rest of my body as it focused down my left arm, then accumulated in my hand. Well, that was new. Or maybe this was the first time I'd been calm enough after a vision to notice.

I was still mist-blind as I rolled forward onto the balls of my feet, then climbed onto the dinette bench seat. I pushed my laptop carefully out of the way and tugged my sketchbook toward me.

My left hand felt as though it was on fire as I found a piece of charcoal in my satchel, then applied it to what felt like a blank page in my sketchbook. Just the act of pressing the charcoal to the page eased the energy burning in my palm.

I wondered when my sight would come back, but then the thought disappeared as I began to capture the vision on paper. Pressing the charcoal to the page was enough to release the magic that had flooded my body and mind. I didn't need to see.

I sketched Ettie, the shattered glass, and what I'd seen of the building and the window through which Beau's sister had fallen. Or been pushed … or thrown.

My sight cleared.

The Brave was dark. I reached for and turned on the nearest light without lifting the fingers of my left hand from the page before me. I was working on a close-up of Ettie's face, smudging carefully to define her skeletal structure. I'd go back and refine the other sketches over the next couple of days.

I still couldn't get her eyes right. Perhaps I shouldn't worry about it, but I felt as if I was missing something.

Ettie was dead. So maybe I couldn't get her eyes right because she no longer existed behind them, filling those murky brown orbs with energy.

Maybe such thoughts were way over my pay grade right now. According to Chi Wen, I was a function of magic, but not simply a tool or a recorder. I was an interpreter.

Still just a cog in the wheel of fate, though.

But how could I believe in fate, in Chi Wen, and even in my otherworldly love for Beau yet not believe — or, rather, not submit — to the notion of my life being controlled or even dictated by a higher power?

What was missing from Ettie's eyes? Her soul? Was I so arrogant to believe that I could see such a thing? That when I sketched Blackwell and Jade, I could capture the pure essence that fueled them?

I was exhausted. I wasn't going to solve such huge questions — questions that had plagued humanity since ... well, forever — with scrawled lines on paper.

I placed the charcoal I still clutched in my left hand down on the lime-green Formica of the table. Every edge of the remaining nub was smooth and rounded.

The door swung open and the Brave dipped to the right.

I flipped the sketchbook closed. Though with both of my hands covered in charcoal from smudging and shading, it would be completely obvious I'd been sketching.

I lifted my gaze as Beau entered the Brave. He was smiling, obviously content from his run. His white teeth were a stark contrast against his smooth mocha skin.

I wasn't going to be able to hide the sketchbook from him. I shouldn't want to hide it from him ... except it was now filled with pictures of his dead sister.

I couldn't shield him. All I could do was be at his side as he suffered the pain, the torment of living. All I could do was see him, love him, and believe in him. He did nothing less for me.

Kandy stepped up behind Beau. Even three feet away, I could feel the energy of their shifter magic. They were awash in it.

Though I was bone tired, a smile in answer to Beau's spread across my face. Sometimes I loved him so much that the joy of it hurt.

His dark aquamarine gaze dropped to my hands. "You've been sketching."

I nodded.

Kandy did an about-face, stepping back out of the Brave before she'd fully entered and clicking the door shut behind her. The werewolf was odd. I knew she'd be able to hear our conversation through the door, but she still wanted to give us the semblance of privacy. Maybe that consideration was a pack thing?

Maybe she wanted the distance for herself. My visions bothered her. The idea of possibly seeing her own future, and of that future not being of her own design, rattled her. I got the feeling that werewolves, or shapeshifters in general, were very careful about being out of control. I was glad that was the case. The mere thought of an out-of-control werewolf was disconcerting.

"Are you okay?" Beau stepped close enough to gently turn my left hand palm up and brush his fingers across my butterfly tattoo.

"I think it's a magical locator," I said. I realized I hadn't told him about the tattoo flitting around when Kandy had shown up. "The tattoo, I mean. When it leaves my wrist and flies. It's showing me magic. Or Adepts, at least. Maybe? I think."

Beau stared down at my wrist for moment, absorbing this information. "Okay."

"I'm not sure I can control it, though. I asked Chi Wen if it was an extension of the oracle powers."

"But his answer was vague."

"Something about my father being a sorcerer. So that means … what? That I have more than just oracle powers? Do you think … do you think that my other tattoos are going to … activate as well?"

Beau looked down at me, his brows drawn tightly together.

"That's cool, right?" I whispered, only half joking. "The weirder and weirder it all gets … it's still cool?"

Beau sank to his knees at the end of the dinette, wrapped his hands around my hips, and tugged me toward him. I curled my arms around his neck and shoulders, pressing my left cheek to the top of his head. I was awkwardly pinned between him, the table, and the bench seat, but I didn't give one shit about it.

Beau's face was crushed to my breasts. I could feel the electricity of his magic through my thin tank top.

"Well, this is always okay," he drawled, pressing a kiss to each of my breasts.

I laughed, but then quickly sobered. "I'm not sure I want you to see the sketches."

Beau nodded, then looked up at me. "Did you get any new information?"

"I don't think so ... except she falls or is pushed through a second-floor window."

"What kind of building? House? Business tower?"

"No. I don't think so. I don't ... obviously they didn't look familiar, but also, I don't have any context. Might have been a narrow alley, but I don't think so. It didn't feel like a downtown sort of area. Some sort of new construction ... newly paved and newly painted, at least."

"So we keep going."

"We'll be there tomorrow."

"Yeah. Fantastic." Beau was less than thrilled. He straightened and turned to the kitchen, seeking food as he always did after a run.

My heart ached for him, which was a relatively new and terribly unpleasant sensation. I didn't want to be responsible for his pain. Maybe his sister was going to die anyway. I was just banking on it being better for Beau that we tried to do something about it beforehand.

Beau found some beef jerky, then opened the door to toss a piece to Kandy. The green-haired werewolf climbed into the RV and eyed my closed sketchbook warily. The two shapeshifters ripped the plastic packages of dried meat open, then chewed while contemplating me.

"Well, that's not uncomfortable at all," I muttered.

Beau grinned.

I mock-scowled at him, standing to tuck my laptop and drawing stuff away so Kandy could transform the dinette into her bed.

"Does getting the visions mean you can change what you see?" Kandy asked.

I glanced over at the werewolf. She looked deceptively relaxed, lounging against the back of the passenger seat. But even I could hear the tension behind her question.

"Did you lift a huge rock off the dowser? Did she think you were dead? Did she almost drown?"

Kandy nodded grimly.

"I saw all that before it happened. Would you have done anything differently if I'd told you?"

Kandy thought about this for a while. Then she lifted her arm, calling my attention to the thick, gold cuff she wore. "The treasure keeper gave me these at the behest of the far seer."

Since Kandy had connected him to Chi Wen, I instantly assumed the treasure keeper was another guardian dragon. "Would Jade have died if you weren't wearing them?"

Kandy didn't answer, but I got the feeling she just didn't want to acknowledge the possibility of the dowser dying.

"And now you're here," I said, feeling slightly more hopeful that I wasn't just leading us on some ill-fated rescue mission. "So the far seer seems to think he can manipulate the future to some extent. And so do I. I'm just figuring out the how part."

Kandy snorted, then stepped toward the bathroom. "He's one of the most powerful beings in the world.

There are nine of them. I've really only met three. And they all scare the shit out of me. I learned a long time ago that nothing was scarier than me in the dark. I was wrong." She stepped inside and latched the door behind her.

I looked at Beau.

He shrugged. "At least they're on our side, right?"

I clicked off the light — Kandy could see perfectly fine without it — and crossed to the rear of the Brave to climb into bed. Beau followed me.

I pulled down the covers and tucked up onto the far side of the bed. It was too hot to snuggle, but Beau stretched out beside me and lightly touched his fingertips to mine.

We listened to Kandy move around in the dark, clicking the table out of the dinette and shifting the cushions to make it a bed.

Just as I was drifting off to sleep, Beau whispered, "They are on our side, right?"

I didn't answer. I wasn't sure how to answer.

He grunted and rolled on his side, forcing me to do the same to accommodate his bent knees. He was too tall for the bed. We spooned about a foot apart. His magic danced across the back of my bare legs, arms, and neck, only abating as his breathing deepened and he fell asleep.

I was exhausted but I didn't sleep. It bothered me that I couldn't answer Beau's question utterly truthfully. Dating a shapeshifter who could smell lies made me wary of being flippant.

A week ago I would have said 'yes' unequivocally. Wouldn't I? Of course the guardians were on our side. They were the good guys, right? But what did that mean exactly? Why did I hesitate to answer Beau? Was I assuming Chi Wen would put us in harm's way if it served some greater purpose? And how would that even work? We were inconsequential, weren't we?

Except Kandy … and the cuffs she wore. They weren't inconsequential.

Beau shifted in his sleep, turning to face the other way. I snuggled closer, pressing my knees underneath his legs and my face to his back despite the heat. Only then did I drift off to sleep.

CHAPTER FIVE

"I'll be back," Kandy said.

"What? When?" I shielded my face from the already-warm morning light cutting through my sunglasses. Obviously, lenses that were dark enough for Vancouver weren't meant for Kansas. We'd risen around dawn to unhook the Brave from the water and electricity of the campsite, then to empty and fill our holding tanks. Our immediate neighbors were apparently still asleep.

"We've been in the territory of another pack for two days." Kandy crossed to the SUV where she'd parked it snugly against the front nose of the Brave.

"That's illuminating," I muttered with a glance at Beau. He appeared to be checking the front tire pressure, even though I was fairly certain he'd already checked it earlier.

Leaving the driver's door of the SUV hanging open, Kandy paused, glaring down at the back of Beau's head. After a long-suffering sigh, she elaborated. "Driving through is one thing, hanging around is another. I'll have to run down to New Orleans and check in with the Gulf Coast pack and Francois."

Beau grumbled something under his breath that sounded like, "Racist pig."

"In person?" I asked at the same time, but my question went unheeded.

"Stand up and face me, kitten," Kandy snarled.

Tension rippled through Beau's shoulders. Though he stood and pivoted his body toward Kandy, he appeared to still be examining the tires of the SUV rather than looking directly at the easily triggered werewolf.

"You have something to say?" Kandy asked.

"Wolf pack," Beau spat.

"The Assembly has mandated that all packs are open to all shapeshifters. Wolves just happen to be the dominant species. Are you saying you sought admission with Francois and were denied?"

"No."

"Then what?"

Beau didn't answer. Kandy narrowed her eyes at him but didn't move closer. The silence stretched out so long between the two of them that I began to get antsy, glancing anxiously around the mostly still-sleeping campsite. We'd wanted to pull out early, before many people woke.

"My mother ..." Beau trailed off.

Kandy waited, then prompted. "Your mother?"

"This is about Ettie, not her."

"It wasn't me who brought her up," Kandy said. "Your mother what?"

"Was abused by her pack master."

"Francois?"

"No."

"Who, then?"

"I don't know."

"Cats are very rare. Tigers, more so. But no one recognizes your last name, Jamison. It's not pack. So was your mother bitten, not born?"

"Jamison was my father's name. And no."

"Wait," I said, uncharacteristically injecting myself into the tension-filled conversation out of pure curiosity. Knowledge was power among the Adept — even I learned that lesson quickly. "Shapeshifters aren't just born?"

Kandy shrugged. "He mentioned abuse. Another type of Adept might become a shifter if they were systematically bitten over a long enough time to inject enough magic into the bloodstream. If the shifter was powerful enough. If the victim didn't die from the foreign magic. It would take months, and would get the shifter instantly blacklisted with the packs and the Assembly. But I doubt a tiger could be created that way. Not one who would then be powerful enough to breed a shapeshifter with Beau's magic, especially with a non-shifter mate." Kandy then turned her attention back to Beau. "So? Your mother's last name?"

Beau shifted uncomfortably. "I don't know."

Kandy frowned.

"She doesn't want to be pack," Beau continued, his words stilted as if they were painful to speak. I brushed my fingers lightly across the small of his back. He pressed into my touch.

"She's in hiding?" Kandy asked, incredulous. "Why not go to another pack and confront her abuser? Why not go to the Assembly? She raised you outside of a pack? That must have been near impossible. And in Francois's territory? Did you move a bunch? How does she manage her transformations?"

"She doesn't," Beau growled.

Kandy snapped her mouth shut on whatever questions she was planning to continue to pummel Beau with. "I see," she murmured. "I won't mention you or your mother, then, when I check in."

MEGHAN CIANA DOIDGE

"And if he asks your business directly?" Beau sounded seriously doubtful.

"I'm not his wolf," Kandy said. "I'm a pack enforcer. You think anyone can take something from me that I don't want to offer, kitten?"

"No. Sorry."

Kandy nodded. Then she turned her glare on me. "Try to stay out of trouble while I'm gone."

"Make it quick, then," I said. Yeah, I got snarky when someone I loved was being worked over. So ... that was only when Beau was attacked, obviously.

Kandy bared her teeth at me, then laughed. Her mirth was a wild sound that was sure to wake everyone nearby. She sobered quickly, glancing back at Beau again. "I have the address."

He nodded. "If Ettie isn't there, I'll text."

Kandy climbed into the SUV and pulled away far too quickly.

I waved the plume of dust the werewolf left in her wake away from my face. "How far is New Orleans?"

"Twelve hours or so."

"How close are we to Southaven?"

"Eight hours. Probably more in the Brave."

"But she'll catch up?"

"It's five hours back. And if she drives like that ..." Beau shrugged, turning to open the door to the RV.

I could have sworn I heard the squeal of the SUV's tires as Kandy hit the paved entrance to the campsite, then roared over to the highway, but I was only imagining it. Somehow, her leaving made the idea of meeting Beau's family worse. As if I'd lost a buffer between me and the shitstorm that was coming.

The Brave dipped as Beau stepped on the lowest step.

"This is going to be bad, isn't it?" I mumbled.

"Yeah." He reached back for me.

"Understatement of the year?"

"I don't know." Beau grinned. "The year's only half over."

"Great," I groused. Then I grabbed his hand and let him tug me up the steps.

Southaven, Mississippi, wasn't particularly interesting. At least not the parts I saw of it. I mostly noticed how dusty and brown it was everywhere as Beau cut off the interstate into a suburb. He'd taken over driving at the last gas station we filled up at.

We'd stopped for breakfast, lunch, and a really early dinner. I'd never seen Beau eat so much or spend so much money on food. My shrink would have said he was fortifying himself. The supposedly eight-hour trip took us ten hours. I didn't care if Beau wanted to make it twenty-four hours, or even two extra days. My heart was a wedge of pain in my chest the entire time. I bought him more treats at the gas station and chattered like an idiot to cover my anxiety.

It was late afternoon as we drove by row after row of sun-bleached bungalows with plastic kiddie pools on the front lawns. Every second house either had an RV, a spot for an RV, or a pickup truck in its driveway.

"Is that the high school you graduated from?" I asked as we crawled passed a large campus. The sports fields surrounding the sprawling, single-level, orange-brown brick building were huge. Three portable classrooms were set up in a concrete playground area.

"Barely."

Beau was driving slower and slower. I didn't know how close we were to his childhood home. But he'd been keeping under the speed limit since we'd gassed up, his foot seemingly barely touching the accelerator now.

We turned the block, keeping the school fields on our right. The grass was dry, but even I could tell that the high school put more money into their recreational facilities than their educational ones. Huge banks of expensive lights hung over the bleachers, which a crew of students and parents appeared to be painting despite the late-afternoon heat.

"Did you play football?"

"Badly. And carefully."

"And under the bleachers? Smoking, drinking, and drugs?"

Beau snorted. He hadn't even glanced over at the high school while we'd been talking. "Rarely. Shifter metabolism hardly makes the wasted hours worth it."

"And sex?" I asked, wagging my eyebrows in his direction. "Maybe in the middle of the football field?"

Beau clamped his jaw tightly. I instantly regretted my playful question.

"I was —"

"No," he said, interrupting me. "No sex on the football field." He looked over and attempted a smile. "But I'm open to the suggestion."

I laughed somewhat stiltedly, choosing to listen to his words rather than his tense tone.

Silence fell between us as we navigated another corner. Vehicles were parked on both sides of the street now, forcing Beau to slow even further.

"Should I stop asking questions?"

"No."

I couldn't think of anything else to ask him as we rolled by a corner store. "We could get some ice cream."

"Do you want some?"

"Not really."

"Rochelle …"

"It's okay, Beau. I get it."

"I used to steal candy from that store," he said awkwardly, as if he was forcing himself to communicate. "Even after I had the money to pay for it."

"Yeah? Pop Rocks and sour chews?"

"Sure. Licorice. Gummy bears. Small stuff."

"Easy to pocket."

"Yeah."

Beau slid the Brave to a stop in front of a gray house with black trim. No. Correction. The main color of the house used to be off-white. Sunburned grass was encroaching on the concrete path that led to the front stairs and the black-painted front door. The double carport was occupied by what appeared to be the rusted husks of two cars, with another car sitting on blocks between the carport and the neighbor's fence. The neighbor's exceedingly high fence.

"Home sweet home," Beau muttered. He didn't turn off the engine.

I glanced around the neighborhood. It looked fairly cookie-cutter, but most of the houses were kept in better condition than the one we were currently parked in front of.

"Cy is a mechanic?" I asked. "Those are muscle cars?"

"No," Beau spat. "And yes."

"They're your cars?"

"No, Rochelle. No. Just … give me a minute."

95

I laid my hand on his arm. He was clenching the steering wheel too tightly but I didn't say anything. His skin rippled at my touch. I'd seen him involuntarily transform once, when Blackwell had used an amplifying device at a restaurant the first time we'd met the sorcerer face to face. But now I wondered if anxiety or anger could trigger the same result.

Beau's tiger wouldn't be terribly comfortable in the driver's seat of the Brave.

"I swore I wouldn't come back," he finally said.

"Okay. Okay. We can leave a note with my cellphone number."

Beau growled and shut off the engine. Then he climbed out of his seat as if forcing himself to move.

I followed.

He paused with his hand on the exterior door, closed his eyes, and took a few measured breaths.

I wanted to wrap my arms around him, but I didn't. I wanted to wrap my arms around myself and fall to the floor in a fetal position. But I didn't.

Beau reached back for me without opening his eyes. He pulled me tightly against him, cupping his long body around and over me. I curved into him, reaching up to wrap my hands around the back of his neck.

He pressed his lips to my forehead.

"You're hot," I said. "Feverish, even."

Beau shook his head in response. "Ask me more. Ask me more questions."

My mind blanked. Then I blurted out the first thing I could think of. "Did you have any pets?"

"No. I … found a stray dog once. Brought him home …" Beau's entire body shuddered and he didn't continue the story.

"You don't have to do this," I whispered. "I can go alone, find Ettie, and tell her what to avoid or where not to go. That sort of thing. Or convince her to hang with us for a few days. It's my vision, my responsibility."

Beau pressed a fierce kiss to my lips, darting his tongue into my mouth without a hint of his normal playfulness. I dug my fingers into the back of his neck, submitting to and participating in his passion. Our teeth knocked together and he pressed his hands to the back of my head to hold me steady. Then he broke the kiss the moment before it turned into something more, before our hands began roaming and removing clothing.

"You see me." Still cupping the back of my head, Beau brushed his thumbs across my cheeks. He didn't need to be holding me. I wasn't going anywhere. I was completely ensnared in his dark aquamarine gaze.

"No matter what else I see today ... or tomorrow ... or the next day," I said. "I see you. As you are."

"As I am with you." Beau sighed and dropped his hands. "Okay." He spoke to himself, then met my gaze again. "Okay?"

"Okay."

Beau opened the door to the RV. Then, climbing down the steps, he crossed the sidewalk onto the brown, untrimmed lawn of his childhood home.

I followed, instantly feeling as if the late afternoon sunlight was frying my skin. Though I was sweltering in jeans and a tank top, I was glad I didn't own any shorts. Not only did I hate the way they looked on me, but I also didn't need the nasty burn that much exposed skin would result in.

I squinted toward the house after I locked the Brave, shielding my already-covered eyes from the sun. I couldn't see any evidence that anyone was at home.

I wasn't sure what we were about to see, about to confront.

I wanted to pull Beau back inside the haven of the Brave and drive away. But I didn't.

Ada Harris was a piece of work. Except for her striking blue eyes, I couldn't see any bit of Beau in her long, bony face. Though with the heavy curtain in the living room pulled against the heat of the sun, I really couldn't see much of Beau's mother except for the cigarette dangling from the same fingers that loosely held a bottle of some dark-colored bourbon. Or so I gathered from the label.

The house hadn't been locked. The front door opened onto a hall that stretched back inside. The living room was on the immediate right. A closet that was missing its doors and crammed with broken sports equipment stood to the left. A quick glance put the kitchen behind the living room at the back right side of the house, with the bedrooms on the opposite left.

The place wasn't dirty, but it wasn't well tended either. A pile of car mechanic magazines took up the dull-grayish-blue carpeted area between a recliner and the wood-burning fireplace. Ada was sprawled length-wise on a faded floral-print couch on the far side of the room. Books were strewn across the coffee table along-side her — romance novels, to judge by the amount of skin tone on the covers.

Ada's almost-feverish gaze had locked on Beau the moment he stepped into the living room. She'd muted the TV.

She didn't even glance at me, which was okay. I was happy not being noticed.

Ada had one of those modern, Japanese-influenced aromatherapy diffusers misting on the white-painted mantel. Its sleek black exterior and mesh top looked out of place and expensive. I couldn't smell whatever essential oil it was burning … or melting, or whatever the thing did. The mist the diffuser created looked uncomfortably like the kind that filled my mind before and after I had a vision. I looked away before it could trigger me, though I had no idea whether that was even possible.

"Beau." Ada's voice was rough, as if she hadn't spoken in a few days. The long ash of her cigarette dropped onto the carpet between her and the leg of the coffee table. I eyed it, ready to leap into action if the carpet caught fire. It didn't. "Who's the girl?"

Ah. So she had noticed me.

"You aren't bringing her here for my blessing, are you?" Ada laughed harshly. "Ugly thing, isn't she? For my handsome Beau. Your neighborhood ladies won't be so free with their cash with her tagging at your heels."

Beau flexed his fingers, curling his hands into fists, then keeping them that way.

"Or maybe I'm wrong," Ada said, continuing her vitriol. "You've grown. Your bitches might like the manlier you, even if it comes with a pale-faced nothing of a wife."

"I'm looking for Ettie," Beau said, grinding the words between his teeth.

Ada rolled up into a sitting position on the couch. Her oily dark hair tumbled around her gaunt face as she leaned forward to snub the cigarette out in an ashtray alongside two other butts. Either she didn't actually smoke much or she emptied the tray frequently. Hunched over her knees, she tilted her head up to look at Beau, then tilted it farther back to take a swig from her bottle.

Beau made a pained, disgusted noise that sounded as if it had torn from his chest involuntarily. I squeezed my eyes shut at the sound, but I didn't falter any further in front of his terrible excuse for a mother.

"Come for Claudette, have you, Beau?" Ada laughed again. The noise was so grating I actually had to stop myself from trying to brush it away from my ears. "Going to ride her success now?"

Beau sighed, then scrubbed his hand across his face. He half-turned to include me in the conversation. "Ada, this is Rochelle. If you weren't completely blitzed, you'd smell her magic."

"I'd have to be at least two more bottles deep not to smell the stink of a witch."

"She's an oracle."

Ada looked at me then, narrowing her eyes as if that would help her see me better.

I didn't smile. I didn't offer any pleasantries. But I did remove my sunglasses, so I could meet her stare without wavering.

Shapeshifters didn't hold each other's gazes. To do so was a challenge, though not necessarily one of aggression. But I wasn't a shapeshifter, so I didn't play by their rules.

One of these days, that was going to get me seriously injured.

But today, it won me Ada's fear.

Beau's so-called mother recoiled back from me. Her lips pulled away from her teeth in a terrible grimace as her shoulders hit the back of the couch.

Yeah, my pale gray eyes were freaky. And paired with the declaration of my magical prowess, they were even otherworldly. Though obviously, that was only if magic scared you, as it did Ada. According to Beau, she never transformed if she could help it.

"What … what …" Ada stuttered.

"Where is Ettie?" Beau repeated.

"School," Ada spat. Her fear slowly melted into anger.

Yeah, we were really ruining her afternoon buzz. Wait until she heard our news about the impending death of her daughter. Though I wouldn't put it past her to not give a shit.

"When was the last time you spoke with her?"

"A couple of hours ago. She checks in every couple of days. Like a good child should."

"Still okay," Beau murmured to me.

Ada's mounting anger dissolved into confusion. "What do you mean, 'still okay'?"

"I'm taking care of it," Beau said. "What school? Did she get into college?"

Ada snorted. "College. Keep up, Beau. She's at Ole Miss."

"Which campus?"

"Oxford."

Beau turned his back on his mother, completely dismissing her. "University of Mississippi. We need to go to Oxford. It's about an hour and a half from here."

"What is she doing there now?" I asked. "Summer classes? Will she still be on campus by the time we get there?"

Beau glanced back at his mother, who folded her arms and glowered at us. "She's taking evening classes through the summer for extra credit," Ada spat. "On Tuesdays she has elementary organic chemistry." She raised her chin and her voice. "She graduated top of her year and got a private science scholarship."

"Yeah, good for her," Beau said. "Maybe it'll get her out of this hell someday."

We'd barely moved into the living room, so it took us only two steps to get back to the front door.

"At least she isn't some whore!" Ada screamed after us. "With a juvie record as long as my arm!"

Beau faltered, turning back. I threaded my fingers through his and tugged his arm toward the open door. For a moment, I thought he might not follow me. I wasn't going to be able to drag him.

But then he stopped resisting me. Instead, tucking me behind him, he jogged down the gray-painted, peeling concrete steps to the front walk.

"Well, look what the cat dragged in."

A man snickered, drawing my attention over Beau's shoulder to the driveway. A short, stocky guy — dressed in a white wifebeater replete with beer and ketchup stains — slammed the driver's-side door shut on an old Mustang parked in the driveway.

The guy was balding, or about to be. His thin, dark-blond hair covered the top of his head so sparsely that the next breeze was liable to blow it off. His prison tats looked seriously cheap and cheesy.

"Just can't stay away? Can you?" The guy snickered again, glancing over his shoulder at the Brave as he sauntered across the dead lawn to place himself on the front path between the RV and us.

I hadn't ever heard a man snicker like that. It was seriously creepy.

"What do you want? Money? Tricks ain't paying like they used to? Or did Byron send you?"

"No," Beau spat.

"Heard sweet Cy was in the green, did you?"

"Again, no."

So this was Cy. Ettie's dad. Beau's stepdad. I had assumed he was the reason Beau didn't want to come back to Southaven, but after meeting Ada, I'd reconsidered that.

"No?" Cy echoed mockingly. "Who's the slag?" He jutted his chin in my direction.

I was exceedingly aware that the door to the house was still open behind me, only a quick dash up the stairs away. Apparently, Beau's training was having an effect. Though with Ada in the living room, I wasn't sure that was the best escape route.

Beau stepped threateningly toward his stepfather. Cy's smile widened in response. The guy was seriously stupid or insane. Only a moron goaded a shifter like —

Cy was close enough to me now that I could see his eyes. They were beyond bloodshot. The inside edge of his eyelids were a step away from full-on bleeding.

I threw my weight forward on my toes, clapping my hand to Beau's shoulder as a warning.

"Beau," I whispered.

"I see," Beau said, stepping back to me. "I smell."

Cy's smile turned rabid.

"Crystal meth?"

"Probably. Plus he's just an inbred asshole."

Cy laughed at the insult, then flexed his hands.

"Let's go," I whispered.

Beau nodded. Never taking his gaze off Cy, he reached around and tucked me against his right side — as far away as he could keep me from Cy while crossing to the Brave.

Two short strides along the well-worn concrete path brought us within grappling distance of Beau's stepdad. Cy didn't move to the side.

"But you just got here," Cy said. His voice was now high and whiney, mocking but laced with a creepy needi-ness. "Come on, pretty boy Beau. Stay. Be useful."

"I'm not interested in your line of work."

Cy snickered again. The hair stood up on the back of my neck. There was something seriously wrong with the guy, beyond the rampant meth use. I'd known addicts who were good, kind people just looking for a way to escape the shit of their lives. I'd chosen the Brave instead of drugs. Habitual meth user or not, Cy was not a typ-ical addict.

"Listen, man," Beau said, attempting his soothing tone. "We're just here to see Ettie. She's in trouble. We're going to help her."

Cy narrowed his eyes, all traces of the creepy smile and snicker suddenly wiped from his face. That wasn't a good sign.

Unfortunately, Beau missed it. He was probably just desperate to get me out of the situation, but instead of stepping away from Cy, he stepped in and past him.

Cy pivoted, seemingly to let us by.

Beau took another step.

Cy closed the space behind us, grabbed my free arm, and yanked me away from Beau. He was slyer than I thought, going for me — the weaker link — rather than his shapeshifter stepson.

I attempted to spin away, to disrupt Cy's footing, and slip out of his grasp as Beau had taught me. But I wasn't remotely fast enough.

Pain exploded in my right shoulder as Cy twisted me toward him. I stumbled off the paved front path, twist-ing my ankle on the edge of the concrete and half-falling onto the grass.

After letting me go so I didn't get ripped in half, Beau spun, slamming a punch into his stepdad's gut.

Cy didn't even grunt. He took the blow while yanking me up between him and Beau, until my right arm was twisted behind me and his other arm fell across my throat in a chokehold.

Beau faltered. His fists were raised and trained on Cy, but even as tiny as I was, I was a pretty effective shield.

Now I just had to figure out what kind of Adept took a punch from a shapeshifter tiger and didn't even need to shake it off.

Cy snickered. Inbred asshole, indeed.

"Let's try that conversation again," Cy said. "I have use for someone of your ... attributes, Beau. Come work for me and I won't tear your bitch's head off."

"I don't do that sort of thing anymore, Cy." Beau was scared, but trying to hide it.

I never wanted him to hurt in any way connected to me. Yet here we were.

"It ain't like that now," Cy said, cajoling.

"Man, you're a moron," I said, reaching up to wrap my free left hand around Cy's bare forearm. My arm-sleeve tattoos were a dark, sleek contrast to his shoddy prison tats. "Not only should you learn to shower, because you reek. But you're dumb enough to grab and hold a person whose magic you don't even know."

Cy cinched his forearm tighter around my neck, momentarily cutting off my ability to insult him further. "Oh, yeah, slit? You think a little itty bitty something like you has anything that can hurt me?"

Black dots swam before my eyes. Blinking them away, I focused on the fear in Beau's face and how angry that made me.

"Didn't Beau tell you about me?" Cy whispered, his scummy spittle misting over my ear and neck. "I don't feel physical pain."

"Yeah?" I croaked out. "I'm not that kind of Adept."

I'd never been able to practice what I was about to attempt during my self-defense training sessions with Beau, because apparently I needed to be extremely angry to wield my magic offensively. While Cy had been yammering, I focused on the feeling I got when my oracle magic flooded through my left arm and hand before I needed to sketch. "Feel this, asshole."

Heat seared between my palm and Cy's forearm. Mist exploded in my mind's eye.

I caught a glimpse of something ... slats of light across white-painted concrete walls ... an overturned table, glass and blood littering a gray concrete floor ...

And Cy bleeding from every orifice in his head —

Behind me, he screamed. His hold loosened on my neck. He stumbled away.

Beau yanked me forward. Still sightless, I tripped, tumbling onto my hands and knees in the grass.

Instinctively, I cupped my left hand around my raw diamond. Its magic soothed my tingling palm and the oracle mist faded from my mind. I pivoted on my knees to look past Beau, who was now standing between me and his stepdad.

Cy was still clutching his head and screaming.

"What the hell did you show him?" Beau asked, turning to help me to my feet.

"Something bloody." I reached for his hand.

Cy darted toward us. He was moving way too quickly for someone whose only talent was feeling no pain.

I shouted, "Beau!"

Cy crashed into Beau, who rolled to the left instead of attempting to block or counter his tackle. Probably in order to not crush me underneath them. Beau tumbled across the lawn away from me.

Cy, barely on his feet himself, went after Beau, kicking him over and over again in the chest and head. He was salivating and shrieking incomprehensible obscenities.

Beau curled into a fetal position to protect himself as I scrambled to my feet.

A neighbor across the street glanced out her front door. Then, apparently completely pissed and totally unconcerned, she ducked back inside with a slam. What the fuck?

Cy stumbled a few steps away from Beau. His breathing was ragged.

I ran toward them, tripping over the other side of the front walk as I crossed it. My chin smacked into the dead lawn, but I didn't feel it as I lifted my upper body off the ground, trying to get my feet underneath me again.

Cy did an odd skip, jumped into the air, and slammed his steel-shanked boot down onto Beau's ankle.

Something nasty snapped.

Beau screamed.

I threw myself between them, sprawling across Beau but facing up and glaring at Cy.

He stepped back from me, trying to get his breathing under control. Blood dripped from the corner of his eye, but as far as I'd seen, Beau hadn't laid a hand on him.

I sneered at him. "Took the juice out of your buzz, did I?" I raised my hands before me. "Let's go another round." Yeah, I was a great poker player. Or I would be if I knew how to play.

Beau tugged me back toward him, attempting to clear me to the side but not wanting to simply toss me there. I could hear him panting in pain, but I had to keep my focus on Cy.

I evaded his grasp, rolling forward into a crouch so I could dig my toes in and spring forward if necessary.

"I'm tired of this shit with you, Beau," Cy said. "My job offer is legit. You don't want to be messing with me anymore. For your own safety."

Beau laughed, a hacking, nasty noise that made me shudder.

Cy pulled out a gun that had been tucked underneath his wifebeater in the small of his back. He wasn't wearing a belt.

"Real?" I whispered to Beau.

"Real."

Cy's silver handgun, a snub-nosed six-shot model, stared me straight in the face.

Like in the movies.

Not a vision. Not a hallucination. Not the time to be observing and gathering clues.

I froze.

Beau froze.

"You're just going to shoot me here? On your front lawn?" I asked, completely incredulous when I should have been utterly terrified. "With your neighbors watching?"

Cy grinned. "How many reports do you think the police have on you, Beau? How many complaints? And that last time? I filed a restraining order. I guess you didn't get the notice, being out of state and all."

"What does that mean? That he can just kill us?" I asked Beau without turning away from Cy.

"Depends on what the neighbors see," Beau answered. "And what they're willing to testify to."

"After we're already dead, you mean."

A car door slammed nearby, then someone crossed the street. Their footfalls crunched on dry grass as they stepped off the sidewalk.

Cy and I continued to stare at each other. The gun leveled at my face still didn't seem real to me. Stupid, eh? Probably. But after years of suffering what I thought were debilitating hallucinations, maybe it just took more than threats to rattle me.

"Interrupting a cozy family reunion, am I?" Kandy drawled from the direction of the sidewalk.

"None of your business, bitch," Cy snapped without looking at the green-haired werewolf.

I straightened, raising my eye level closer to that of Cy's. I'd lost my sunglasses in the tussle. Even though he kept the gun steady, he flinched. It was just a twitch of his face, but I saw it.

Kandy glanced between Cy and me. Then she laughed. A low, rumbling, humorless sound. "But it is my business, asshole. We're pack."

Cy glanced over at her for the first time.

Kandy smiled at him. Or, rather, she bared her teeth.

"Werewolf," Cy snarled.

"Bing, bing! The idiot gets it in one." Kandy lifted her arms, sunbursts glinting off the gold cuffs on her wrists. Two-inch wolf claws grew out from the tips of her fingers. "I hear the oracle has a nasty touch, but she's a sweetheart in the depth of it all. How about you and I tangle? Adult to adult."

"Like you can hurt me, gash."

"He's got some kind of invulnerability," I said. "He doesn't feel pain."

"And he's fast. Too fast," Beau said. "And unusually strong. Caught me by surprise."

"Beating you down is old news, Beaumont," Cy said. "But now I know how to keep you there." He moved the gun a few inches closer to my face.

"It's the meth," I offered, ignoring the shit spewing out of Beau's stepdad's mouth.

Kandy tilted her head, regarding Cy like he was a bug. "That's okay with me. I was never a big fan of simply causing pain."

"You wouldn't talk such tough shit if you knew what I was into," Cy sneered.

Beau snorted.

"I bet I can rip your head off before you blink," Kandy said, super casual while discussing murdering Cy to his face. "What do you think, Beau?"

We all stared at Cy.

He widened his eyes, attempting to not blink. Consciously or subconsciously.

"Yeah," Beau drawled. "You're faster than him. Drugs or no drugs."

"But where would we hide the body?" I asked.

No one answered me. Which was fine, because it was a weird, creepy question anyway.

"Let's see you try it with a couple of bullets in you." Cy swung the gun halfway toward Kandy, then checked himself and trained it back on me.

I understood suddenly that I had seriously weirded him out if he perceived me as the bigger threat. It was probably a bad sign how that pleased me on such a visceral level.

Kandy's voice was a low growl. "I'm an enforcer of the West Coast North American Pack, bearer of the cuffs of might that were gifted to me by one of the nine most powerful beings in the world. You think bullets can slow me down?"

Cy eyed Kandy, then looked at the gold cuffs. Sunlight danced across the diamonds and the inscriptions decorating the wide bracelets. His face stretched into a pained, vicious grimace. He lowered the gun. "Fuck you," Cy snarled. "Get off my fucking lawn."

He turned and walked toward the house.

"Move, Rochelle," Kandy said brusquely.

I shifted out of her way. Making sure to face the house, she hunkered down by Beau's broken ankle and prodded it.

He winced. "It's not so bad."

"Right," Kandy grunted. Then she placed one hand on Beau's foot and the other on his lower leg. Before I could stop her — or even figure out what she was doing — she twisted Beau's ankle abruptly.

Beau whelped, but he held back the scream I was sure he needed to voice.

"What the hell?" I cried.

"You a doctor now, oracle?" Sarcasm laced Kandy's pissy tone.

"Are you?"

"Physiotherapist. Plus I've been dealing with shape-shifters since the day I was born."

Well, that effectively shut me up. I gnashed my teeth together and paced, glancing up at the house. I couldn't see where Cy had gone, so he wasn't in the living room. But I was certain the confrontation wasn't over.

Beau tried to catch my eye and smile, but I shook my head at him. I needed my anger if I was going to get through this without melting down. I'd just had a gun, along with a wallop of background information about Beau, metaphorically shoved down my throat.

Kandy prodded Beau's ankle and foot again.

"Bearer of the cuffs of might?" he asked teasingly.

The werewolf snorted. "The guy's a moron. I could make up shit all day and he'd eat it. Let's go. I'll get you into the RV."

"It's okay for him to walk?" I asked.

"Not yet, but I can't exactly carry him out in the open."

"Cy was just waving a gun around."

Kandy shrugged. "Yeah, that's just regular human garbage. Me carrying Beau would make a bigger splash on YouTube. Then we'd be in real trouble." She grabbed one of Beau's arms. "Get on his other side, oracle. I'll do the lifting, but you can make a show of it. Don't put any pressure on your ankle, kitten."

I hunkered down to get Beau's arm across my shoulder, but Kandy was already lifting him up. I tried to pretend I was holding weight that I actually wasn't as we shuffled toward the door of the RV.

"That was a quick trip to New Orleans," Beau said.

"Francois was out of town. His beta met me in Jackson. All is not well with the Gulf Coast North American Pack. They're investigating the deaths of two of their younger wolves, possible drug overdoses. Which just doesn't happen. I'm a complication. They want me gone, and quickly."

Beau grunted. "Happy to oblige."

We reached the door to the Brave, then awkwardly dragged Beau up the steps. He was suffering in silence, but it was obvious we were causing him more pain in the process.

Once inside, Kandy took over. She stuffed Beau in the far corner of the dinette, then lifted his injured leg at an angle that let him rest his calf on the edge of the opposite bench. I had to be careful not to bump his foot when passing through.

"Painkillers?" I asked Kandy as I opened the door of the bathroom.

The werewolf shook her head. "He'd have to down the bottle to make a difference, even if that was enough. We'll hit the nearest gas station for ice." She glanced at Beau.

"Two rights, three lefts," he said wearily.

Kandy nodded, crossing to the door. "Rochelle, you follow me." She took a step down out of the Brave, but then paused. "And Beau?"

"Yeah?"

"That wasn't meth."

Beau swallowed, closed his eyes, and rested his head against the wall. "Yeah, I could smell it."

Kandy nodded curtly, not at all happy. She shut the door to the Brave behind her. I locked it, then stepped back to keep an eye on the house through the window over the dinette while Kandy darted across the street to her SUV.

"I'm so sorry," Beau murmured.

"There's nothing to be sorry about."

"Rochelle …"

"No, Beau. I dragged you here. I feel like a complete asshole for bringing you back."

He shook his head. "I left Ettie here. With them. I took off the second after I graduated. I barely made it out of school or out of town. You heard Ada. Even now any attention from the police would be … extra shitty. That's who I am."

"Beau …"

Outside, the SUV started up. I glanced out the tiny window over the sink, tracking Kandy as she executed a U-turn, then pulled forward to idle in front of the Brave.

"Go," Beau said. "I just need a nap. Fuck them anyway. We get Ettie and we go. End of sob story."

I climbed into the driver's seat, buckled in, and started the Brave. "Beau?"

"Yeah?"

"What could you smell? If not meth?"

I pulled away from the curb, following Kandy's SUV down the street. Beau didn't answer until a block later.

"My mother. He smelled like my mother's magic."

"What do you mean? Like they'd been in contact? That makes sense doesn't it?"

"No, not like that. I don't know. It was like he was sweating my mother's magic. I doubt Kandy could pick it up the same way, because she doesn't know Ada. But that's what it smelled like to me."

"Is that ... how could that be possible?"

"I don't know."

Carefully navigating the tightly parked streets to the gas station, I replayed pieces of the conversation with Cy. I was trying to tie something he'd said, or anything he'd done, to my vision of Ettie lying dead on the sun-softened blacktop.

"Beau?"

"Yeah?"

"Who's Byron?"

He didn't answer. I couldn't look back at him and drive, so I elaborated. "Cy asked if Byron had sent you."

"I know."

I stole a glance over my shoulder as I rolled to a stop at a corner. Beau's head was tilted back and his eyes were closed. I felt bad for poking at him when he was in pain.

"Just some asshole drug dealer who we're going to stay as far as fuck away from as possible," he said. "If Cy is on the outs with him, then that's why Ettie's in trouble. Asshole probably owes Byron money. He's probably using what he's supposed to be protecting."

"Meth? Or whatever you smelled?"

"Yeah ..."

Beau didn't sound so sure, but I let the conversation drop. We weren't there to rip open old wounds. I wanted to be gone even quicker than we'd arrived.

CHAPTER SIX

"Cy is a piece of shit. Too stupid to even deal," Beau said. "His limited magic makes him valuable to the local dealer as a meathead. Nothing else."

"That didn't look like nothing," Kandy said. "And it didn't smell like nothing either." She placed an entire bag of gas station ice on Beau's leg, having bought three bags in the time it took me to park in the empty lot beside the station.

"It has nothing to do with why we're here," Beau said.

"Listen. I'm all for skipping the my-stepdad-is-a-total-asshole preamble. Been there, done that," the werewolf said. "So why don't you just jump to the part where you confess what shit you're into so I can figure out why the hell I'm here."

"Beau hasn't even been in the state for four years," I said.

Kandy turned her glare on me. I folded my arms, jutted my chin out at her, and leaned back against the laminate counter. She wasn't going to intimidate me in my own home.

The werewolf pulled her phone out of her back pocket and scrolled back through her text messages. "So you know what happens when you throw a few bucks the way of an Adept who has a way with technology?"

"What?" I said snottily, though I was exceedingly aware that I was treading a fine line of ignorance. "She can find shit on people like any regular person with Google can?"

Kandy snorted. "She can find a whole lot of shit about an Ada and a Cy Harris, even though all she had was an address to work with, but Beau Jamison doesn't come up with anything at all. Not. One. Thing."

She turned her glare back to Beau.

He sighed. "But Beaumont Harris has a bunch of priors, no convictions. All under the age of eighteen. I reverted to my birth name, for obvious reasons."

"So?" I asked.

"So?" Kandy echoed in disbelief.

"Yeah, so what? You think Beau wants to be here? Hell, I don't even want to be here, but we're here, aren't we?" I yanked my sketchbook out of my satchel. "You want to know why? You want to see why? It's right here in black and white."

"Whoa, whoa, oracle," Kandy said, throwing her hands up in mock-surrender. "We're having a conversation, not a cage match. I'm asking questions because I need to know what I'm protecting Beau from. I'm not accusing or condemning anyone."

I stared at her for a moment, then realizing I was still thrusting my sketchbook out between us, I tucked it back in my satchel. "Fine."

"Okay, fine."

"Cy mentioned a restraining order that I didn't know about," Beau said. "He could have been bluffing. I seriously doubt he went to court for anything permanent. The local police aren't going to be my biggest fans, but I'm not skipping bail or anything."

Kandy harrumphed, not wholly convinced, but then turned her attention to whatever food she could gather in the Brave's kitchen.

Beau eyed me behind her back, then offered me a pleased grin. I narrowed my eyes at him. His grin widened. Apparently, he liked it when I freaked out while defending him.

Kandy started throwing things on the table. A loaf of bread, a hunk of cheese, cold cuts.

I snorted as I gathered the food back onto the kitchen counter. "I'll make sandwiches."

"Finally," Kandy groused. "What were you waiting for?"

She hopped cleanly over Beau's propped-up leg and settled down on the bench seat opposite him.

I clicked the cutting board in over the sink, creating a perfect workstation for sandwich making. Then I crossed back to the fridge for condiments.

Beau reached for me as I passed. I brushed my fingertips against his in response.

Kandy was staring out the window into the parking lot, toward the pumps and the minimart beyond. I didn't think she cared about our PDA, but something was still seriously bothering her.

I'd spread mayo and mustard on the whole-wheat bread and was in the middle of thinly slicing tomato when Kandy finally broke the silence.

"Man, your parents are way worse than mine."

Beau started. He'd been dozing. "Thanks," he said dryly.

"Mine just didn't give a shit, you know? Don't give a shit."

"Right."

"Where do we go from here?"

"To Ettie. Whatever is going on with Cy has nothing to do with warning Ettie."

"Sure ..." Kandy trailed off. "I just don't think that was it."

"Was what?" I slid a plate piled with diagonally cut sandwiches into the middle of the table, then tore three pieces of paper towel off the roll to use as napkins.

"The far seer didn't send me here to stop you from getting a few extra bumps and bruises." Kandy was still looking out the window, but now she was playing with the cuff on her right wrist, twisting it around and around.

I poured milk for everyone. Beau eyed the sandwiches, then looked at Kandy expectantly.

She waved her hand toward the sandwiches. "Eat. Eat."

He smiled at her pleasantly, still waiting.

She snarled, grabbed half a sandwich, and bit into it. "I'm not your alpha." Her words were garbled around a mouth full of food.

I sighed and slid into the tiny wedge of seat beside Beau, careful to not jostle his leg. Shapeshifter games.

Beau twined his fingers through mine and reached for half a sandwich with his other hand. I'd made a veggie sandwich for myself, devoting the remainder of the bread to turkey sandwiches for Kandy and Beau. I could handle touching cold cuts.

"So something else is coming," Kandy said.

"Okay," Beau said. "Maybe it is Cy."

Kandy shrugged. "He's nothing. He's not the threat."

"Don't know, then. Maybe that was it. Maybe Cy would have shot us."

"In front of your mother?" Kandy asked.

"What would she care?"

"She was at the window, clutching the curtains."

Beau eyed Kandy uncertainly. "Over Cy, maybe."

"Maybe."

Kandy looked back out the window. I knew we'd get kicked out of the gas station parking lot sooner than later, even if we filled up the RV and the SUV, so I nudged the plate of sandwiches toward Beau. He squeezed my hand, then ate another two halves in rapid succession.

"So we find Ettie." Kandy finally turned her attention away from the window to grab another sandwich.

"Oxford's only an hour and a half away," Beau said.

"It'll be after six by the time we get there," I said. "And we didn't get an address or phone number."

Kandy snorted derisively. Snapping up two more sandwiches, she climbed out of the dinette over Beau's leg.

"What?" I asked.

"We'll track her," Beau explained. "Get on campus, then track her from there."

"Don't you need a … like an article of clothing?"

"I know what she smells like," Beau said.

"And I know what Beau smells like," Kandy said. "And her dad is really delightful. I know what that pig smells like as well." She left without further comment, shutting the door behind her and sauntering toward the gas station's minimart.

I looked at Beau. "Families smell alike?"

"Shared blood smells similar," Beau said. "Usually. I can't track like a wolf can, though. I wouldn't be able to find just anyone, other than you and Ettie, maybe. Not by scent alone."

I stood to clear the table. "What was with all the staring out the window? Contemplation doesn't seem like a werewolf trait."

Beau laughed. "She was watching for Cy. The Brave kind of stands out. Wolves prefer to run in a pack. Makes them harder to pick out and pick off."

"But cats hunt solo."

"Most of the time." Beau smiled at me.

I grinned back at him over my shoulder, rinsing the milk glasses and placing them upside down in the rack to dry.

Kandy banged on the front hood of the RV as she crossed back to the SUV parked beside us, startling me. I peered out the windshield, seeing the werewolf now carrying a bag of Doritos and a handful of pepperoni. I shook my head, pulled a bag of Oreos out of the upper cupboard, and dropped it in Beau's lap. He grabbed for me at arm's-length reach, wincing in pain as he did so.

"Rochelle? We okay?"

I stepped back to brush my hand over his closely clipped hair, then pressed a kiss to his forehead. "We're always okay. Except you need to sleep. Food and sleep kick-start healing, right? Should I help you back to the bed?"

"Nah, here is good." He let go of me, though not until after he gave my ass an appreciative squeeze.

I laughed. "Later."

"Promise."

"The vow is implied. Always."

"Ah, good." He leaned his head back and closed his eyes.

I climbed into the driver's seat, then once again followed Kandy's SUV onto the main road and toward the highway.

Beau's family had said a shitload of shit about him. By his reaction and his mini confession to Kandy, I gathered that a bunch of it was true. That made me livid.

Not at Beau, though — who I imagined had done what he needed to do to survive — but at his supposed family.

Yeah, I didn't see any Thanksgiving or Christmas family dinners in our future. And honestly, I was more relieved than mournful about that. I wanted Beau away from these poisonous people ASAP. I just hoped Ettie wasn't such a shithead.

"That's her," I said, just seconds after I laid eyes on the two women at the end of the gray-carpeted corridor.

The two twenty-somethings — a blond and a brunette — were standing together in hushed conversation in what appeared to be a study nook. Not that I knew anything about universities, but a couch and some chairs off to the side of a hallway in the science building was pretty obviously a student lounge area of some sort. The lack of snacks or a TV seemed to put it firmly in the 'study' category.

About fifteen or so students milled around, chatting or texting, between us and the two women at the end of the hall. Apparently, an evening session of elementary organic chemistry — if Ada had any idea what she was talking about — had just let out. I'd tried googling the university's schedule but hadn't been able to track down the location of the lecture while driving. Further investigation had been thwarted by Kandy, who preferred 'quick and dirty' tracking, which apparently consisted of wandering through high-traffic areas while inappropriately sniffing people, seating areas, and handrails.

"That's her?" Kandy asked.

"That's her," I said.

Kandy focused her gaze on the two women as we approached. Ettie was wearing a white collared T-shirt and blue cotton skirt. Her shoulder-length blond hair was slightly wavy, and pulled back from her face with a headband that matched her skirt. The other girl, a brunette with her long hair pulled back in a braided bun, was wearing shredded gray jeans paired with a red and orange tie-dyed tank top.

"I thought you said she's a blond?"

"She is blond. Dyed, but blond."

"But the blond's a dud. A normal."

Beau shifted his shoulders uncomfortably. "Yeah."

"The brunette's the witch," Kandy said. "Well, like one-quarter witch."

Ettie was shaking her head emphatically, though she was still smiling at the brunette. The quarter-witch — according to Kandy — shifted her feet, looking like she was ready to start begging over whatever they were discussing.

"But …" I said. "Ettie's not an Adept?"

"Not a drop," Kandy murmured.

I glanced over at Beau.

He looked chagrined. "Talking about it always equaled a beat down from Cy. But yeah, I thought she was just a late bloomer. But, ah …" He shrugged, turning his attention to his sister down the hall. "Apparently, she isn't."

Ettie pulled her phone out of the front pocket of a light-blue backpack, which was emblazoned with the university's red, white, and blue 'Ole Miss' logo. She started texting.

"But the visions," I muttered underneath my breath, knowing that Kandy and Beau could still hear me. "The visions are always about Adepts."

"Not this time, apparently," Kandy said. "Don't you love it when magic gets all convoluted and obscure?"

The green-haired werewolf grinned at me, as if she wasn't being sarcastic. Her smile widened as I stared at her, dumbfounded.

"No," I said. "No one likes that."

Kandy barked out a laugh. "And here I was getting bored."

All the university buildings we'd entered while tracking Ettie appeared to be constructed as blocks of corridors running in a perimeter around and through classrooms and lecture halls. The individually placed buildings were sprawled across and surrounded by what seemed to be miles of manicured green space and a complex network of paved roads. We'd parked the Brave and the SUV in one of the large parking lots situated on the outskirts of the campus, passing by at least two massive sports complexes as we'd driven in.

The science building where we eventually tracked Ettie down — Coulter Hall — looked much the same as the other buildings. Its exterior was constructed out of red brick, though, and it didn't have as many windows as some of the newer parts of the campus.

There weren't a ton of students on campus. I imagined that was because it was summer break and early evening. Any high school acquaintances that I kept vaguely in touch with who'd made it into university had to take the summers off to pay for next year's tuition. And university in the States was even more expensive than it was in Canada, at least as far as I'd ever heard.

"Ettie," Beau called out. We were only a dozen steps away now.

Ettie flinched. Then with the same smile still plastered to her face, she glanced over to see the three of us advancing down the corridor toward her.

I caught the moment she recognized her brother. It took her longer than I thought it would. Her fake smile didn't change.

"See you later then, Sara." Ettie spoke to her friend without looking at her. Her accent was a thicker version of Beau's sweet Southern tone, but not the more lyrical for it.

Sara bobbed her head, glanced at us, and spun on the spot to take off down a perpendicular corridor.

Ettie tucked her phone back into her backpack. "Hey, Beau."

We stopped a few feet away, then stood there awkwardly. Though Ettie barely glanced at me, she eyed Kandy carefully. Resisting the urge to pull my sketchbook out of my satchel and see how accurately I'd captured her likeness, I noticed that she'd opted for a plain gold lip stud rather than the magnolia one I'd seen in my vision.

"This here is Rochelle," Beau said, dipping his shoulder in my direction. "And Kandy."

Again, Ettie didn't even bother to look at me. "Claudette. Or as Beau calls me, Ettie." She reached out to shake Kandy's hand.

Kandy didn't accept it. Ettie curled her fingers into a fist, glanced at me a second time, then dropped her arm.

"Why are you here?" Any pretense of friendliness was gone from Ettie's tone. "I thought you weren't coming back."

"I wasn't." Beau spoke carefully. "Mom said you were —"

"Mom?" Ettie sneered, the expression suiting her much more than her previous smile had. I had a feeling that was the attitude she used around her family the most. I would have. "Mom said? She's 'mom' to you now?"

"She's your younger sister?" Kandy asked casually.

"By eighteen months."

"Then what gives her the right to talk to you like that?"

Beau sighed. "Maybe now isn't the time —"

"Now is always the time."

"So what that I'm younger than him?" Ettie was glancing back and forth between Kandy and Beau. "He lost any respect I had for him when he left. That's what gives me —"

Beau interrupted his sister, glancing at a few students who appeared to be settling into the study nook. "We need somewhere private to speak, Ettie. Then we're gone."

Ettie snapped her mouth shut, spun on her heel, and took off down the same adjacent hall Sara had used. We followed.

"There you go," Kandy said. "Much clearer."

Ettie glanced over her shoulder to glare at Kandy. The werewolf bared her teeth in one of her smiles that wasn't really a smile. Ettie quickly looked away.

As we followed Beau's sister deeper into the building, the air conditioning became oddly more oppressive than the heat. It was as if I was having sudden difficulty filling my lungs with the cool air. Or maybe I was drying out from the inside with each breath. Also, I was really cold in my tank top. The contrast between the extreme heat outside and the dry cold inside was screwing with my head, making me uncomfortable simply while walking down the hall.

I tried not to notice that Beau was limping.

Ettie led us through two sets of doors, one of which she unlocked, and into a lab. Though I'd never set one foot in a laboratory of any kind, the science equipment stacked on shelving along one of the walls was a dead giveaway. Long metal tables between the door and the heavily frosted high windows on the opposite wall were so clean they reflected the overhead fluorescent lights that Ettie flicked on as we entered.

Kandy, who was trailing behind us, glanced around the classroom and closed the door.

Ettie dumped her backpack on a table, then turned to Beau with her arms crossed and chin jutted out. "So?"

Beau cleared his throat but said nothing, eyeing Kandy as she walked the perimeter of the lab. She tested the door on the opposite corner. It was locked.

"Lecture hall," Ettie said in response. She turned her attention back to Beau. "I work here."

"Oh, yeah? First-year chemistry, huh? That's —"

"Second," Ettie interrupted. "Second year. Why are you here?"

"Are you sure it's her?" Kandy asked me. She was leaning against a table behind and to the right of Ettie, effectively blocking Beau's sister from bolting toward the lecture hall.

"It's her," I said, though I was seriously mystified as to why I would be having visions of anyone who wasn't magical.

"It's her what?" Ettie snapped.

"In my vision," I said. "You know, getting … hurt."

"Or, you know," Kandy said mockingly. "Getting dead."

Ettie snorted, then looked at Beau for confirmation.

"Rochelle's an oracle," Beau said. "She sees you."

Ettie paled. "What?"

"Yeah, I see you dead."

"When? How? What?"

"I don't know. Soon, by the weather and the color of your hair. You dye it, right?"

Ettie reached up to touch her hair, seemingly more concerned that I'd accused her of being a bottle blond than by her impending doom.

"Brilliant." Kandy laughed.

"There's no need to be nasty about it," Ettie said.

"No one is being nasty, Ettie," Beau said. "We're here to …"

"To help me?"

"Yes, ah … that's Rochelle's territory." Beau glanced sideways at me.

"Do you own a sundress with blue flowers on it?" I asked Ettie.

"Doesn't everybody?"

"Burn it. Dye your hair brown. Don't hang out in commercial areas, specifically around freshly paved asphalt —"

"I'm not dyeing my hair or burning my clothing because some crackpot says she sees my death," Ettie said, dismissing me completely and returning her attention to Beau.

"That's some really detailed and personal info for a supposed crackpot," Kandy sneered.

I reached into my bag. "I could show her my sketchbook …"

"No," Beau said, sharper than he'd ever addressed me before. "No one should see themselves like that."

My heart pinched. Beau and I never discussed the vision I'd had of him dying. A vision I'd only managed to thwart through pure ignorance. I'd never shown him, or anyone else, those sketches. But that didn't mean he hadn't looked for himself.

I left my sketchbook in my bag. I'd pull it out as a last resort. "Okay, I get it sounds crazy," I said to Ettie.

"I'm just figuring all this fate, destiny, and future stuff out myself.

"Great," Ettie said nastily.

I gritted my teeth. I just had to keep reminding myself that I had a function to perform and that with parents like hers I'd be an asshole too. "How about we … go camping somewhere cold. Hang out. Maybe the vision changes?"

"I can't just hang out with you," Ettie sneered, running her gaze up the length of me. It wasn't a long look.

Kandy laughed again. "A fate worse than death, hey?"

Ettie rounded on the werewolf. "And just who the hell are you? Beau always had a thing for older women —"

"That's enough!" Beau yelled.

A row of glass vials hanging in a metal test tube holder on the shelf beside us shattered. Ettie flinched, but I was pretty sure I was more shocked than she was. I hadn't known that Beau's voice could somehow break glass. Maybe that was some aspect of his shifter magic?

"You misunderstand the situation," Beau continued, his voice low and steady now. "I don't want to be here. I wouldn't be here, not without Rochelle's insistence that we try to help you somehow."

Ettie stared at me, her brow furrowed with confusion.

"I imagine Cy is in some shit. And that shit is going to bleed over onto you."

"But —"

"We're not staying any longer than we have to," Beau interrupted. "This is not a conversation. I would have preferred to call, but I didn't have your number. You'll stay quiet and listen."

Ettie closed her mouth, shook her head, then lifted her arms in a 'whatever' sort of gesture.

"Finally," Kandy grumbled. Pushing away from the table she'd been leaning against, she sauntered past Ettie toward the main doors. As she passed Beau's sister, she leaned in and took a long sniff of her neck.

"Oh, ick!"

Kandy ignored her, locking gazes with me. "A dud," she said. "Through and through."

"How dare you call me that— " Ettie began.

The door behind me slammed open.

Kandy stepped in front of me as I spun around. Then Beau stepped to her side. They formed a wall, giving me just a glimpse of the men funneling into the room.

"Normals," Kandy snarled. "Watch your strength. Guns."

The men formed a semicircle about ten feet in front of Beau and Kandy, deliberately standing out of arm's reach.

Beyond the broad shoulders blocking my view, I could see the two men nearest to us on either side. The newcomers were bruisers — previously broken noses, gold chains, hairy arms, and all. I was fairly certain there were five of them. They stood with their backs to the main entrance. If they had guns tucked underneath their loose shirts, I couldn't spot them.

Ettie stepped up beside Beau. "What is going on?"

"Claudette," some guy I couldn't see drawled. His accent was an odd mixture of lyrical vowels and sharp consonants. French influenced, maybe? "A lazy birdie said I'd find you here. And you, Beaumont. It's been too long … for my pocketbook, at least."

"I don't know where Cy is, Byron," Ettie said. She didn't sound remotely worried about the five guys who'd just occupied the lab as if it were a country they'd invaded.

Byron? I peeked around Beau's shoulder and caught a glimpse of a beefy guy with a faded scar across the right side of his too-tanned face. He was wearing a collared, short-sleeved silk print shirt loose over his beige shorts.

"What you know, Claudette, doesn't really factor into our visit," Byron said. "You'll come with us, and Cy will come get you. Ada will make him. You always were your mother's favorite." The men around Byron snickered.

Beau shifted his feet.

"Not yet," Kandy said. Her voice was a low growl.

Ignoring Beau and Kandy, Byron continued, "And then he'll have to answer a few questions about the new shit he's dealing behind my back to get through the door."

"She's not going anywhere with you," Beau spat.

"Why don't you introduce me to your friends, Beaumont?" Byron said. "Why hide the littlest one behind you? What's so important about her?"

"Maybe we're protecting you from her," Kandy said.

"I doubt that. But since I'm not inclined to stand around a university campus for longer than I have to, why don't we move this chat somewhere more ... amenable to me."

The guy closest to Ettie grabbed her arm. She shrieked, more affronted than injured.

Beau reached over and broke the grabby guy's hairy wrist.

"Fuck!" the guy screamed, definitely in pain. He let go of Ettie and backed away from Beau.

Someone coughed ...

No, my painfully slow brain informed me ... that was what the bark of a silenced gun sounded like.

Before I could react, Beau was on the floor before me and Kandy was standing in his place.

The werewolf was holding Byron's gun aloft, standing nose to nose with him.

Beau rolled to his feet but stayed hunkered down. He was assessing the situation.

Kandy had just saved his life.

My limbs felt heavy, sluggish. As if I were mired in a large tub of nasty processed cheese. Weapons were being drawn, bad guys were shifting around me, and I couldn't move.

That was the moment Chi Wen had seen.

That was the moment I'd almost lost Beau.

"Nice dog bite," Kandy sneered, nodding toward Byron's scar. "Bet I can do better."

Then she crushed his gun as if it were made out of brittle candy.

With his free hand, Byron reached underneath his loose silk shirt and pulled a stun gun out from a body harness. He wore two. He jammed the electric weapon into Kandy's gut. She snarled and broke his arm.

He screamed, even as he somehow managed to hit her with the stun gun's shock again.

Beau picked me up, threw me over his shoulder, and ran for the locked lecture hall door.

"Stop," Ettie screamed from behind him, but she wasn't talking to her brother. She threw herself on the guy with the broken wrist who'd swung his gun to follow Beau's movement.

Well, points for Ettie.

The other three assholes mobbed Kandy alongside Byron, slamming her with their stun guns and practically frying her with electricity. She didn't go down, but she wasn't in control of all her limbs anymore.

"Beau, no!" I cried. "Kandy!"

Beau smashed through the door, stumbling into a huge auditorium. A hundred or more metal-framed gray vinyl seats rose up before us.

"Meth ragers!" someone yelled from the lab.

"Don't kill them!" Ettie screamed.

Beau dropped me to my feet.

"Beau!"

"Run, Rochelle," he said. "You promised." Already turning back into the lab, he glanced back at me, his eyes blazing green with his shapeshifter magic. "You promised."

I nodded. Then, not wanting to waste time thinking about it, I spun left toward the stage area, away from what I assumed were the entrance doors. I went for the windows, not wanting to get caught in the maze of hallways.

Furniture splintered and glass shattered behind me as I snagged a wooden chair from behind a brown folding table. Once I cleared the lectern, I flung the heavy chair through the far windows, which appeared to overlook some trees growing in the green space between the buildings. The safety glass of the middle window shattered. The chair dropped over the exposed ledge.

Running over the escape scenarios Beau had drilled into me for eighteen months until they were just a jumble in my head to block out the grunts and groans emanating from the lab, I grabbed the ledge, scrambling to find a solid grip among the pebbles of glass littered there.

I flung my leg over the window frame. It was a high drop to the grass below. Well, for me at least.

A man screamed in pain behind me. Not Beau. I couldn't help but smirk nastily at the sound. If it wasn't for the stun guns and protecting Ettie and me, Beau and Kandy would have cleared the lab in two minutes.

I lowered my body over the edge. My satchel got caught up on the ledge above me. I tugged at the strap until the bag fell, whacking me painfully on the hip. Thankfully nothing appeared to fall out. I hung there for a moment, scraping my palms on the red brick of the exterior ledge. Then I dropped to the ground before I could talk myself out of it.

I lay there, stunned on the well-watered green grass, and staring up at the broken window ten or twelve feet above me. The wooden chair was on the ground beside me, but even if I dragged it underneath the window, it wouldn't raise me high enough to climb back into the lecture hall.

Muffled grunting filtered down to me, shot through with pain.

Then a ferocious snarling growl.

Then nothing.

"Where's the little bit?" Byron asked, sounding as if he was moving into the lecture hall. I still couldn't place his accent. It was Southern, but definitely not the same as Beau's and Ettie's.

I rolled over onto my stomach, then pulled myself to my hands and knees. I was fairly certain I hadn't hurt anything in the fall, but I didn't feel like testing that notion right at this moment.

Footfalls crunched through glass on the other side of the window. "Hey!" someone shouted.

I wasn't going to have much of a choice.

So I ran.

I ran.

It was sweltering. And, though the sun was dipping in the sky, it was not yet setting.

I wanted to turn back, but I didn't.

I ran away, as I'd promised so many times in so many training sessions over the past year and a half. I should never have persuaded Beau to go home. I should have been happy with a phoned-in warning ... if only we could have found a working number. Obviously, if we'd tried harder, we could have found a working number. Everyone was online these days ...

But I hadn't been happy with the idea of a phone call. Had I been so convinced of my own abilities that despite Chi Wen's warnings to observe and interpret — to not get involved — I had pushed Beau until he'd relented?

Had my arrogance and my childish need to claim my magic gotten Beau mentally screwed by his mother, beaten by his stepfather, and almost shot?

Oh, God. That had been the moment Beau was supposed to die. The moment Chi Wen had seen ... and thwarted.

If nothing else, that was crystal clear. The far seer had just manipulated the future he'd seen. He'd just saved Beau's life via Kandy.

Though I was clear on one other thing. I was running away while an asshole drug lord tortured Beau with thousands of volts of electricity. Of that, I was sure.

I blew by the next two buildings, startling a few students as I jogged past. Then I remembered that Beau had always said that I should call 911 and circle back in this sort of situation.

I cut right, then right again.

Actually, I wasn't sure that calling the authorities was a smart move just yet. With Beau's juvie record — plus whatever his connection to Byron was — a police presence might make everything a bigger mess.

Slowing my pace, I fell in behind a group of other twenty-somethings on a sidewalk that ran parallel to a road cutting through the campus. They were chatting about what cafeteria to hit for dinner while my boyfriend was being assaulted two buildings away.

A gray van drove by in the direction we were walking, then turned right across the sidewalk up ahead.

Finding the road made me realize I wasn't sure I could backtrack to the parking lot where we'd left the vehicles. What happened if I couldn't make it back to the Brave? Would it be towed?

Stop. Stop. Stop thinking.

Following the van, I left the shelter of the students heading for dinner, then jogged across the lawn to round the corner of red-bricked Coulter Hall.

I crossed to the wide front walk leading to the entrance of the building, ducking in behind a group of four girls. By their endless stream of chatter, they seemed years younger than me. But by the discussion they were having about fall classes, they were actually two years older, at a minimum.

A small crowd had gathered before a paved area adjacent to the side road and before the front doors of the science building. It wasn't a parking lot, so I guessed it was an area for delivery vehicles and whatever.

"What's happening?" asked one of the girls I was tagging along behind when our forward progress was impeded by a wall of students.

"Some sort of campus security training exercise," a guy answered back from the middle of the crowd.

I pushed my way through the students until I stood just behind the first row. Someone had thrown a couple of battered red cones on the sidewalk. Everyone around me was chattering and pulling out their phones.

About twenty feet away, Ettie was being pushed, none too gently, into the back of the gray van that had just passed me on the road. The guy with the broken wrist was doing the shoving. He was also limping, bleeding from a cut on his forehead, and wearing a navy windbreaker with the word 'security' emblazoned in white capital letters on the back. It was the sort of jacket that the bouncers or security guards wore at big events.

"That's not campus security," one of the girls said behind me.

Mr. Fake Security climbed in the back of the van after Ettie as I pushed my way through the crowd sideways in an attempt to see more of the interior of the vehicle.

Byron and a third meathead hustled out of the building, carrying Kandy between them. Apparently, the tiny werewolf was too heavy for just one of them. She appeared to be out cold. The sight made me seethe. At least, Byron's right arm was tied in a makeshift sling.

They swung Kandy, dropping her — hard — into the back of the van. The meathead eyed the crowd nervously, stuffing his hand deep in the right pocket of his fake security jacket as he yanked the sliding door shut with his left.

I caught a glimpse of Beau and the two other bruisers in the back just before the van door latched closed. All three of them were out cold. And, even from this far away, I could tell that Byron's thugs would have been better off being loaded into an ambulance. Beau's head had been in Ettie's lap, which made me feel slightly better about her.

"Are they … are they kidnapping those people?" another woman asked from my left.

"The real campus police are on their way," a guy right beside me said.

The meathead crossed around to the driver's side of the van as Byron turned to address the crowd. "No worries, guys," he called. "Just a training exercise." Then he flashed some sort of badge.

"Like that's legit!" the guy beside me cried, stepping forward as if to confront Byron.

I grabbed his arm. "No," I hissed. "Let security handle it."

The guy shook me off, but he opted for pulling out his phone and taking pictures of the van instead of pushing forward.

Byron climbed into the passenger side of the van. The vehicle pulled away before he got his door fully closed.

The muttering and fretting of the crowd grew, but it was just a wash of useless noise.

Beau had drilled me with contingency plans, over and over again. I was supposed to call Audrey if we got separated. I was supposed to make it back to the pack if anything ever happened to him.

I cleared the crush of the crowd, but stayed nearby on the grass in the shadow of the brick building. I dug my phone out of my satchel and pulled up Audrey's contact info.

Except … if I went to Portland, that meant I had to just let whatever was happening with Beau … with Ettie … with the vision … happen.

Beau would be pissed if I didn't follow the plan he'd painstakingly drilled into my fiercely independent brain.

But how long would it even take Audrey to get to Mississippi? And then what? She'd call the police, or she'd at least ask for assistance from the Gulf Coast pack, and neither of those things was good for Beau. Well, I wasn't sure about the pack thing, except I got the sense that Beau was protecting Ada from them for some reason.

I scrolled from A to B with a flick of my thumb. I had a dozen entries total, at most.

I stared down at the contact I'd selected.

Blackwell.

I didn't trust the sorcerer. Beau didn't trust the sorcerer. But he and I had formed a pact over a year and a half ago. Blackwell's end of the bargain had included a 'friends' clause, one that meant he'd come to my aid if it was in his power to do so.

As far as I'd figured, sorcerers didn't get much more powerful than Blackwell. Which was probably why most of the other Adepts I knew hated him. That, and he had a habit of collecting things that didn't belong to him.

As he'd collected me.

I opened a text window and typed.

I'm in trouble.

I hit send. Then I heard sirens, so I backed farther away from the crowd, tucking myself behind a large tree to watch the campus police pull up to the building. As the first of the security guards stepped from their car, the crowd surged forward as one entity to voice their version of the events they'd just witnessed.

My phone pinged. I glanced down at a new text message.

> *Where are you?*

Oxford. University campus. Mississippi. I'm unharmed.

> *Can you get to shelter? Somewhere private?*

I glanced around. Campus security was pushing the crowd back, requesting that students head to their dorms or to the cafeterias. The guy who'd wanted to stand up to Byron was talking animatedly with a guard who was taking notes. Another guard was collecting cellphones.

I wasn't sure where 'shelter' and 'private' would co-incide, but I knew I'd figure it out eventually. I applied my thumbs to my keyboard.

Yes.

> *Go. I'll need an address and a picture.*

I tucked my phone in my purse, thinking over my options. I clung to the anger evoked by watching Byron haul Kandy around like she was a bag of garbage. That fury overrode the fear that made me sluggish. It galvanized me, even if it was a false bravery built on adrenaline rather than ability.

Looking around at the still-gathering crowd, I was surprised that so many students were on campus for the summer semester. Perhaps the regular student body was just larger than I realized. Either way, some of the campus buildings had to be closed after hours or even for the entire summer. I just didn't know how to identify them.

A dark-haired girl was watching me from around the corner of Coulter Hall. She ducked back when I saw her. But then she stuck her head out again, beckoning me.

Ettie's friend from the hallway. Sara.

I glanced around but didn't see anyone else paying attention to me. So I jogged around the corner of the building.

Sara had disappeared.

I crossed the short strip of lawn to a sidewalk that ran parallel to the main road, noting that students and security personnel were gathering behind Coulter Hall where I'd broken the lecture hall window.

I turned the opposite direction, heading back toward where I hoped the parking lot was … where I hoped I'd find the Brave. The RV had to be private enough for Blackwell, right?

"Are you okay?" Sara fell into step beside me, ducking out from behind a few other students as I passed by a bus stop.

"Why do you care?"

"Well ... you're friends with Ettie, right?"

I glanced over at the quarter-witch. She looked nervous and really tired. Maybe even strung out.

"Sure," I said. "I'm friends with her brother."

"Oh, even better."

We continued walking down the sidewalk toward what I assumed was the center of campus. The university was just a maze of buildings and roads to me. At least I knew the parking lots were on the outer edges.

"Even better for what?" I asked.

Sara shrugged. "You know."

"I don't. Do you take classes with Ettie? Are you roommates?"

"Nah, not like that. Oh! We took first-year English together."

The conversation was going nowhere, and I had everywhere else to be. "Listen. Sara, right? I'm looking for a ... quiet spot."

"Yeah, to lie low. You need to lie low, right? I saw them take Ettie and your friends, but not you."

"Right. Yeah. Do you have a place in mind? Nearby?"

Sara bit her lip, then nodded. "Follow me."

She turned abruptly, walking swiftly away at a ninety-degree angle.

Err, okay.

I hesitated. I'd never been stupid enough to follow strangers anywhere. Though Sara wasn't exactly raising any stranger-danger flags, besides the possibly strung out thing. And whatever she had going with Ettie was strange. Strange enough that it might actually have something to do with the vision. Or possibly just be a lovers quarrel. Both options could be potentially useful, though.

The quarter-witch glanced back, frantically waving for me to follow her as she darted between two campus buildings.

So I did.

If I believed in magic, shouldn't I believe it would steer me right when I needed direction?

I snorted. Even I couldn't go that far. And I was supposed to be the damn oracle.

CHAPTER SEVEN

I'M OKAY. I'M GETTING HELP.

Half-lying by text message was almost as bad as thinking about lying to Beau's face. I was getting help. Just not the help Beau wanted me to get. Byron's flunkies had probably confiscated his and Kandy's phones, but I figured a text message couldn't hurt.

As I followed Sara across the campus, I kept replaying the scene in the lab in my head.

The moment of Beau's almost-death. The moment Chi Wen must have seen, but I hadn't. Why hadn't magic warned me? Or had Chi Wen already changed the future before he opened the pathway in my mind for the visions to return? And while I was thinking about that — it was scary as fuck that the far seer could mess with my brain like that.

Stop.

I didn't need to think about that right now. It wasn't remotely relevant to my current situation.

What I needed to be thankful for — and to focus on — was that they'd switched to stun guns. After Kandy saved Beau's life and crushed Byron's gun, they'd switched to nonlethal weapons. I had no idea why, except Ettie was in the mix and maybe they didn't want to hurt her. But it meant they didn't want to kill Beau and Kandy either. Not on campus, at least.

"Chi Wen said we'd survive," I muttered to myself, willfully ignoring that I was currently bent on changing the future and potentially causing ripple effects myself. I didn't know what the far seer had seen. Maybe this was all a part of his vision and I was simply fulfilling it. Yeah, I'd go with that.

I closed the space that had lengthened between me and Sara.

We crossed through a sports field of some kind and jaywalked across a road. Then suddenly we were walking between regular-looking houses.

Quicker than I would have thought possible, Sara had led me to what appeared to be off-campus housing. Or at least a couple of blocks of two- and three-storey houses that were adjacent to the campus and appeared to either have been converted into apartments or set up for groups of students to rent.

Sara hadn't spoken to me since she'd agreed to take me somewhere safe. So when she darted through a lopsided open gate between two high sections of an overgrown holly hedge, I hesitated. Peering up at the house beyond the spiny-leafed bushes, I reconsidered involving Blackwell.

Maybe the sorcerer was just an added complication? Maybe I shouldn't be so quick to dismiss Beau's carefully constructed contingency plans?

But I trusted my instincts.

I eyed the three-storey house. It was skirted along the front by a covered deck supported by narrow white pillars, and edged with a rickety railing. Blankets instead of curtains appeared to be pinned up over the interior of the lower windows. Twin mounds of cast-off shoes were piled on either side of the front door. The house had a distinct drug-den-in-the-making sort of feel.

"Come on," Sara urged from the deck. "I have a room upstairs."

The tall hedge hid the house from the street. Empty pizza and Chinese food boxes littered the area around the garbage bins, and I couldn't see anyone else nearby. Blackwell had requested privacy, but this might be tipping the scale into secluded-serial-killer territory.

Sara was definitely jittery. But was she more on edge than normal for someone who thought she was helping someone on the run?

I spotted a decrepit two-car garage set back on the right side of the house. "What about the garage? Does anyone use that?"

Sara frowned, then followed my gaze as she stepped over to the edge of the deck. "What? No. It doesn't work. I mean, you can't park cars in there. It doesn't have one of those doors, you know. And it leaks."

"Perfect." I stepped toward the side of the house, batting a cluster of hydrangea bushes out of my way to follow the cracked and crooked path.

"I don't have a key."

"Okay." I kept moving.

Sara watched me, her expression now pained for some reason. "I ... do you mind if I go inside first? Sam might be back ..."

"Sure. Don't worry about me. I probably won't be here for long. I just need to send some texts, you know."

"Okay. I'll bring you a granola bar later."

Sara darted inside as I crossed around the house. The derelict garage was even creepier the closer I got to it. That was okay, though, I'd seen a lot of creepy in my life. Creepy couldn't hurt me.

"Oh!" I heard footsteps scuttle across the front porch, and I turned back from the side door of the garage to see Sara hanging over the deck railing behind me. The old painted wood groaned under her weight and I grimaced, worried I was about to watch her take a face plant on the path. "What's your name?"

"Rochelle."

"You'll put in a good word for me, hey, Rochelle? With Ettie? She wouldn't hold out on you."

I had no idea what Sara was talking about. But it sounded suspiciously as if she might have been trying to score from preppy, science-scholarship, backpack-wearing, better-than-all-of-us Ettie.

"Right. What's Ettie selling these days? Just the crystal meth?"

"No, no. She's got this new line on something called crimson bliss."

"Right."

"Who doesn't want to feel invulnerable?" she said, as if she was quoting some sort of advertising tagline.

"Totally."

"So you'll talk to her for me? I just want to be near the top of her list, you know? She sells out so quickly, and ... well, you get it."

Apparently I looked like I understood what it was like to need an in with a drug dealer. "Completely. I'll see what I can do."

Sara grinned, gave me a double thumbs up, then slipped back into the house.

Great. Beau's sister was a drug dealer. That was going to make him feel even better about leaving her to fend for herself at seventeen.

I had a sinking feeling that Ettie was on the road to her own destruction by choice. And that diverting the vision wasn't going to be as easy as asking nicely. Or going camping.

I'd worry about that later. Beau and I could talk it all out, right after I got him back.

I tried turning the rust-challenged garage doorknob. As attested to by Sara, it was locked.

Keeping my left hand curled around the knob just in case the door miraculously opened under continued pressure, I momentarily gave in to the terror that was suddenly having a party in my belly. I pressed my right hand flat against the wooden door to steady myself. Old paint curled and crunched underneath my palm, but I ignored it. I refrained from pressing my forehead to the door as well, but only by reminding myself that I had no idea who was watching me from the house.

Beau would be able to pick this lock. Hell, Beau would be able to snap this lock with a twist of his wrist.

I gave the doorknob a jiggle, wondering if I had any bobby pins in my satchel. I'd never used a bobby pin in my life, so I was being utterly irrational, but at least I was still standing.

For the last year and a half, I had constantly wondered if I would be strong enough to keep moving without Beau. My knees actually buckled as that thought slid through my mind again.

Think, Rochelle. Break a window? Go into the house instead? But how private would that be?

I just needed to pop the lock.

An unfamiliar shock ran down my left forearm. I almost let go of the doorknob, but that wasn't what had shocked me. I looked down at my tattoo of a skeleton key. The one Chi Wen had touched a couple of days ago. It looked … more rounded?

"I need to pop this lock," I murmured.

Energy ran down my forearm again like a rippling muscle spasm. Then the key … shifted. It was still entwined in my tattooed barbed wire, so maybe it couldn't lift free as the butterfly had. But it could slide, twining down my arm and into the palm of my hand.

Nothing else happened.

Then I tried turning the doorknob again.

The lock clicked.

I didn't bother to question this newfound ability — because if I questioned it, I might start wondering whether any of this was truly real, and I didn't need to get caught in that loop again. Instead, I walked into the dark garage as if I owned the place ... and not like I was breaking and entering by magical means.

I closed the door behind me, digging into my satchel for the keys to the Brave. Beau had attached a tiny Maglite to my keychain. Then I remembered that Blackwell had said something about needing an address as well as a picture.

I had no idea where I was.

Damn it.

I dashed back out to the sidewalk. Noting that my key tattoo was back in its proper place, I used my phone to take pictures of the street sign, the front of the house including the address, then the garage.

Now the neighbors would definitely think I was crazy. Though this close to the university, maybe they'd just assume I was majoring in photography.

I made my way back into the garage, where a bit more exploration revealed that it featured a bare bulb overhead that actually worked. I texted the pictures to Blackwell. Then I looked around.

The garage floor was only half-complete, as if someone had dumped quick-dry cement on the dirt floor, doused it with water, then pushed it around until it ran out. Old workbenches covered with random hand tools and dusty mason jars of nails and screws ran along the paved side of the garage.

Like Sara had said, no car was parked inside. I wasn't sure the double doors on the wall that led to the overgrown driveway running alongside the house could even open. They looked nailed shut. A few bikes were stored along the opposite wall, but they looked forgotten.

Blackwell arrived in a rush of electric magic that blew past me, then immediately faded. He cast his dark gaze around the derelict garage, then tilted his head in my direction.

I scuffed my feet in the dirt, then stopped myself. His gaze dropped to my necklace. I was clutching it — though I hadn't realized I was doing so.

"You said private," I said.

"And you provided." Blackwell's dark hair was a bit longer than usual. It fell over his high forehead but was otherwise perfectly coiffed as always. He was wearing his signature dark suit and a pressed white dress shirt, but no tie. The suit was charcoal gray with a white-and-gray-striped silk handkerchief in the pocket. His face was almost gaunt, his cheekbones more sharply defined than usual. He might have lost weight since I'd seen him last.

"Are you done?" Blackwell asked, opening his hands to the sides with his palms facing me. He was smiling, but it was a tight-lipped, almost tense expression.

I'd been seeing him in my head since I was sixteen. But seeing him in person was still surreal. I knew every inch of him … in a completely nonphysical way.

I knew he constantly wore a ruby-and-gold amulet underneath his perfectly ironed shirt. That with one touch, that amulet could transport him anywhere in the world … and that apparently, he needed only an address and a few pictures to guide him. I was also fairly certain he'd stolen that amulet from a dragon many, many years ago.

I'd seen a vision of that … the first vision I ever had. All the gold decor and other artifacts were a dead give-away — or at least they were now, because I now knew about dragons. I had visions of the child of a guardian dragon. Yeah, Jade Godfrey, who was always surrounded by a halo of gold herself, and who was prone to seeking out and constructing artifacts.

Plus, Blackwell was fearful of dragons in general. Which made sense if he'd stolen something from them.

Also, he either loathed or loved Jade Godfrey. Maybe at the same time.

But even with understanding all that, I didn't know even the simplest details about him, including his age or anything of his background.

"How old are you?" I blurted.

The sorcerer raised a perfectly black, arched eyebrow at me. "Thirty-four."

"You look about that," I said. "But you feel older."

"Did you ask me here to talk about what determines how old we seem at any given time? Perhaps it is the accumulation of knowledge. Or perhaps reincarnation."

I stared at him, then slowly shook my head.

"Well, then …" He spread his hands in that palms-open gesture again, though with bent arms this time.

Was he trying to be … accessible? Amenable? It didn't suit him.

"Beau and Kandy have been taken."

"By whom?"

"I don't know. A drug lord, I think. Some guy who has a beef with Beau's stepdad."

"And the werewolf? She just went willingly? With a human?" Blackwell appeared far too amused by the idea of Kandy being kidnapped. But then, the sorcerer played fast and loose with the pack.

"They had stun guns. You know, electric shock weapons. Tasers. A lot of Tasers."

"And why are you in Mississippi?"

"A vision of Beau's sister, Ettie, brought us here."

"Ettie doing what?"

"Dying."

Blackwell mulled over this information. Then he asked the question I had expected to be the first thing out of his mouth. "And what does the dowser have to do with it? Why is the werewolf here?"

"Nothing. Kandy was tasked by the far seer."

Blackwell rocked back on the heels of his insanely expensive-looking black leather shoes. Any discussion of Chi Wen always muted the sorcerer. Even by text message, which was how we usually communicated.

"Call in the pack."

I squared my shoulders. "I don't want to. You are …"

"I am what? Certainly not more ruthless than the pack."

"More clandestine. More precise."

A smug smile spread across Blackwell's face. He was the sort of man who didn't mind being called sneaky. Maybe it was a sorcerer thing. I didn't know. I only knew him.

"And we have a bargain, you and I," he said. "You understand our boundaries. You don't really know where you stand with the pack … or even with your own mentor."

We hadn't spoken much in the past year and a half. I hadn't had anything but older sketches to finish and sell to Blackwell. But apparently he asked the right questions when we did talk or text. "Don't head-shrink me, sorcerer."

Blackwell barked out a laugh, as if I'd surprised him.

"Also," I said. "No Hoyt." The last time we'd all been in the same place hadn't gone well. The creep, Hoyt, had attacked Beau, burning him badly with some sort of magical silver ball bearings.

"The spellcurser has many uses. And is currently otherwise occupied. But I agree he is best kept out of this situation."

"Beau would tear him apart."

"Indeed. Your shifter's ... enthusiasm was expensive enough to clean up last time."

"That was your fault."

Blackwell inclined his head, not really agreeing with me but willing to move on with the conversation.

"And don't think I trust you," I said.

"Of course not. As I said, we have a bargain."

I loosened my grip on my necklace, reaching down to unclip the tiny glass vial that hung next to the raw diamond. I held it up for Blackwell to see. The liquid within appeared black in the yellowish glow of the overhead incandescent light.

The sorcerer's smile took on a wicked edge.

"You'll only need a drop to trace him," I said, making sure it didn't sound like a question. I didn't know much about magic — and knew less about sorcery specifically — but I wasn't simply handing Blackwell a vial full of Beau's blood.

"I assume he wears one containing your blood as well?" Blackwell asked.

I didn't answer. The sorcerer's smile widened to reveal his exceedingly straight, blindingly white teeth. I hadn't seen him face to face in over a year, and I already knew he wasn't a toothy smiler. But then, I'd had him in my head since I was sixteen, so I knew exactly how dangerous the man standing before me was. Whether he was playing at being friends or not.

"The shifter's idea?" he asked as he reached for the vial.

I nodded.

"Smart boy. He's been training you as well, I see." His dark gaze swept over me, then he glanced around the garage. "This will do."

Disrupting an intricate series of dust-coated spiderwebs, Blackwell grabbed a red plastic broom that I hadn't noticed propped in the corner. He proceeded to sweep clean a five-by-five space in the center of the floored area of the garage. Then he pulled a piece of white chalk out of his suit pocket and expertly drew a pentagram on the concrete.

A puff of magic brushed me as he joined the final point. I shivered, wrapping my arms around myself and taking a step back. For some reason, standing on the bare earth closer to the door steadied me.

Blackwell stepped into the pentagram. He crouched down and carefully allowed a single drop of Beau's blood to fall onto the concrete at the center of the chalked star. Still hunched, the sorcerer tilted his head to meet my gaze. "I'm glad you texted me, Rochelle. Of all the numbers you must have on your phone, you chose mine."

I lifted my chin, mimicking his gesture. Even though we'd already touched on this point, I somehow knew that how I responded to his statement was terribly important. "You said you'd come. You're the only one I know who will put me, and Beau, first."

"Over justice, you mean? Or rescuing any innocents?"

"Exactly."

Blackwell chuckled to himself. Then he dug what looked like a badly tarnished nickel out of his pocket and placed it over the drop of Beau's blood. "If the blood is older than a week, this might not work."

"It isn't."

"Smart boy," Blackwell repeated. Then, as he murmured to himself, his attention shifted to calling whatever magic he commanded into the pentagram. Not that I could feel anything, but I could see something … an almost transparent gray-blue shadow shifting around Blackwell's feet as he continued to murmur to himself in a language I didn't understand. Gaelic, maybe. The sorcerer's accent thickened as he spoke. His tone turned commanding.

The shadow coalesced around the coin. Then, in a flare of green that I associated with Beau's magic, it disappeared as if it had been absorbed into the metal.

Blackwell picked up the tarnished nickel. Not even a hint of blood remained on the concrete. The sorcerer straightened, scuffed the chalked edge of the pentagram with his foot, then stepped out to stand a few steps away from me.

He dangled the vial of Beau's blood before me. "Blood magic, by your command, oh oracle," he said. His tone was mocking, yet a seriousness I didn't fully grasp lurked underneath it.

Forcing myself to not simply snatch the vial from him, I took it carefully, making sure the stopper was secure. I was careful to not touch Blackwell as I did so. The last time I'd touched the sorcerer while he was performing magic, I'd burned him somehow. I hadn't mentioned that side effect to anyone but Beau, who thought that maybe it was some offensive aspect of my oracle magic. Except I hadn't burned Cy today, nor had I meant Blackwell any harm at the time it happened, so I wasn't sure.

I clipped the vial back onto my necklace and kept my questions to myself. Now wasn't the time for magic lessons. Now was the time to find Beau, hopefully unharmed.

Blackwell's gaze snagged on my mother's gold chain as I clipped the vial back onto it. For a split second, I saw his dark magic roll over his eyes.

I shuddered at the sight, tucking the chain underneath my tank top to hide it. The sorcerer's gaze lifted to mine.

He tossed the coin up in the air. It glinted with green as it fell back into his palm.

"Since you don't trust me," he said without malice. Then he tossed the coin up for me to catch.

I snatched it out of the air, afraid to touch it but also afraid to let it hit the ground. The metal was cool in my palm. Up close, I could see that it actually wasn't a nickel, though it was too small and thick to be a quarter. I didn't recognize the coin or the letters etched into it.

"Hotter, colder," Blackwell said. "A child's spell, learned at my grandfather's knee. Effective but short-term."

"Okay."

"Fix your mind on your boy and lead the way, oracle."

I swallowed my fear, wrenched my gaze away from the sorcerer, and gripped the coin in my left hand. I held this hand palm up, elbow bent at ninety degrees, and waited.

"The butterfly ..." Blackwell furrowed his brow at the tattoo on my left wrist. The butterfly wasn't moving, so I wasn't sure what had drawn the sorcerer's attention. But I didn't wait for him to complete the thought or question me further.

I exited the garage, quickly crossing past the house and through its overgrown holly hedge to the sidewalk. Then I waited to see how the coin would lead me to Beau. Apparently, it was my turn to rescue him. It was a good thing we alternated.

Having a powerful sorcerer at my back gave me a confidence that I never would have had on my own. Based on Blackwell's reputation with the pack and Jade Godfrey, that feeling might get me blacklisted in the Adept community. But I didn't care.

Magic had brought me to this place.

And I wasn't leaving without Beau. For better or worse.

"The coin?" Blackwell prompted as he stepped up beside me to survey the block of suburbia in which we were standing. He had to be sweltering in his suit, but he appeared cool and collected as he withdrew a pair of metal-framed sunglasses from his pocket. "Any change in temperature?"

I eyed his suit suspiciously. First chalk, then the coin, and now sunglasses? Yet not one unseemly bulge in the fabric?

Blackwell was grinning at me. "I'm an open book, Rochelle. For you. Ask me anything."

I kept my mouth shut. The suit jacket was obviously spelled somehow. Asking the sorcerer about it would only serve to stroke his massive ego.

Blackwell chuckled to himself. He held up his hand, appearing to randomly flag down a car driving along the street. The gleaming black luxury sedan slid to a stop before us, parking between a beat-up coupe and a mini-van along the sidewalk.

A young redheaded guy jumped out of the sedan, leaving it running. He half-waved, half-saluted at Blackwell, then hopped into the passenger side of a second car that had pulled up alongside the first. The second car drove off.

I stared at Blackwell as he casually stepped forward to open the passenger door of the sedan.

Sorcerers.

Man, they liked their tricks.

I climbed into the car without remarking about its sudden appearance.

Blackwell slipped into the driver's seat, then pressed a button that appeared to automatically shift the seat and adjust the rearview and side mirrors so everything was perfectly aligned for him. He looked at me questioningly.

I made sure my face was completely blank as I leaned forward to turn down the fan. The air conditioning was way too intense.

Blackwell raised an eyebrow at me.

I held the coin up in my open palm. "Nothing."

Blackwell nodded. "We're not close enough to the trail perhaps. Lead me back to where the kidnapping took place."

Okay, easier said than done. I'd been pretty freaked out when I followed Sara off campus, and she hadn't exactly been using the main roads to get us here.

"Okay," I said. "It happened at Coulter Hall at the university." I glanced around, attempting to get my bearings, but everything looked different from the perspective of the passenger seat.

"Coulter Hall." Blackwell spoke as if addressing the interior of the car, activating the GPS. He glanced at the map that appeared on the screen on the console.

"It won't continue to work for long around us." He put the car in gear and drove up the street.

"What won't work?"

"The technology. You haven't noticed?"

"No."

"I can see how you get by with the Brave. It's older, and I gather Beau keeps it in good shape. But magic wears on technology. I would have thought your computer and phone would be a problem."

"They're new. Used, but pretty new to me."

Blackwell glanced down at the hand in which I held the coin. Then he checked both ways before turning the corner.

He was looking at my butterfly tattoo, not the coin. I quashed the impulse to hide my inner wrist from his sight. If Beau had taught me anything, it was to never show fear in the face of a bigger predator. It always cracked me up that he said 'bigger' like that, as if I could be a threat to anyone.

The coin warmed in my hand. I might have missed it if the car hadn't been so chilly. "Warmer," I said, as relief flooded through my limbs.

Blackwell nodded and kept driving.

We kept driving as the sun set, following the path the coin set out for us and circling back every time it cooled. The path took us from the university and along the highway, heading back to Southaven, which wasn't surprising given that Byron seemed to be gunning for Cy. But we exited farther south than I remembered having turned off for Beau's old house.

Following the main streets, we found ourselves in the midst of a pocket of shops within a residential area. The coin led us to the gray van, which was parked along with four other cars in a lot behind a brick building at the edge of the retail zone.

We circled the block, approaching the building from the front.

The neighborhood wasn't scuzzy. Just older and beginning to get run-down. By the general age of the buildings, it might have been the neighborhood's local commercial center at one point. But all that was left now were a few mom-and-pop shops, a couple of cafes, and what appeared to be an old bank in a brown brick building.

Yeah, the drug lord who'd kidnapped Beau had inexplicably parked his getaway van behind a bank.

The streetlights along the block flickered on to herald the evening as Blackwell pulled up across from the bank, parking in front of a closed used bookstore. Both sides of the streets were lined with parked cars; Blackwell had scored the last open spot. A few pedestrians wandered the sidewalks, but the cafes appeared to be the main draw this late in the evening. The sorcerer carefully checked the parking restrictions, but then he stopped me from exiting the sedan when I went for the door handle.

"Wait."

"The coin is burning up. Beau is near."

"The vehicle's coated with a weak distraction spell, but opening the doors and getting out is too much of a disruption for it to fully cover," Blackwell said. Then he nodded toward the brick building.

A couple of guys were loitering outside the front doors, but I didn't recognize either of them from the university lab. A night deposit box had been cut into the brick at some point. I couldn't see much of the building's interior beyond the well-lit reception and waiting area, but the bank appeared to have been recently renovated into office space.

"Humans," Blackwell said as he rolled down his window.

Despite the fact that it was now after dark, stifling heat swamped us like an electric blanket on overload.

"So?"

"So, Adepts don't tangle with humans. Well ... I won't with you in tow."

He fished his cellphone out of his pocket and snapped a couple of pictures of the bruisers. One of them was sipping from a huge soda cup. "That tattoo is distinctive."

I squinted at the loitering muscle. They both had tattoos, but I couldn't see anything distinctive about their ink. Maybe I needed my eyes checked. A nearsighted oracle. Now that was ironic.

Blackwell attached the pictures he'd taken to a text message he was about to send to some guy named Marshal. He showed me his screen, zooming in on the tattoo on the neck of the nondrinker.

"A swastika?"

"Prison tattoos."

Blackwell added the address of the bank to his text message and hit send. Then he went back to observing the building.

"So we just wait?"

"We wait."

"But —"

"What do you see across the street?"

"An old bank."

"And?"

"Two guys. Both smaller than you."

Blackwell snorted.

"So?" I challenged. "What do you see?"

"An armored building in the middle of suburban America, possibly filled with human thugs working for your possible drug dealer. Humans who have the will and the capability to capture two shapeshifters in full sight of a campus filled with students, then bring them here. Not some clandestine location down by the river where the alligators roam."

"I think that's Florida. And they didn't know they were shapeshifters."

Blackwell ignored me. "Two guards out back watching a fortified door. Two guards out front, plainly packing. They have absolutely no concern about local police. Plus, the vehicles in the parking lot put the minimum count of hired guns up to five."

I tried to come up with a snippy response, but I honestly hadn't seen the guards at the back, or the fortified door. I'd honed in on the van, wanting to simply rush the building and find Beau.

Blackwell's phone pinged. I read over his shoulder.

>*Both pictured have outstanding warrants. But why do you care?*

Blackwell texted back. *They work for a possible local drug dealer and are currently holding a shapeshifter who is under my protection.*

>*Since when do you work for the pack?*

Consider it a favor.

>*I'm hours away.*

I'll come get you.

>*Yeah, it'll be easy to explain that one to the office.*

Blackwell didn't text back. He handed his phone to me and started the car.

"Wait," I said.

"Pay attention, Rochelle." Blackwell pulled away from the curb. "Even shielded, if we linger, we'll draw attention. A sorcerer is only as good as the tools he wields."

"I'm not a sorcerer."

Blackwell smiled, then deliberately eyed my butterfly tattoo again. This time, I turned my wrist away.

The sorcerer's phone pinged. Flipping the phone up to read the text would put my wrist back into the sorcerer's questioning view. Though I really wasn't sure why I was attempting to hide anything from him. Instinct, maybe.

He slowed the sedan a few blocks down from the bank, indicating left into the parking lot of a Chinese restaurant. Then we waited for oncoming traffic to clear.

"The text?" Blackwell prompted.

I glanced at the phone.

>*Ah, shit.*

" 'Ah, shit,' " I repeated as another text appeared with a ping.

>*This will void our debt in full.*

I repeated the message to Blackwell, who sighed. "Text yes."

He pulled the sedan into the parking lot.

I texted. *Yes.*

>*Then meet me where I had the unfortunate experience of meeting you the 1st time. 15 minutes.*

I read this message to Blackwell as he backed the sedan into a spot across from the front door of the restaurant.

Blackwell laughed. "Not everyone likes me as much as you do."

"I don't like you at all."

"Exactly."

Only a single table situated at the front window appeared to be occupied. But judging by the bags being loaded out of the kitchen door into an idling red hatchback, the place did a brisk takeout business.

Blackwell shut off the car, then turned to face me. "You will stay in the car."

"Ah, really?"

The sorcerer made a show of dropping the car keys into his suit pocket. "You will not wander back to the bank. You will not call attention to yourself in any way."

"This guy owes you something?" I asked, avoiding acknowledging his orders to stay put.

"Yes. And now he won't," the sorcerer answered pointedly. I ignored the implication that he was wasting a favor owed to him on Beau and me.

"And he can help us how?"

"He's a United States Marshal."

"A U.S. Marshal owes you a favor?"

"A sorcerer owes me a substantial favor."

I thought about this for a while. Adepts had to have jobs, obviously, but I hadn't had much reason to think about what those jobs might be. Beyond Beau working as a mechanic or Jade running a bakery, I mean. Now Kandy was a physiotherapist and some other guy was a U.S. Marshal.

"I thought magic didn't work on humans?"

"Mind magic such as yours wouldn't work on a mundane, nor could a mundane be turned into a fully realized werewolf or vampire. But sorcerers can wield other magic. Can't they?"

He reached over and deliberately tapped my butterfly tattoo, hard. An electric shock accompanied his assault on my wrist.

"Care to tell me about the butterfly?"

"No."

He laughed. "We have years and years to discuss such things, oracle. A long and fruitful collaboration. Do you think the pack can train you to wield magic?"

I didn't answer.

"Stay in the car."

He waited for me to respond. I grunted in acknowledgement.

Blackwell got out, locking the doors behind him, then sauntered over to the restaurant. The red hatchback zoomed out of the lot, laden with its load of takeout. It blew between the sorcerer and me, tires squealing as it hit the street.

I watched Blackwell as he pushed open the front door and entered the restaurant. Neither of the diners or the waiter appeared to notice him. He immediately turned right, crossing into the men's room.

He didn't come back out.

CHAPTER EIGHT

>*Why isn't Kandy answering her cellphone?* D.

I stared for so long at the text message that had popped up on my phone that the oil coating the veggie spring roll I'd been about to eat started burning my fingers. I dropped the roll back into the takeout container, then sucked on my sizzling digits. I'd bought the spring rolls simply to prove to Blackwell that I could come and go from the car if I wished. But once I'd opened the container, I realized I was actually hungry.

At first, I'd hoped the text was from Beau, but it came from a number I didn't recognize. Then the 'D' tag was a nasty shock to my adrenal gland.

D for Desmond?

Was the alpha of the West Coast North American Pack texting me? How did he get my number?

My phone pinged again. I flinched. I really needed to put it on silent. Yeah, I was twenty turning sixty-five — or at least my fried nerves were.

>*Answer me.*

So yeah, it was Desmond. And I had no idea how to answer him. Lie? Tell the truth? Ignore the message? But if we were all ignoring texts, wouldn't that confirm that something was wrong? We didn't need the pack descending on Southaven. Not yet. Not without first understanding what was going on with Beau's family. And certainly not now that Blackwell was involved.

The red hatchback zoomed back into the parking lot, drawing my attention away from my phone. As the car stopped by the kitchen door, the driver jumped out to grab more takeout orders.

Inside the restaurant, Blackwell finally exited the bathroom, glancing back to confirm that the man behind him was keeping pace.

That didn't read as kinky at all.

I checked the time. It was 8:46 P.M. The sorcerer had been gone for twenty-one minutes.

I applied my thumbs to my phone's keypad and messaged Desmond back. *Just about to go pick her up. I'll tell her to check her phone.*

The alpha didn't reply.

I tucked my phone away and gobbled down one of my spring rolls as the two sorcerers exited the restaurant and crossed toward the sedan.

The U.S. Marshal was a cowboy — wiry frame, hat, boots, and all. He wore blue jeans paired with an unbuttoned suit jacket, a white dress shirt, and a skinny tie. The badge attached to his belt glinted as he paused to scan the parking lot. And I could see then that he wore a gun in a shoulder holster. I imagined him wearing one at his ankle as well.

He narrowed his eyes in my direction, then resumed following Blackwell to the car.

A cowboy sorcerer marshal. Huh.

I stepped out of the sedan as the two of them approached, yielding the front seat as I noisily crunched on my second spring roll. The rolls were pretty tasty for something I hadn't really wanted but had bought to spite the sorcerer. As if he could lock me in the car. Sure, I hadn't wandered back to the bank unaccompanied.

But that was just from good sense, not because I was following his orders.

Blackwell ignored me.

The marshal held out his hand for me to shake. "Henry Calhoun," he said, in a heavy but lyrical Southern accent. So maybe the cowboy thing was genuine.

I eyed him, thinking about dropping my sunglasses to do my intimidation thing. But I couldn't be bothered.

"Henry," I said, as cordial as I was capable of being while wiping greasy fingers on my jeans. "Thank you for helping me."

Henry tilted his head to the side. His hair was dark underneath the cowboy hat, which also shaded his cobalt-blue eyes. He wrapped his hand around my outstretched, degreased palm.

Electricity passed between us.

"Rochelle Saintpaul," I offered, using my legal name. Not my birth name.

"Rochelle," Henry repeated. "You are not a witch."

"No, I'm not." I smiled, not really knowing why as Henry continued to hold my hand. I instantly liked him. That was weird.

Henry grinned back at me. "The tattoos are a good disguise."

"Are they?"

"The whole goth thing."

"I'm not a goth either."

He laughed, finally dropping my hand. Blackwell, who'd been watching our exchange without comment, climbed into the driver's seat and shut the door behind him.

Henry Calhoun eyed me. "You keep bad company, Rochelle Saintpaul."

I nodded. "Wait until you meet the other two."

The marshal laughed again. "Fair enough."

He reached over to open the back door of the sedan for me. I settled into the seat, scarfing my last two spring rolls before we'd driven out of the parking lot. I couldn't help but think that if I was that hungry, Beau must be starving.

Or maybe not. Because maybe he was dead.

No.

I wasn't going to start letting my mind control me. Beau wasn't dead, because the coin was still warm. The magic in his blood was an active part of Blackwell's tracking spell, so if the coin was still tracking him, then he was still alive.

Right?

I desperately wanted to confirm my reasoning with Blackwell, but his earlier odd mention of blood magic made me think I should keep my mouth shut about the spell around Henry.

Instead, I squeezed the coin in my left hand — so firmly that it cut into my palm — and focused my attention on the sorcerers in the front seats.

The marshal was riding shotgun, which was an ironic position for a cowboy. Or maybe in this case, 'appropriate' was a better word.

Because we were riding to a rescue.

Right?

We circled the block around the renovated bank, switching directions for a second pass. And, while I desperately sought a glimpse of Beau out the back window, Blackwell and the marshal had a muttered argument about the strength of the shielding on the sedan. Henry snapped blurry pictures of the new guards posted by the reinforced door at the rear. Apparently, he had some photography app on his phone that was good in low light.

We parked about two blocks away, down a side street where we still had an angled view of the rear of the bank. The houses on either side of us were lit with the glow from their flat-screen TVs.

"The van's gone," I said, unable to keep my dismay in check.

Henry was texting. "Make? Model?"

"Ford Econoline," I said, surprised that I could remember. "Medium gray. No rear windows."

"Maybe 2008," Blackwell added. "Larger grill, longer hood. Diesel."

Henry continued to text. His phone pinged multiple times as he did so. "Records," he said, referencing the text message he'd just received. "But no outstanding warrants on the two new guys." He nodded toward the bruisers loitering by the back door. One of them wore a black cast on one arm.

"Beau broke that guy's wrist," I said proudly. "What idiot asks for a black cast?"

"A shapeshifter revealed his strength in front of a human?"

Err, maybe I'd shut up now.

"Their attackers used force," Blackwell said. I had filled him in on the details of the kidnapping while we were tracking Beau and Kandy to the bank. "As someone would with a person under the influence of drugs."

"They saw their strength and assumed they were in a meth rage?"

"So I gathered."

Blackwell met my gaze in the rearview mirror. I looked away.

Henry's phone pinged again. "Shit. I told you the office would question how the hell I got here so quickly."

"What will you tell them?" I asked, honestly interested in how a sorcerer worked with humans and technology all day.

"I backdated the tip. I'll just say I was on my way and hope no one thinks to double-check." The marshal looked up from his phone, then pivoted around in his seat to pin me with his cobalt-blue gaze. "Tell me about the drug connection."

Neither Blackwell nor I answered.

"I'm about to execute drug possession and drug trafficking warrants. Drug lords don't generally go around kidnapping innocent people."

He paused, waiting.

Again, neither of us spoke.

"I'm going to need to call the local authorities."

"But the locals are in Byron's pocket!" I cried.

"Byron who? And you know this how?"

"Blackwell ..."

The marshal turned to look at the sorcerer.

Blackwell sighed. "It was a guess, based on their open display of fortification and force."

"Accusing the locals of being on the take isn't going to be helpful."

"We just need you to occupy the humans while we free the shapeshifters," Blackwell said.

"It's not just a badge," Henry said stiffly. "And I'm not drug enforcement."

"Beau and Kandy aren't involved," I said. "But Beau's family might be into something. We've just gotten in the way."

"Adepts running what? Meth?"

Blackwell glanced at me in the rearview mirror. Then he raised his eyebrow, making it my choice as to how much I wanted to tell a U.S. Marshal. Problem was, I didn't know what — if anything — I needed to be circumspect about.

"Apparently not," I mumbled. "Beau and Kandy think it's something similar, but different. Cy, Beau's stepdad, was amped up enough that he was faster and stronger than Beau thought he should be." I kept the tidbits about Cy smelling like Ada's magic and that Ettie was selling something called crimson bliss to myself, hoping it wasn't relevant to the current situation.

The marshal stared at me hard for a long moment. Then he nodded. "Fine. But I'm not covering up any crime."

"You won't have to," Blackwell said. "You deal with the humans and I'll deal with the Adepts."

"You're not a member of the League, Blackwell."

"And we're not dealing with sorcerers."

Henry pointedly glanced at me over his shoulder. "No?"

"No," I said, though I wasn't actually a hundred percent sure about my magic anymore.

"Just the pack," Blackwell said. "They can police themselves."

"Let's hope," Henry muttered, returning his attention to his phone. "Okay, I think I have enough to go in. Blackwell, you'll create a distraction out front."

"Obviously."

"That'll pull these guys from the back so I don't have to mess with the door. I'll head in and arrest everyone on the premises while you look for the shapeshifters. You'll exit through the rear. I'll ignore you leaving, then call in the locals to sort out the warrants."

"Who do I go in with?" I asked.

"No," Henry answered.

Nothing else. Just 'no.'

"She'll come with me," Blackwell said.

"Absolutely not. It'll be bad enough to have drug dealers yammering about a guy in a dark suit wandering around the place. I'm not exposing a tiny teen covered in distinctive tattoos to this. A teen without offensive magic."

"As far as you can tell," Blackwell said.

Henry cranked around in his seat, frowning at me. "It'll be your funeral."

I bared my teeth at him, mimicking Kandy's smile. Though the marshal didn't flinch, so apparently I didn't pull it off. "I'm valuable to the sorcerer."

Henry snorted. "Good luck with that."

Blackwell laughed, then climbed out of the car.

I followed, wishing I'd worn long sleeves or had a hoodie to throw on over my tank top. I hadn't really thought about how distinctive my tattoos were. Apparently, I hadn't planned well for a future of jacking drug dealers.

As we strode through pools of triangular light cast by the streetlights that sporadically illuminated the residential sidewalks, Blackwell tucked his hands casually into the pockets of his dress pants, causing his suit jacket to buckle. Any time before that, I would have thought him completely incapable of marring his appearance. Maybe I didn't know him as well as I thought.

I was practically having to jog to match his long stride. It was never this awkward walking next to Beau, even though he was easily four inches taller than the sorcerer.

The marshal was currently circling one block over in the opposite direction from us so he could approach the bank from the back.

As soon as I thought Henry was out of earshot, I hissed, "I think the tracking spell on the coin is fading."

"Yes, effective but short term, as I said." Blackwell was systematically scanning the quiet neighborhood as we crossed between a couple of parked cars to the opposite side of the street.

I wanted to say something pissy back, but I was too jittery and nervous to come up with anything appropriate.

"So our main concern," he said, "specifically when figuring out how we're going to penetrate these defenses, is why hasn't the werewolf or the shapeshifter freed themselves?"

"The van is gone. Maybe they've been moved to another location?" No matter how rational I was attempting to be, I couldn't stop the hitch of fear I felt over the idea of Beau being taken again.

As we left the shadow of the houses to pass alongside the parking lot at the back of the bank, Blackwell glanced down at something hidden in his left hand.

The van might have been gone, but five cars still remained in the lot. So according to Blackwell's logic, there was at least one person inside the building. Two guards at each entrance plus one inside equaled five cars. That was as long as the bad guys didn't prefer to carpool or park on the street.

"The werewolf is an enforcer of the pack," Blackwell said. "I'm actually surprised she isn't the beta. She leaves a trace … leading to the rear entrance of the bank but not back out, based on the fade of the residual."

"You have something that traces magic?"

"Of course. Adepts of a more ... animalistic connection to their power don't take well to captivity." The sorcerer didn't appear remotely concerned about the bruisers at the reinforced back door, though they were eyeing us aggressively as we walked by. "They tend to ... forget themselves when under stress."

The guy whose wrist Beau had broken barely glanced at me, focusing his attention on Blackwell. I probably should have told the sorcerer of the possibility that he might recognize me. Oh, well. Next time.

"Like Beau in the restaurant?"

"Admittedly, the boy got caught in the amplifier in that case."

"So, your mistake?"

"I wouldn't say that." Blackwell's tone was easy. Amused. He didn't seem remotely tense.

"Your point?"

"There is a reason the pack operates as it does, with such a tight structure and zero tolerance for human-witnessed violence."

"Because it happens."

"Yet these guards and this building appear undamaged. Which makes me wonder how humans are holding two shapeshifters. Both of them powerful. One of them is young and separated from his chosen mate, whose fate he must be unsure of and concerned about."

"So Byron, the drug lord, isn't human?"

We turned left around the corner of the building and onto the sidewalk of the main street. So much light was streaming through the front windows of the converted bank that I actually had to squint my eyes even behind my tinted glasses.

"Perhaps." Blackwell lowered his voice. The two guards posted by the front entrance were about a dozen feet in front of us, but both were peering down at their phones. The sidewalk was otherwise empty of pedestrians. "Yet I feel no evidence of other Adepts at work here. No wards, no spells."

We kept walking, crossing directly in front of the bank and the two guards. Blackwell lifted his hand from his pocket, touched his forehead, and said, "Cheers," as we passed.

"Cheers?" I said mockingly. I was wondering when Blackwell was going to get to the distraction part of our mission.

The sorcerer wrapped his right hand around my forearm, squeezing way too tightly. I instantly leaned my weight away from him and opened my mouth to protest.

Then a bomb went off behind us.

I jerked forward, and would have done a face plant onto the sidewalk if Blackwell hadn't been holding me.

A sudden wave of pressure boxed my ears, making me so disoriented that I couldn't find my footing for a second. I managed two more awkward steps before the feeling passed.

Blackwell let go of me. "I didn't know you were so sensitive to magic."

I wasn't a fan of intriguing the sorcerer. At least not any more than he already was. I grunted my pissed-offness, but I couldn't find the will to articulate it with actual words.

Not a bomb, then.

Magic.

Blackwell casually spun around to face the entrance of the bank. The two guards were slumped on the ground on either side of the glass door. They'd been knocked out cold. They'd also dropped their phones on the way down, presumably smashing them in the process.

That probably shouldn't have been my first concern.

"Jesus, everyone is going to …" I glanced around. Granted, there weren't many people out this late at night in a mostly residential area, but no one appeared to have been drawn out of their homes to point and shout. You'd think having drug dealers hanging out in the old bank on the corner would be of constant interest in and of itself. And then two meatheads suddenly collapsing for no apparent reason should have been an even bigger draw. But nope. The sidewalk and street remained empty. That was … weird.

Blackwell stepped forward.

I followed.

Two steps later, I shivered as a tingling coolness slid over me. More magic.

I glanced around again. Now the street appeared fuzzy, and everything was weirdly warped if I turned my head quickly. Apparently, whatever spell Blackwell had dropped with his 'cheers' as we passed the bank had knocked out the guards as well as cloaking the takedown. So that explained the lack of people rushing to investigate.

Blackwell yanked open the door to the bank and flung what appeared to be a tennis ball inside. He quickly shut the door and stepped back.

I was still staring like an idiot, watching the tennis ball through the front windows. It bounced once as a man ran into the front entranceway. He raised a gun. The ball bounced a second time. And he … he just … fell asleep.

"Did you learn that one on your grandfather's knee?" I asked, reaching for snark to cover my ignorance.

"Practically," Blackwell said.

He grabbed one of the downed guards by the shoulders, then dragged him toward the entrance.

The tennis ball just kept on bouncing farther into the room, taking out another guy. Then it continued into the central corridor and out of my sight.

"Some help?" Blackwell asked.

I stepped over the guard's sprawled legs and pulled open the oddly heavy door. Blackwell dragged him inside, tucking him along the base of the wall underneath the window, near a massive cherrywood receptionist's desk.

The sorcerer brushed by me to step outside for the second guard. I continued to hold the door open for him, though I seriously just wanted to rush in and start screaming Beau's name. However, though love might make me silly, I wasn't going to let it make me stupid.

The front room of the renovated bank was set up like a waiting area in a fancy lawyer's office. A gorgeous deep-purple orchid perched on the right corner of the receptionist's otherwise spotless desk. The plant was still wrapped in plastic, as if it had just been delivered from the florist that afternoon. A matching orchid sat on a cherrywood-framed glass side table beneath the corner window of the seating area to my right.

I moved as far as I could into the lobby and still hold the door open. The receptionist, an impeccably made-up redhead, was curled underneath the desk. She must have taken shelter when she saw the guards drop outside. Blackwell's shield spell, or whatever it was, appeared to work only in one direction. Then the redhead must have been taken out by the tennis ball spell. At least she hadn't hit her head on the way down.

"It's weird, isn't it? That the receptionist is still here? At what? Nine thirty at night?"

Blackwell didn't respond. It was an inane, irrelevant question. But I felt the need to answer it, so I did so myself. "I guess drug dealing is a 24/7 sort of business."

"Or they were expecting someone," Blackwell said as he dragged the second guard inside.

I allowed the door to swing closed behind him.

The sorcerer tucked the second meathead along the wall underneath the window on the opposite side of the door, so that he was hidden behind one of the reception area's overstuffed dark leather couches.

Blackwell straightened. Crossing back to the entrance, he pulled a slender six-inch-long metal box out of his apparently bottomless pocket and placed it across both door handles. The etching on the box was reminiscent of the design carved into Kandy's cuffs. I'd seen similar markings on Blackwell's amulet, but I had never been able to fully capture them in my sketches.

"Are those … runes?" I asked.

"That is how a sorcerer typically articulates his magic."

Ignoring Blackwell's snark — I was willing to take as much as I dealt — I pressed him for more information. "A lock?"

"Yes. We'll collect it before we leave." He glanced at something in his hand again, turning as if he was following a signal. As he pivoted, I caught sight of a platinum box about the size of a deck of cards cupped in his palm. Symbols swirled and shifted over its smooth face. More runes, maybe.

"And that wasn't a tennis ball."

"What? No. Is that what it looked like to you? It's odd how the mundane part of your brain tries to interpret magic."

"Thanks for calling me stupid, asshole."

Blackwell barked a laugh, then strode past a set of brand-new high-backed wing chairs in the seating area. Ignoring the two meatheads who had collapsed in the middle of the tiled floor, he crossed through to the central corridor. This appeared to bisect the recently renovated building, and was the path the not-a-tennis-ball had taken.

"This way."

Skirting the wall, we slipped along the corridor. I was pleased that my sneakers made no noise on the pristine low-plush cream carpet. Blackwell was likewise silent, though I would have bet every cent in my satchel that it was magic that made him so, not the Italian leather lace-ups he favored.

The closed space of the hall reeked of new paint. If the offices we passed were going to be used for some sort of paper shuffling in the future, they certainly weren't being used now. Blackwell barely bothered to glance through the open doors as we slipped by.

Some sort of scuffle sounded from up ahead, consisting mostly of muffled grunts of pain. Then a wispy breeze of some sort of magic brushed by me, tingling oddly at my wrists.

Blackwell grunted, sounding pissed as he shook his hands as if trying to rid himself of something clinging to them. "His one true talent," he grumbled under his breath.

"The marshal?" I asked in a whisper.

Blackwell dipped his chin in a slight nod.

"What does he owe you for, anyway?"

The sorcerer paused to retrieve the tennis ball that wasn't a tennis ball — but which still looked like a tennis ball to me — from where it had rolled to a stop against a doorjamb. He tucked the device in his jacket pocket, then looked back along the hall behind me.

My question hung unanswered. Granted, it was none of my business and certainly not the best time to ask.

Blackwell continued forward. The corridor branched off at right angles at the rear of the building.

A long hallway with multiple doorways stood to our right. To the left, six feet of corridor ended at a large steel door. This hung open a few inches, but the gap wasn't wide enough to see the room beyond.

Blackwell consulted his tracking device, then opted for the long hall to the right.

I followed him, wishing I had the ability to see, or taste, or feel residual magic, so I would know if Beau was near. I rubbed my thumb across my butterfly tattoo, but the butterfly didn't seem inclined to take flight and lead me to Beau. I wondered what triggered it. That was another question for the sorcerer before me. However, despite what I had boasted to Henry about being valuable to Blackwell, I was concerned that my morphing tattoos would make me even more collectible to him. In a snatch-and-grab sort of way.

Yeah, I still didn't trust Blackwell. But then, I didn't trust anyone but Beau. So that wasn't news.

Bathrooms that appeared to be under construction stood to our right as we continued down the hall.

Henry Calhoun stepped out from a doorway farther ahead on the left. He flipped what appeared to be two interconnected gold bangles in his hand as he exited the doorway, then paused the motion when he recognized us.

"Impressive handcuffs," Blackwell said as we walked toward each other. "I'd heard rumors."

"They were difficult to source," the marshal replied, grinning. Yeah, sorcerers liked their toys.

"An alchemist you know?" Blackwell's question was smooth and completely barbed at the same time.

"Nah. They're a couple of hundred years old."

"Ah, those cuffs."

"Yep."

"I have no idea what you're talking about," I said, interrupting what was apparently degrading into a sorcerer gab session.

Henry grinned at me, flipping what I now recognized as rune-carved golden handcuffs in his hand again.

"There are five more in the entrance," Blackwell said. "Your casting didn't stretch that far."

"No. I usually have to be in the room."

"It brushed by us in the hall."

"Really? The cast tried to grab you?" The marshal directed the question to me.

I shrugged. I'd felt the tingling at my wrists in the hall by the offices, but I wasn't interested in chatting about it.

"So the tattoos are more than just decoration," he mused.

I shrugged a second time.

Blackwell continued down the hall, glancing into the room the marshal had just exited.

I moved to follow. Henry ran two fingers across my bare left shoulder as I stepped past him.

"Hey," I said. "Hands."

"Hmmm," Henry replied, rubbing his forefinger and middle finger together with his thumb. "I'd like to meet your tattoo artist."

"I'm the artist," I snapped.

"You ink the designs yourself?"

"Well, no … I …" Realizing I was answering questions about magic I was still figuring out myself, I stopped talking.

Henry laughed. "Even more intriguing." He raised his hand, palm facing me. A light-blue effervescence dusted his fingertips.

I glanced down at my shoulder, cranking my neck back to see matching effervescent lines fading away from where he'd touched me.

"What's that? A spell?"

"A talent," Henry replied as he moved away, heading toward the central corridor.

Blackwell stepped back out into the hall, crossing over to me. "Not there," he said. "I was fairly certain that was Calhoun's trail, but I wanted to check."

I stepped forward to peer into the area Blackwell had just exited. It appeared to be a break room. A trashed break room, currently strewn with garbage and food.

Four men were knocked out cold in front of a sink filled with coffee mugs. They were crammed side by side, arms interlocked, and cuffed to each other behind their backs with what appeared to be multicolored industrial zip ties. I recognized two of them from the university, but Byron was still unaccounted for. The room's table and chairs were all knocked over, as though at least some of the men had been dragged away from their seats. The fridge was hanging open. A half-made sandwich sat on a cutting board beside the sink.

Wow. Magic didn't usually turn my head. Mostly because I'd spent the bulk of my life ignoring the unusual for fear that I was crazy and seeing things. But if the marshal's handcuffs helped him secure this many armed bad guys with a flick of his wrist? Well, that was impressive.

"Rochelle," Blackwell hissed from farther down the hall.

I turned away from the mass trussing in the break room and jogged after Blackwell, heading back the way we'd come.

A quick glance to my left as we crossed into the hall's left-hand wing and toward the steel door revealed the marshal as he steadily made his way to the entrance.

Blackwell pushed the steel door fully open. It looked as if it had been recently installed. The steel studs on the other side hadn't been walled over yet.

The door opened into a small, mostly empty room that was still under construction. The walls and ceiling were framed with more steel.

The antechamber to the old bank vault lay beyond an arched doorway. The thick vault door was wide open, but bars set just inside the door blocked the doorway.

A cherrywood magazine table that was a match to the waiting-area furniture stood to one side of the barred doorway. The marble-floored antechamber was otherwise bare of furniture.

On the table, completely incongruently, a diffuser that looked identical to the one I'd seen in Beau's mother's living room was misting merrily away.

I could see Beau just over Blackwell's shoulder, standing within the barred vault. He was frowning at the sorcerer.

Instantly elated, I tried to step past Blackwell.

He held me back.

"Wait. Something isn't right." He glanced at the tracking device in his hand again.

"Well, now I know what the far seer meant by his 'But you're not going to like it' prediction." Kandy's voice rang out, followed by a string of imaginative curse words. "It had to be you."

I leaned around Blackwell to see the green-haired werewolf was standing beside Beau with her arms crossed, glaring viciously at the sorcerer.

"You could stay behind bars, werewolf," Blackwell said. "You seem to be coping."

Kandy wrapped her hands around the thick metal bars penning her and Beau into the vault. She strained as if she were attempting to pull them apart. And, even though she was still wearing the thick gold cuffs, the bars didn't bend. "Magic," she spat, "doesn't appear to work in here."

Blackwell scanned the antechamber. He hadn't set one foot onto the marble floor, and he was still blocking me from entering.

"Hey." I offered Beau a smile.

He grinned back at me. "Hey."

"Let's not get all mushy here," Kandy snarled. "You should have stayed away."

Still grinning at Beau, who appeared unharmed, I ignored the finger Kandy pointed at me — and noticed instead a number of nasty red marks on her neck.

"Kandy isn't healing properly," I said to Blackwell. "Are those welts from the stun guns?"

Kandy dropped her hands from the bars with an unconcerned shrug.

"I see it," Blackwell murmured. "I just can't feel a spell or ward that could possibly be dampening their magic in this way."

"You have to think like a mundane," I said, pointing past him toward the diffuser.

"The … aromatherapy?" Blackwell stumbled on the word.

"Aromatherapy that doesn't smell like anything?" Kandy snarked.

"Who placed it there?" Blackwell asked. "A witch?"

"We were out cold when we were brought in," Beau said. "Also this." He extended his arm through the bars. His inner elbow was bandaged, as it would be if he'd given blood.

Blackwell hissed.

Kandy snorted, not happy. She was bandaged on both inner elbows as well.

"What?" I asked.

"Blood magic," Kandy spat.

"What?"

"We have to go," Blackwell said. "The shifters need to be behind wards." He stepped into the room but crossed to the diffuser, not the vault.

"Oh, yeah?" Kandy asked. "You going to protect us? From who? Yourself?"

Blackwell ignored her, scanning around the table. Then, seemingly satisfied, he unplugged the diffuser.

I crossed to the vault, reaching out for Beau. He mimicked my movement so we could link arms through the bars.

"Hey," I said.

"Hey," he replied.

"Cute," Kandy said. "You will not make me beholden to this asshole sorcerer, Rochelle."

Blackwell picked up the diffuser. "Have it your way, werewolf. Perhaps whatever is in this will wear off before the police arrive."

He exited the room without another word.

Kandy snarled at his retreating back.

"Sorry," I said. "I couldn't figure out a quicker way."

"Try the pack," Kandy said.

"A call to Audrey might have brought in the local authorities or the Gulf Coast pack," I said. "And I thought we were avoiding them both right now."

Beau shifted his feet uncomfortably.

I steadfastly held the green-haired werewolf's gaze.

"Someone has taken our blood," she said. Her tone was low and intense. "Whatever else is happening, that is a huge affront. I'll protect you and Beau and hold your secrets. But I won't allow the pack to be compromised or harmed while doing so."

"We understand," Beau said. "We're grateful you're with us."

Kandy kept her gaze locked on mine until I nodded. Then she shrugged and stepped back from the bars. "Fine. But Blackwell is always the wrong choice."

Ignoring her, I withdrew my hands from Beau's warm embrace. I focused instead on the large latch that locked the barred door. With them placed just behind the vault door as they were, the bars must have been a secondary security measure. I was seriously glad I didn't have to figure out how to open the vault itself.

"One of the guards must have the keys," Beau said helpfully.

I nodded. But instead of leaving to track down those keys, I wrapped my left hand around the lock. I concentrated on the skeleton key tattoo on my forearm. The magic that somehow animated my tattoos came easier this time. The key shifted down the tangle of tattooed barbed wire and into the palm of my hand with minimal effort.

The cage clicked open.

Kandy swore.

"What was that?" Beau asked, pushing the barred door wide to sweep me up into a fierce hug.

"New trick," I answered. Then I kissed him.

"Ah, great," Kandy groused, though she didn't actually sound unhappy as she crossed out of the vault. "New magic. That's always fun. Let's keep moving, kiddies."

"Have you found Ettie?" Beau asked as he placed me back on my feet.

"Not yet."

"I need you gone." Henry was talking to Blackwell as we followed Kandy into the back hall. The marshal eyed us as he passed the magical lock from the front door back to the sorcerer. Blackwell tucked the device in his suit pocket. "I've called the local authorities. They'll help me clean up here and arrest anyone with outstanding warrants. But I need you to not be here."

"Nice meeting you too, sorcerer," Kandy said.

Henry laughed, reaching out to shake Kandy's hand. Surprisingly, she accepted the gesture.

"These two need to be behind wards," Blackwell said. "They've had blood stolen and I'm concerned about repercussions."

Kandy snorted.

"And I'm taking this." Blackwell lifted the diffuser so Henry could see it clearly.

"It's of Adept origin?"

"Apparently."

"Fine."

"No," Beau said. "Not fine. My sister is still here."

"The building is cleared of sisters," Henry said. "We five are the only Adept here."

"She's not like me," Beau said, starting to explain.

"The redhead at reception is the only female in the vicinity, other than the two by your side, shifter. Sorry."

Beau turned to look at Blackwell. "We need to track her."

"We will. But not until I figure out what's in this." Blackwell tucked the diffuser underneath his arm. "And who has your blood."

"Use the back door," Henry said. He reached his hand out to Blackwell. "This clears my debt."

Blackwell eyed the marshal's outstretched hand. Then with a shallow nod, he shook it.

"Oh, I like you so much better now," Kandy said.

"We'll talk," Henry replied with a wink.

Kandy barked out a laugh, then gave Beau a shove so he'd follow Blackwell out the back of the building.

"Wait," Beau yelled after Henry. "At least tell me you got your hands on that Byron bastard."

"Byron who?" the marshal called back without pausing or turning around.

"Redmond. He runs this crew."

"I'll let you know who I've got when I've booked them." The marshal gave us a wave but continued on toward the entrance.

"Rochelle?" Beau asked me as we found the back door and tumbled out into the parking lot hand in hand.

"I don't know, Beau. But I didn't see him."

CHAPTER NINE

"Taking us back to some sleazy motel and shoving us behind wards accomplishes nothing, asshat," Kandy snarled at Blackwell. We were back at the sedan, and the two of them were currently wrestling each other for the right to open the driver's door.

I glanced at Beau. He shrugged his shoulders. As we'd walked back from the bank, Blackwell and Kandy had argued the entire time.

"It's your blood, werewolf," Blackwell snarled back. "You want to be an idiot about it, it's your funeral. But I won't have the pack place the responsibility for your death on my marker."

"Speaking of the pack," I said, not even remotely loud enough for Kandy to hear me through her ranting, "Desmond texted —"

"I should rip your head off," Kandy growled at Blackwell. "Call in that 'marker,' you evil son of a bitch."

"You currently appear practically too weak to move, wolf," Blackwell spat back. Then he grimaced regretfully.

Kandy let go of the car door. Blackwell stumbled back a step, caught himself, then closed his eyes for a moment as if reining in his emotions.

Sirens sounded, not that far away.

Blackwell opened his mouth.

"Shut it!" Kandy snarled. Then she stalked around the car to the front passenger side.

I grimaced at Beau. He nodded, silently agreeing with me. Calling a werewolf weak was a really, really bad idea.

We climbed into the back seat together. I scooted across until I was sitting behind Kandy, tucking my satchel between my feet.

Blackwell folded his long frame into the driver's seat.

"I blame you." Kandy didn't glance over her shoulder, but it was obvious her vitriol was now directed at me. "I owe you nothing, sorcerer."

"Apparently, that is the way of the pack." Blackwell's tone was once again smooth and cultured.

"I have no idea what you're referring to. This is about you and me. There is no debt to be wiped between us. There's only blood on your hands."

Speaking of having no idea what anyone was talking about, I still didn't have a firm grasp of what the pack — or Jade Godfrey — held against Blackwell. I glanced at Beau. He shook his head, just as ignorant as I was.

In the early visions I'd had of the dowser, I'd often seen her in conflict with Blackwell. But I was fairly certain their 'bad blood' had something to do with her sister, Sienna, who'd gone dark. Actually, 'blood frenzied' was the term Audrey had used when I asked her. The beta had been more open to answering questions than anyone else in the last year and a half. Apparently, Adepts didn't talk about magic. How that was supposed to be healthy, I had no idea.

"Getting you behind wards would be the best next step." Blackwell started the car, continuing the conversation from outside as if it hadn't been interrupted.

"You don't give a shit about us," Kandy spat.

"But I do give a shit about Rochelle. And I'm more than a little intrigued by this." The sorcerer set the diffuser into the dashboard shelf in front of Kandy. The werewolf leaned away from him as he did so.

He ignored her to pull away from the curb as the approaching sirens got louder. Flashing lights were accumulating around the bank two blocks away.

Blackwell awkwardly turned the car around in the narrow street, driving away as Kandy fumed.

Beau reached over and folded my hand in his. I shuffled as close to him as I could with my seat belt on, laying my other hand on his forearm.

"So much to talk about," he murmured to me.

"And no time to talk about it," I whispered back. Then I smiled at him.

Looking relieved, he pressed a kiss to the back of my hand.

"It doesn't smell like magic." Kandy spoke up again from the front seat, begrudgingly opening up a discussion about the diffuser.

"No?" Blackwell responded. "How did it make you feel?"

"Like nothing at first."

Obviously, the two of them had mutually and silently decided they were going to act professional now.

"But we were knocked out, like Beau said."

"Then super groggy," Beau added.

"Yeah, and it never really wore off."

"It's easing now," Beau said.

Kandy touched her neck. The welts from the stun gun were looking less red and puffy. "Yeah, a bit."

"And those cuffs of yours?" Blackwell asked, not quite managing to keep his greed from seeping into the question. "They made no difference?"

Kandy twisted the cuff on her left wrist as she eyed Blackwell's profile. The sorcerer didn't take his eyes from the road. He'd negotiated us back to the main street.

Beau and I cranked around to watch the scene at the bank through the sedan's back window. Police cars, ambulances, and a fire truck had blocked both lanes of traffic, but I couldn't see any movement from the bank itself, or the marshal.

Kandy not answering the sorcerer's question seemed to confirm my suspicion that Adepts didn't like talking about their magic. What the werewolf probably didn't know was that Blackwell had seen all my sketches. In fact, the sorcerer owned the bulk of them. Well, any that he decided were relevant to him. So he'd seen the cuffs in action. I was fairly certain werewolves didn't lift thousand-pound boulders off their friends, namely Jade Godfrey, without some extra magical help.

We were now a few blocks down from the bank, the view growing smaller behind us.

"Fucking Byron," Beau muttered, turning away from the back window.

"Does he know you're a shifter, Beau?" I asked.

Beau shook his head.

"Then why place the diffuser in the room?" Blackwell asked. "It would have been smarter to simply lock you in the vault." He glanced at us through the rearview mirror. "Why take your blood if he doesn't know what you are? If he isn't a practitioner himself?"

No one answered him.

Blackwell negotiated the sedan around a corner just past the Chinese restaurant where he'd picked up Henry. The diffuser slid to the other side of the shelf as he did.

"We've seen a diffuser like that," I said.

"Yeah. That essential oils store on West Fourth in Vancouver sells them," Kandy said.

I looked at Beau. "No. Today."

He frowned, uncertain. So he hadn't noticed the diffuser in his mother's living room. I wasn't surprised. He'd been livid.

"Where?" he asked.

"Ada's," I whispered.

"Ada's," he repeated hollowly. Then he slumped back in his seat. "Cy."

"Cy what?" Kandy prompted, turning around in her seat to look at Beau.

"Cy's new gig," Beau said, his mouth twisted with scorn. "The one he was pitching me this afternoon. The shit he's selling behind Byron's back. I shouldn't have assumed it was nothing."

"Selling diffusers?"

Beau looked at me. His expression was so pained that my stomach twisted just looking at him, even though I wasn't the one who'd hurt him.

"Maybe selling something that can be used to suppress a shapeshifter's magic," I whispered, putting the pieces together.

"If they're willing to sit around on the fucking couch with it running all day, smoking and drinking ... and watching fucking soaps," Beau snarled.

"Your mother tries to suppress her changes?" Blackwell sounded shocked by this idea.

"Yeah."

"And this Cy is an Adept?" the sorcerer asked.

"Barely," Beau growled.

"Sorry, Beau," Kandy said, then she turned back to face out the front window again. "Forget the motel. Take us back to the highway. I'll tell you where to turn."

"It's your choice," Blackwell said with a shrug. "Your blood."

"Yeah. And I want it back."

Beau leaned over and pressed his lips to my temple. "This is crazy," he whispered. "We warned Ettie. I don't want you around this shit anymore. We should just get to the Brave and go."

Regardless of the prone-to-judgement adults in the front seats, I reached up and ran my hand down the side of Beau's face and neck. "Yeah, I know you're right," I whispered. "But I need to see this through. I need to understand why I was shown what I saw. Plus we kind of got Kandy into this. And ... well, Blackwell is ... intrigued. Which can't possibly be good left unchecked."

Beau half-growled and half-sighed. Then he turned away to look out the side window at the houses and buildings blurring by. He wasn't mad at me, but he was viciously mad with himself.

Again, I couldn't fix anything. I could only be with him.

Or that was what I kept telling myself ... over and over again. Because I was trying to ignore another reedy voice attempting to creep into my thoughts. It was bringing my well-cemented fears of being delusional, of being crazy, into the forefront of my consciousness. Once, I'd thought this voice sounded like my shrink, but it was just my id in disguise.

And right now, my id was whispering to me about how I made everything worse just by being there. Just by existing.

I tightened my grip on Beau's hand and shoved the thought away ... but once it had been articulated by my mind, I couldn't unhear it.

"Listen, it's getting super late," I said from the back seat. The moon was high in the sky as northern Mississippi blurred past outside along the edges of the interstate. We either weren't far enough away yet from the light pollution of the city to see many stars, or they weren't out. I was becoming increasingly and uncomfortably aware of how far away we were from the Brave. "You guys should eat something. And sleep. We should head back —"

"No," Kandy said from the front passenger seat. She'd been texting furiously — from my phone — for the last thirty minutes. She didn't even raise her head as she shut me down. "Next exit," she said to Blackwell. "The house is a couple of blocks off the highway."

The sorcerer obligingly changed lanes.

"You'll heal faster."

"Lean and mean is a thing, oracle," Kandy growled. "Kitten knows what I'm talking about."

I looked at Beau. He shrugged. "The sooner we lay hands on Cy, the sooner it's done."

"Left up ahead," Kandy said.

Blackwell lifted his gaze to the rearview mirror, but I caught only a glimpse of the dark shine of his eyes.

I shuddered. "This isn't how it's supposed to be," I whispered to Beau. "This is supposed to be about saving Ettie … not everything else."

"I know," he whispered back.

Then the vision crashed down over my head and shoulders with no warning.

I convulsed with it, drawing my knees up, then slamming my feet into the back of Kandy's seat.

"What the fuck?" the werewolf snarled, but I was beyond caring.

I clawed at my neck, attempting to pull my necklace free of my tank top, but was thwarted by the continued convulsions. The vision didn't appear in a hazy mist. It was a blizzard, an avalanche.

Beau reached across me to undo my seat belt. "Pull over, pull over!" he was shouting.

I tried to breathe through it, but all I could see and feel was white, white, terrifying white. I was fighting the magic, though I knew I shouldn't be. I had to calm down.

Beau pulled me into his lap, gently easing my sunglasses off.

"Is she having a seizure?" Kandy asked.

"No," he said.

Kandy let out a string of curses. "There, there. That's the house."

Blackwell was muttering something in another language. The car abruptly swayed to the side, then stopped.

"I can't see!" I cried. In the comfort of Beau's arms, I had tried to calm down and let the magic have its way, but all I was getting was endless, driving white. "Why can't I see?"

My door clicked open. The evening heat instantly blanketed me. The relentless white storm in my mind eased, though not enough for me to see. I seriously loathed air conditioning.

Beau tightened his arms around me. A low, rolling growl rumbled through his chest.

"Easy, shifter," Blackwell said. "Getting her out of the car might help."

"Are you crazy?" Kandy snarled from the front seat. "The neighbors will take one look at her, then at us mauling her, and call the cops."

"We're shielded, werewolf," Blackwell said. "Try using all your senses."

"You're such a dick."

Blackwell didn't answer. I felt his cool hands on my upper arms, coaxing me forward. "Being on the grass might help. Even just your feet."

"I've seen her have a vision in a freaking house, sorcerer," Kandy said.

"Sealed into a metal box? Completely surrounded by man-made materials and recycled air?" The sorcerer was tugging at my shoelaces, pulling off my sneakers and socks.

Kandy didn't answer, but Beau spoke up. "In the Brave …"

"Do the visions come easily in the RV? Or just better than now?" Blackwell's tone was gentler as he addressed Beau than when he'd spoken to Kandy.

Beau didn't answer.

I lowered my feet onto the grass, feeling Blackwell step away. I was already sweating in the residual heat of the day, but I felt instantly more settled with the dry grass underneath my feet.

"It's okay," I whispered. White mist flooded my mind for a brief moment, then parted, leaving me looking at a large room. Sunlight flooded in from the bank of windows to my right.

Not the alley? Was this a different vision?

Ettie was standing before a steel counter situated underneath the middle window. The counter was strewn with broken glass, twisted metal, and crushed plastic. Boxes, all featuring pictures of either diffusers or electronic cigarettes, were knocked asunder, half of them on the counter and half on the floor around Ettie's feet. Beau's sister was picking through the broken glass on the counter as if looking for something.

She was wearing a white sundress with the blue flowers that I thought might be forget-me-nots.

Same dress. Same day.

I squinted at the windows. They weren't the type any-one could accidentally fall through. Ettie would have to climb up on the counter just to open one … if they even could be opened, which didn't appear to be the case.

Muffled voices sounded through the closed door across from me. So there was a room beyond this one.

Ettie found whatever she was looking for. She dropped it into an undamaged diffuser, then quickly plugged the diffuser into the wall.

Her eyes were bloodshot, as if she'd been crying for hours and hours. Or as if she was really, really amped on something. I'd heard the look called 'booted,' 'red,' or 'razed' before, but it all meant the same thing. Ettie was under the influence of some drug. I'd pegged her all wrong. Not Miss Goody-Goody now.

She was looking directly at me. Except I couldn't have been there. Chi Wen had said I couldn't have vi-sions of myself.

She was looking through me, not at me. I turned.

Beau was hunched against the far wall. His T-shirt was torn and bloody, and one of his eyes was swollen shut. He straightened with effort, as if some of his ribs were broken. Then he reached out and smashed his fist into a diffuser that was smoking away on a nearby metal shelving unit.

"You always ruin everything, Beau," Ettie cried.

Beau collapsed onto the concrete floor.

The door banged open behind Ettie. We both whirled around at the sound as it was half-ripped off its hinges.

"Dad!" Ettie cried, more ticked off than worried.

Something was wrong with Cy. His face was bleed-ing. No, correction — his eyes, nose, and ears were bleeding. He was looking beyond Ettie, beyond me. He was focused solely on Beau.

Then before I could blink, he tossed Ettie through the window like she was a piece of trash in his way.

It happened so fast. Even within the vision, I nearly missed it.

Ettie had been standing between her father and Beau. Cy had taken the straightest route to his intended target.

The mist of the vision swirled through my mind's eye, blotting out the sight of Ettie crashing through the window. Blotting out her fall onto the sun-softened asphalt two floors below. That was fine with me. I'd already seen that part.

I became aware of the sound and feel of the real world around me. Beau's warm hand creating a pool of sweat on the small of my back. The blanket of heat the earth still held from the hot day. The dry grass underneath my bare feet. Dogs barking, sirens in the distance, cars … the noise of a suburb.

"Why wouldn't the far seer have told her?" Kandy asked. "About needing to be near the earth?"

"I don't know," Blackwell answered. His tone was distant and thoughtful, yet still tinged with wryness. "Perhaps because oracle magic doesn't affect a guardian dragon the same way."

I loosened my grip on my necklace, having no idea when I'd managed to grab it. Oddly, the diamond was still cool in my sweaty hand. Whether that was because of the necklace's magic or simply a characteristic of the gem, I didn't know.

"Okay?" Beau's whisper brushed against my neck.

"Getting there," I replied. "Sorry … that was … different." My hand started itching. "Beau —"

He pressed my sketchbook into my right hand, along with a pristine piece of charcoal. He must have been waiting, ready with the items I would need when I surfaced from the vision. Warmth flooded my chest, sometimes I just loved him so crazy much that all I could do was wait it out until I was a normal, functioning human being again.

Well, not a human, or anywhere near normal. An oracle. An oracle with a vision ready to bust out of her head.

By the feel of the paper, the sketchbook was already open to a blank page. I slipped into the back seat of the sedan again, already hunched over the sketchbook. I'd regained my vision enough that I could see a blur of green as Kandy placed my sneakers on the floor beside my bare feet.

I pressed the charcoal to the paper so fiercely that it broke. I caught and held the second piece without missing a stroke.

"I'll be back," Beau said.

I nodded, falling into the vision as I replayed it in my mind. There was so much to record. So many little details I could miss. And missing something might cost Ettie her life.

So I just wasn't going to miss anything.

When I finally became aware of my surroundings, I'd worn both pieces of charcoal down to nubs and it was full-on dark.

I flipped through the last three pages I'd drawn. Ettie's bloodshot eyes … dropping a cube of something into a diffuser … Beau unconscious with his cheek pressed against what looked like broken concrete.

I always drew more detail than I necessarily remembered seeing. It was too much information to process quickly. Hell, it might take me days to go over the sketches one by one, refining them and pulling out clues.

Beau at the scene of Ettie's death. Beaten and angry, then collapsing on broken concrete.

And Cy, as Beau suspected, being the person who was going to accidentally kill Ettie while attempting to kill Beau. Or, at least, attacking his stepson.

And Ettie possibly using whatever she was selling. Plus her being complicit. At least with whatever was in the diffusers.

I shut the sketchbook. I just couldn't look at it anymore. I was already trying to figure out how to tell Beau about Sara wanting to buy crimson bliss from Ettie. And now … this vision.

A dog barked, drawing my attention outside. We were still parked outside of Beau's mother's house.

Cy's muscle car — the Mustang he drove, not the ones he parked — wasn't in the driveway. The lights in the house were all ablaze. The living room curtains were wide open.

Inside, Beau appeared to be ripping apart the recliner.

"Jesus." I set my sketchbook aside and scrambled out the open car door.

"Leave it." Kandy's hiss came from behind the sedan. I straightened, blinking away hazy splotches as my eyes adjusted to the shadows and the bright haze of the streetlights.

Kandy was leaning against the trunk of the car, cellphone in hand and arms folded as she watched the drama play out in the living room.

"Like hell I will." I slammed the car door behind me.

Inside, Beau seemingly paused at the sound. He turned to look out the window.

"He's handling it."

"Yeah? And he shouldn't have to handle it alone."

I took off across the front lawn, only realizing I was still barefoot when I stepped onto the uneven front path. Blackwell appeared from the deep shadow of the hedge, crossing in to follow behind me.

"Fine," Kandy said. "I'm always up for making things worse."

The front door was open. Nothing looked immediately different, but the house smelled like fried grease. I veered right into the living room.

Ada was all but insensible on the couch. She appeared to be watching Beau, but I wasn't sure she was actually in a state of understanding.

Pieces of the recliner, the car magazines, and the TV were strewn about the room.

Beau looked terrible. His face was a mask of pain and hate. I actually stopped short at the sight of him. He reached out as if to catch me, though he was too far away to do so.

"This the mind reader?" Ada asked. So she was more cognitive than I thought.

"Oracle," Beau snapped.

Kandy leaned in the archway behind me and whistled. "Jesus, what is she on? What the hell could take down a tiger like that?"

Ada started laughing. It was a low, creepy, burbling noise that made the hair stand up on the back of my neck.

"I don't know. This maybe." Beau tossed a plastic sandwich bag toward Kandy. It was light, and the werewolf had to step into the room to catch it before it hit the ground.

"Be my guest," Ada said. "It takes all the pain away."

Kandy opened the bag, starting to sniff the red powder it held. Blackwell snatched it away from her. "Bad idea, wolf."

Kandy snarled, but more at the situation than the sorcerer. Then she fiercely rubbed her nose.

Blackwell stepped over to a lamp that had somehow managed to avoid Beau's tantrum. In its light, he peered at the contents of the bag.

"Smells like magic," Kandy said.

"Looks like magic. Mixed with or bound to something else. Crystalline ..." Blackwell trailed off thoughtfully.

"Is this what you're using in the diffuser?" Beau asked his mother, pointing to the bag that Blackwell was holding.

Ignoring him, Ada leaned forward, shuffling the romance novels around on the coffee table and looking for something.

"No," I said. "That's cubed shaped. In the vision, Ettie ... I mean ..." I trailed off. Beau was staring at me as if every word coming out of my mouth was another betrayal.

"You saw that in the new vision?" Beau asked hollowly. "Ettie with the stuff in the diffusers?"

I nodded.

"Shit," Kandy muttered.

"And that ..." I glanced over at the baggie that Blackwell was holding up to the light. "Well, it's red. So ... that might be crimson bliss."

"And did you see that in the vision too?" Beau asked.

"No," I whispered. "I heard it from Sara."

"Ettie's friend at the university." Beau's face was utterly blank, devoid of emotion.

I nodded instead of speaking. My throat was closing up, and I could feel myself starting to shake. I shouldn't have said anything, not in front of other people.

"Who doesn't want to feel invulnerable?" Ada screeched in a singsong voice.

"Would you shut up?" Beau bellowed at her.

"I thought you wanted me to talk to you, little Beau." Ada reached out a limp arm. Then she suddenly scratched Beau's leg viciously.

He leaped away from her, knocking the coffee table tumbling toward me as he did so.

I froze, knowing I couldn't jump out of its way fast enough.

Right before the table took my legs out, Kandy nudged it to the side. It spun toward the windows and embedded its legs into the wall.

Beau stared at me, looking as if he was going to be sick. Then he whirled around and put his fist through the diffuser that was still happily smoking away on the mantel. In fact, he put his arm right through the drywall and snapped one of the two-by-four studs behind it.

He withdrew his arm, cradling his bleeding hand.

A moment after Beau locked his gaze to mine, I realized I was covering my mouth with my hands. I quickly dropped them. But just for that split second, I'd been scared … scared of Beau.

"Walk it off," Kandy ordered.

Beau brushed by me and exited the house before I had a chance to reach for him. Before I could speak a single word.

"Give him a second," Kandy said. "Then go out."

Blackwell crossed over to pick up the pieces of the broken diffuser, examining each section as he did so.

"Who the hell are you?" Ada said, struggling to sit up.

"Have you got anything to make her talk?" Kandy asked Blackwell.

"We'd have to wait for whatever she's taken to wear off. Or risk scrambling her brain further. Unless you know of a reader nearby."

Kandy shook her head.

I stepped out of the living room, crossing through the front door to sit on the concrete steps. I couldn't see Beau anywhere, but I knew if I sat there long enough, he'd come back. So I gazed out at the well-lit street and waited.

"Do you think this crimson bliss could be deadly?" Kandy asked from inside the living room.

"Well, I suppose that depends on what crimson bliss is," Blackwell said. "And where you've heard about it."

I could practically hear Kandy clamp her mouth shut. The werewolf had obviously forgotten who she was talking to for a moment.

"I see. Pack business," Blackwell said. "And what's in the diffuser, pray tell? Have you got that figured out too?" The sound of his voice faded as he moved farther into the house.

Kandy didn't answer the sorcerer, instead turning her attention to Beau's mother. "You understand we're trying to help your little girl, right Ada?"

"I don't know you," Ada mumbled. "Cy will take care of Claudette."

Kandy snarled. "Cy probably got her into this in the first place."

Ada didn't answer.

I felt oddly ill about invading her home like this. Harassing her in her own living room. But the echoes of my recent vision still reverberated around in my head. Beau beaten badly. Ettie turning on the diffuser to further incapacitate him. Cy busting through the door in a rage.

Ada was culpable in all of that, even if only by willful ignorance.

"I would never hurt you." Beau's voice was a whisper from the pocket of darkness at the corner of the house.

"I know." I reached my hand through the wrought-iron railing to my right.

"Your face …"

"I know. I'm sorry. I'm not scared of you. I'm just terrified of the situation …"

Beau touched my hand lightly. Then he crossed to sit at my feet with his back to me. I rested my hand at the base of his neck. We stared out at the sporadically lit houses of the neighborhood, listening to Kandy moving around the living room. I thought the werewolf might be tidying.

"This is not who I want to be," Beau whispered.

"This is not who you are."

"Ettie …" He trailed off.

"It doesn't change anything, Beau. The drugs, the diffusers. We still try to save her. She doesn't deserve to be killed. Why else would I be getting the visions?"

"Is it Cy? Did you see that too?"

"Yeah. It's Cy."

Beau cradled his head in his hands. Thinking the worst of Cy, then having it confirmed were two different levels of torture.

Blackwell stepped out from the carport. He must have crossed around to it from the back of the house. He glanced over as he spoke. "Nothing. No more drugs, no evidence of spell work. Other than a diffuser in each and every room."

"Can you do a tracking spell?" I asked.

"I don't have access to potent genetic material. Beau is only Ettie's half-sibling. I might be able to make something work with his blood. But my understanding is that Ettie is nonmagical, not a shapeshifter. So even though they're siblings, the magical connection between them is most likely weak. Ada is her mother, but ..." Blackwell looked away.

"She's too fucked up," Beau said matter-of-factly.

"Indeed. I don't know for certain that this drug does anything to her bloodstream, but it seems a safe bet."

"I'll track them," Kandy said from behind us.

I pivoted around to see that she was carrying some loose articles of clothing.

"I really, really don't want douchebag Cy in my nose, but I think his scent will be more reliable. Judging by Ettie's scent, she hasn't been here in a week or so."

Blackwell nodded. "Starting from the bank?"

"Seems like as good a point as any."

"It might be difficult to access right now. I'll contact the marshal."

"Whatever."

Kandy jogged down the steps beside us. As she passed Beau, she lightly touched the top of his head. The gesture of comfort was seriously out of character for the werewolf, but it appeared to settle Beau further.

He sighed, nodding as if he'd come to some decision. Then he stood up and held his hand out to me.

I took it, actually forcing him to drag me to my feet in an attempt to be playful. He grinned, then dropped my hands to follow Kandy to Blackwell's sedan.

"I would like to look at your new sketches," the sorcerer said, falling into step beside me on the front walk.

"They're not finished."

"I would still like to look at them."

I nodded. Saying no wasn't really an option. Without Blackwell, I'd still be figuring out how to get to Beau and Kandy.

"Beau?" Blackwell called ahead of us.

Beau turned around, catching the keys that the sorcerer had tossed to him in the same motion.

"Back seat," Kandy said as she climbed into the sedan. "I want my car back ASAP."

"Me too," I said.

I slid into the seat behind her, retrieved my sketchbook, and passed it to Blackwell as he climbed into the front seat.

The sorcerer took the sketchbook reverently.

I knew he wouldn't deface it in any way, but my stomach still ached for the entire time it was in his hands and not mine.

CHAPTER TEN

"Six Big Macs, four double Quarter Pounders with cheese, two chocolate shakes, and four fries. Supersized." Kandy barked her order at the blurry-eyed cashier behind the glossy white laminate counter.

"We don't supersize anymore," the cashier said. "I can upsize."

"Then do that," Kandy growled.

"A southwest salad, please," I said, interjecting before Kandy climbed over the cash register and ripped the kid's head off. "Oh, and a baked apple pie. Thank —"

"Make that three pies," Kandy said. Then she elbowed me harshly in the ribs when I went for my wallet.

I could practically hear the skeleton-crew kitchen staff groaning as I took off for the bathroom. They'd probably been cleaning up in anticipation of closing. A few of the tables in the restaurant were still occupied, but it was ten minutes shy of midnight.

Despite Kandy's insistence on being 'lean and mean' and keeping their edge, she and Beau had to eat. He had opted for McDonald's. Blackwell refused to even enter the fast-food place, choosing instead to stay in the car and pore over my sketchbook.

Beau and Kandy had eaten three Big Macs each by the time I made it back to the fire-engine-red booth. Beau looked apologetic, then dug into his Quarter Pounders.

"That is not enough food," Kandy said as she watched me squeeze the lime wedge that came with my salad over the greens. "That is not enough food," she then repeated to Beau. He only shrugged.

Beau looked terrible, and it wasn't because of the horrible overhead lighting or the garish mishmash of red, orange, yellow, and white on the floor-to-ceiling tiled wall behind him. His face was haggard, lacking any of the joy I normally associated with his everyday attitude. But then, I'd never seen him so ... assaulted. Not as badly as he had been today. He looked as if he'd been mentally battered, multiple times.

And it wasn't over.

Kandy downed a large fries in two mouthfuls, then reached for a second helping. "We get rid of the sorcerer next," she said between masticating mounds of deep-fried potato.

"How?" Beau asked.

"We cite family business."

"He won't go," I said.

"Then I'll make him," Kandy snarled.

I glanced at Beau. He was watching the green-haired werewolf, wary but not overly concerned.

"You see the way he's poring over my sketchbook?" I asked.

"So?" Kandy asked. "He's obsessed with you ... and Jade."

"He's not obsessed with me, and these visions don't have anything to do with the dowser."

"Then what?"

"The drugs," Beau said grimly. He was carefully wiping each of his fingers with a napkin.

"Yeah," I said. "The stuff in the diffuser and the drugs."

Kandy glanced sideways at Beau, then answered somewhat carefully. "I could text Alain, the beta of the Gulf Coast pack. See if Byron's or Cy's names come up, and figure out how deep this shit runs."

"Why?" Beau asked.

"She's worried that those two young werewolves dying is connected to this all somehow," I murmured.

"What? How?"

"It's just … instinct," Kandy said. "Timing. And Ada. Werewolves don't overdose, but Ada was high as hell tonight. If it turns out that this crimson bliss is what killed the Gulf Coast's fledglings, it's better to get out ahead of it. Better for Beau."

"Not yet," I said. "What if calling in the pack is what makes everything explode? And results in Ettie's death?"

"What if not calling in the pack results in Ettie's death?" Kandy asked.

Beau scrubbed his head so fiercely I was worried he'd hurt himself.

"I can keep my mouth shut a bit longer," Kandy said. "But your family is about to get caught up in a world of shit."

"If they're involved," Beau growled. "If they're not just victims."

My heart pinched at Beau's continued defense of absolutely horrific people. I looked down at my salad to cover my reaction.

Kandy shrugged her shoulders and stuffed an entire hot apple pie in her mouth. "He's a sorcerer, not a chemist," she said as she chewed.

It took me a moment to realize she had returned to the subject of getting rid of Blackwell. "He's a collector," I said.

Kandy jabbed her finger at me. "You. You got us into this."

"Hey," Beau said.

"She can fight her own battles," Kandy snarled.

"Yeah, she can. But you won't like it," I snarled back before Beau could step in to defend me further.

Kandy snapped her teeth together, eyeing me. Then she started to laugh.

And laugh. And laugh.

A few nearby patrons found the werewolf's laugh creepy enough that they got up and changed tables. Two groups of twenty-something diners actually left.

Kandy stopped laughing as abruptly as she'd started. She locked her gaze to mine, deadly serious. "I like you, Rochelle. And Beau ain't half bad either. But I loathe the sorcerer."

"I made a choice."

"That you did."

"It wasn't like I could call the far seer. And you know Audrey would still be going through proper channels to get you two back. Channels we've agreed aren't a great choice right now. Did you want me to call the dowser?"

"God, no. She'd hate the heat. It would melt all her chocolate. Plus, she travels with a small army these days. No. It would be over by now if you'd called Jade, but there'd be a body count."

"The dowser wouldn't kill humans," Beau said.

"I wasn't talking about the dowser." Kandy grabbed the last of the fries, then picked up the trash-filled trays. "You can eat that to go, right?"

I grabbed my salad and apple pie protectively. I was hungry and tired. We'd been up since before dawn and were about to see another sunrise in a few hours. If I couldn't sleep, I sure as hell was going to finish the only greens I'd eaten all day. Plus, I had a thing for apples. That would keep me going.

Blackwell took over driving for the next leg of our trip, and we returned to the bank in silence. It seemed funny that with so much to talk about, there wasn't a single conversation the four of us wanted to share.

Blackwell would want to talk about the vision and dissect the sketchbook, which I'd safely tucked back in my satchel. But neither Beau nor Kandy would want to talk about the future I'd seen as it continued to unfold.

Beau would want to talk about ... all the things his family had accused him of doing. They weren't terribly subtle with their insults. The fact that they would hold something so desperate against Beau was agonizing. Painful enough that I was trying to not think about it ... other than the fact that he'd gotten over it. He'd made it through. But he wasn't going to discuss his past in front of the sorcerer or an enforcer of the West Coast North American Pack.

Kandy wouldn't want to talk at all. The werewolf was so angry that I could feel the energy rolling off her, even with a generously sized middle seat between us. She kept lifting the clothing she'd found at Ada's to her face and inhaling, alternating between a yellowed wifebeater and a pink head scarf.

Beau reached back alongside the front passenger seat, reaching down to wrap his fingers around my ankle. I leaned forward, pretending to root through my satchel, but instead curling my right hand around his wrist. He squeezed me and I reciprocated. Some of the tension he carried in his muscles eased slightly.

I straightened in my seat, offering Kandy a rectangle of spearmint gum. Beau kept hold of my ankle.

Kandy curled her lip derisively at my offering. "Tracking," she said, but with less heat than I'd expected given her mood.

I nodded and popped the gum in my mouth, leaning forward to offer the package to Beau and Blackwell.

"No. Thank you, oracle," Blackwell said.

Beau took a moment to pass his thumb across my butterfly tattoo. I gathered he needed to keep his senses clear as well, though werewolves were better at tracking by scent than tigers.

Blackwell found his way back to the bank without assistance from any of us or the GPS, proving that the sorcerer had a way better sense of direction than I did. Though honestly, I wasn't sure I wanted to remember anything about this part of Mississippi. Nothing against the state. It would just be a way nicer place without Beau's family in it.

But I had known that going in, hadn't I? And I had pushed us to this point, in that self-righteous, quiet way I had of pushing. Because I was still hoping that magic was ... something. That there was some reason behind it. Not necessarily fate, or destiny, or any of the shit that I couldn't really quantify. Just ... right and wrong, good and evil. If I had this power, then I wanted to do good. Yeah, me. The moron who was friendly with the sorcerer everyone else said was evil incarnate.

We circled the bank, parking at the rear on the side street. The houses surrounding us were mostly dark now. It was that late. Though I could see the reflections of a few TVs through half-opened curtains farther down the road.

I'd expected the doors of the bank to be crisscrossed with crime-scene tape, but they weren't. If you didn't count the drug dealers kidnapping and imprisoning Beau and Kandy, it seemed that we were the only criminal activity that had taken place in the bank that evening. The marshal would have executed his arrests on the outstanding warrants. I found myself wondering if that included searching the place for drugs.

"Stay here," Kandy said to both me and Blackwell as she climbed out of the car. "I don't need you muddying the trail. Beau and I will go for a walk."

"That should go over well with the neighbors," Blackwell said, obligingly settling back in his seat. "A hulking stranger walking his wolf in the middle of the night. What could be more normal?"

Beau snickered as he exited the car. Kandy slammed her door shut. Blackwell rolled down his window as the werewolf stepped over to the sidewalk. "The bank isn't empty."

Kandy whirled back. "What am I, an idiot? I can see!"

Blackwell nodded, not bothering to roll his window back up. Though there wasn't any breeze, I preferred the warmth of the evening over the car's air conditioning. Up ahead, a dim light glowed through one of the rear windows of the bank. Someone was in the break room, or maybe one of the bathrooms. I tried to remember the interior layout correctly.

"They won't go inside, right?" I asked.

"She'll just try to pick up Cy's or Ettie's scent around the exterior," Blackwell said. "They want me gone, then?"

I had been thinking about distracting myself from the urge to follow Beau and Kandy by pulling out my sketchbook, so the sorcerer's quick change of subject took me a moment to process.

"Yeah."

"And you?"

"I'm grateful for your help."

"When you refine the sketches, do you add to them?"

"No. I mean, I just heighten them. Sharpen them, you know? And then I decide which ones to take to a larger scale. For the shop."

"So everything that you remember is in those rough drafts?"

"Yes."

"Then Ettie knows the location of the lab where crimson bliss is being produced. As does Cy, of course."

"How did you deduce that? I saw the diffusers …" I pulled my sketchbook out of my satchel.

"You've already figured it out, Rochelle." Blackwell's tone was uncomfortably kind as if he was babying me somehow. "Beau won't appreciate being kept in the dark. He isn't that … type."

"I'm not lying to him."

"But you're not fully seeing either."

"It's been a shitty day, sorcerer," I snapped.

Blackwell waved his hand, acquiescing.

That just pissed me off further. "You weren't just looking at the sketches while we were eating," I said.

"No."

"So just tell me what you know."

"I know what you know, that this drug lord … Byron, Beau called him … is interested in Cy, so he's interested in the drug. Crimson bliss, you called it. And the crystalline drug Beau found at his mother's is indeed red. So Cy must be involved somehow. Otherwise, why would he be avoiding his former employer?"

"Plus according to one of her clients, Ettie is selling crimson bliss. So that's a double connection back to Beau's family."

"And ... the drug has been deadly to a few Adepts. Though, apparently there haven't been any nonmagical deaths. Not yet."

My heart sank. "How could you possibly know that?"

"I know a great many things, Rochelle Hawthorne," he said. "And if I don't, I find out."

"How many deaths?"

"Five so far. Two werewolves and three spellcasters, as far as I could ascertain."

"Don't tell Beau," I blurted without thinking. "Not yet, please."

Blackwell lifted his gaze to the rearview mirror. I could barely see his deeply shadowed face, and I doubted he could see much of mine.

"Why do you think we're here, oracle?" Blackwell's whispered question chilled me despite the warmth of the night air.

"Not to save Ettie," I whispered back, finally voicing the secret I'd been trying to hide from myself since sketching the last vision. "At least that's not why I'm seeing what I'm seeing. But it doesn't mean I can't still ... try."

"I agree."

"You think the visions are about the crimson drug? Because it can kill Adepts?"

"We won't know until it's all over. But yes, I would assume that you've been given these visions in regard to the drugs, not Beau's sister. You say she's not magical?"

I shivered again, wrapping my arms around myself as I ignored Blackwell's question. "Given by whom? Where do you think the visions come from?"

The sorcerer returned his gaze to the street. He was silent for so long that I assumed he wasn't going to continue the conversation. I was trying to figure out how to question him further when he finally spoke.

"That's not for me to answer. Only you will come to know that, Rochelle Hawthorne."

"Do you believe in God, then? That your magic comes from some divine providence?"

"No. I believe in genetics."

"So I'm genetically predisposed to see glimpses of the future? My brain is simply capable of operating on that level?"

"Yes. I believe that you ... that we ... have evolved."

"But magic goes deeper than that. It's older than that. Older than the far seer, even ..." My voice trailed off. Sharing too much of anything with the sorcerer was a bad idea. We weren't friends.

Blackwell snorted.

I let the subject drop. This was the path we were on. I could try to make the right choices as we went, but I wasn't the only one making decisions now.

Henry Calhoun slid into the front passenger seat of the car before I even knew he was anywhere nearby. Blackwell didn't so much as flinch.

"The wolf isn't picking up anything significant," Henry said.

"I see she's circled three times." Blackwell's reply was coolly polite, as if maybe Henry had worn out his welcome.

I'd flicked on the overhead light to work on the sketches, undoubtedly calling attention to the fact we were parked on the side of a residential street for no legitimate reason. But Blackwell hadn't said anything, so I hadn't turned it off.

Unfortunately, no matter how I shaded or smudged the charcoals, I didn't glean any new information as to a location. Obviously, the goal was to find Ettie elsewhere before the moment of her death. But as the night dragged on, I was starting to feel as if the realization of the vision was exceedingly imminent.

Henry cranked around in his seat to look at me. "I figured you out, Rochelle Saintpaul."

"Oh, yeah?"

"You're a seer."

Blackwell snorted. "She is not some dime-store psychic replete with tarot cards and crystal ball."

"No?" Henry asked, his tone playful. "Then you aren't going to tell me when I'm going to die?"

"It doesn't work like that," I mumbled, stuffing my sketchbook away and rubbing at the charcoal still coating my fingers.

"While your help was appreciated, marshal," Blackwell said, "I wonder why you're here now. I would think you would be well on your way."

"Well, you know how I like to hang out with you, buddy," Henry replied. "But yeah, it's more than that. It's this Byron Redmond and what he's looking for."

"Did you find him?" I asked.

"No. Nor have I heard a single truth about Ettie or Cy Harris, either. Byron's boys are very mute on the subject, as in not one word. They didn't even ask for a lawyer. The four with outstanding warrants are being shipped out in the morning. And the others are just waiting out the twenty-four-hour hold. Not a word." Henry eyed Blackwell, then looked back at me. "I only caught the name because Beau asked after him in the bank."

"But the name alone is intriguing enough to bring you back here," Blackwell said blandly.

"Well, no. Rochelle is intriguing enough to bring me back. I wondered what it costs to commission one of those tattoos."

Blackwell clenched his jaw. Henry was looking at me, but his smile still widened at the sorcerer's reaction.

"It doesn't work like that," I repeated. Though I wasn't sure what I was really denying, because I did sell some of my tattoo sketches in my online Etsy shop.

Henry's gaze dropped to my arms, then to my fingers, which I was still rubbing together. "Maybe not yet," he said. "What do you think, Blackwell? Do you think she would have to ink the designs?"

"I think that Rochelle Saintpaul is none of your business, Henry Calhoun."

"But Byron Redmond and his multiple outstanding warrants are. We maybe have twenty-four hours to stay ahead of the feds on this. If Beau ties Byron to Cy, then I can get a trace on Cy's cellphone. All legal-like. It's a gray area of jurisdiction, you understand, so we'd have to move quickly to contain the situation."

"Beau would have to testify?" I asked, already knowing that I wouldn't want him to do any such thing.

"It's not going to get to that," Blackwell said. "Adepts don't go to human court."

"Byron isn't an Adept."

"But Cy is," Henry said. "Yes?"

"Of some sort."

"Either way, it'll be over in twenty-four hours," Henry said.

"And if we don't want your help?" Blackwell's voice was still coolly professional, but the question was edged with a warning.

"You don't have any choice, sorcerer," the marshal said smugly. "You're in my territory now … unless you want to call in the Convocation or the pack?"

"Those are my choices as you see them, Calhoun? Witches, the pack, or you?"

"Yep. Plus, you need me to keep your asses out of jail." Henry opened the car door and stepped out. Then he poked his head back in. "I booked us rooms at the Motor Inn."

"But —" I started to say.

Blackwell shook his head at me.

I stopped talking.

Henry eyed us both, then nodded and slammed the door shut.

"You didn't want me to mention the Brave?" I asked. "I don't think we can park where we left it overnight." Technically, it was actually the next day now, so it was possible we'd already gotten a ticket.

"I assumed you might wish to maintain some anonymity," Blackwell said. "And I took care of the Brave while you were deep into sketching the vision. It'll be all right parked by the university for now."

Kandy opened the side door behind Blackwell and flung herself into the seat beside me. "Can't pick up anything of Ettie past the parking lot," she growled. "Not even the car she must have gotten into. Too many people coming and going around here today. Her scent isn't distinctive enough. And not a whiff of the asshole either."

Her hair was an odd, mottled mixture of green dye and light ashy brown. I opened my mouth to comment on it.

"Shut it," Kandy said preemptively. She reached up and flicked off the overhead light.

Beau and the marshal were standing next to the streetlight about a half block down. Beau's head and shoulders were hunched forward, his hands in his pockets as he listened to whatever Henry was saying to him.

"We're not getting rid of the marshal either," Kandy said.

"Obviously," Blackwell said.

"This is pack business, sorcerer. Family business. You aren't wanted."

"Yet I'm not going anywhere, wolf," Blackwell snapped. But then he added, almost kindly, "This is too big for you now. Too many factors. The pack will decide it's messy, then attempt to contain it. I imagine, though he loathes them, that Beau would prefer his family survive, if possible."

"What are you saying?" I interrupted. "The pack would just kill everyone?"

"Someone has stolen blood from two shapeshifters," Blackwell replied. "Someone is creating drugs that dampen or enhance Adept abilities. Drugs that appear to be lethal."

"Lethal?" Kandy asked. "You've gotten confirmation?"

Blackwell nodded.

"Ah, shit," Kandy muttered, pressing her head wearily back against the headrest and closing her eyes.

"The witches would do the same as the pack," Blackwell continued. "Though their solution would be much cleaner. Perhaps the humans involved would survive with their memories wiped. Though that sort of magic has a tendency to destroy the minds of the magically lacking."

"Oh my God," I whispered.

"The Adept don't stay off human radar easily," Blackwell said.

Outside, Beau nodded to Henry, then turned to wander back to the sedan.

The marshal, who'd been making notes or texting during the latter half of his conversation with Beau, lifted his phone to his ear as he jogged over to a car. It appeared to be a duplicate of Blackwell's sedan, except it was navy blue as best I could tell in the low light.

"Henry Calhoun will keep you out of jail, at least," Blackwell admitted begrudgingly as we watched the other sorcerer drive away.

Kandy snorted. "Like you'd ever be taken, Blackwell."

"That's why I said 'you,' werewolf. Rochelle and I would be halfway around the world."

Beau ended the conversation by opening the passenger door and climbing into the sedan.

He glanced around at all of us. "So what did I miss?"

Kandy grimaced. "The sorcerers are the least of our problems. Blackwell says he's confirmed that the drug is killing Adepts."

The words were out of the werewolf's mouth before I could intervene. I wanted to deny it, to rally Beau and say everything would be okay. But I couldn't. So I didn't.

"Jesus," Beau said. Then he fell silent.

"Yeah," Kandy said. "You want to have a chance of coming out of this alive, and with your family alive, we're going to have to put up with the sorcerers. Or we could take you back to the Brave and you two could get your asses out of town."

"And leave you to clean up my mess?" Beau said.

"How is any of this your mess?" Kandy asked, her voice uncharacteristically soft.

"I left. And before I left, I was … complicit. I worked for Cy … and Byron."

"As a minor," Blackwell said. "Even the pack with their draconian laws don't hold the sins of a father against a child."

Kandy muttered something under her breath that sounded suspiciously like, "I'll rip your draconian head off."

Beau had turned to catch and hold my gaze. "Rochelle?"

He was leaving the decision to go or stay up to me. Staying could mean more mental and physical torture for Beau — especially if the vision ran the course I'd seen. Running away would be easier in the short term, but possibly way, way more difficult in the long term.

I nodded, through a fear that felt like it had been boiling in my belly for days. "We see it through now."

"It's complicated as fuck," Kandy grumbled, pulling my phone out of her pocket and beginning to text.

Blackwell started the car. "The Motor Inn?" he asked Beau.

Beau must not have known the place. He leaned forward to type the name into the GPS.

"It's glitchy," Blackwell said. "Four Adepts and less than twenty-four hours. Magic has had its way."

My stomach churned at Blackwell's pronouncement. Which was odd for something said with such flippant ease, but the notion of magic having its way just felt like too … much. Too much uncertainty. Too much potential chaos.

I was glad that everyone else apparently knew the next step to take. Because for someone who supposedly saw the future, I felt completely blind and completely out of my depth. Though neither of those were terribly new sensations. It was just the location and the fine details that were different.

The marshal was waiting for us at the Motor Inn, along with an SUV for Kandy that — other than being charcoal — looked identical to the behemoth she had parked at the university with the Brave. Apparently, the marshal took special requests, though maybe only for snarky werewolves.

The motel was a classic two-storey deal, where you could either pull up and park in front of your room or take the exterior stairs to the second-floor balcony. Not that I'd ever stayed in a motel before.

Blackwell parked the sedan in the last available spot, in front of unit eleven.

The marshal dangled car keys in Kandy's face as she pretty much bolted from the vehicle. The werewolf snatched them with a grumbled, "Thank you." Then she grabbed a motel key from him and disappeared into unit thirteen without another word.

Apparently, the red neon 'No Vacancy' sign didn't include us. Free Wi-Fi and 'retro' massage beds were listed as amenities below the grammatically challenged 'You'll Be Glad You Motor Inn' welcome sign. Even though I wasn't sure 'retro' was the right term for describing something that was unintentionally super old, I was already digging through my satchel to see if I had any quarters.

"Any word?" Blackwell asked as he took two more motel keys from Henry.

"When Cy turns on his cellphone, we'll be the first to know," Henry said. "Thanks to Beau."

Beau nodded but didn't say anything.

"I'm in number fifteen if you need me," Henry added, turning away.

Blackwell watched him go. Then, after a quick glance at the room numbers on the plastic tags attached to the keys, he slowly scanned the walkway between the parking area and the doors of the ground-floor units.

"One of those ours?" Beau asked.

"Yes." Seemingly satisfied with his exterior scan, Blackwell unlocked the door to unit eleven and looked inside. "Stay here."

The sorcerer entered the room and began to prowl, not touching anything as he looked around. When he crossed into the bathroom, I could hear him pull the shower curtain back. Then he returned to where we were obediently waiting by the door.

"Clear," he said, passing the key to me. "Though I imagine you'll want to check yourself."

Beau stepped past Blackwell without replying. He conducted a more thorough search of the room, which included lifting the mattress and then the entire bed frame.

"You think Henry would plant something?" I asked Blackwell.

"I think he's a sorcerer. Younger and less powerful than me, and in a position to ... accumulate assets."

"Like you accumulated me?"

Blackwell smirked. "I'm next door." He stepped past me to exit the room.

I closed the door behind me, threw the night lock, and was snatched into Beau's arms before I could turn back.

He lifted me off my feet as he pressed my back against his chest, his face into my neck. "Don't hate me," he whispered into the sensitive flesh just behind my left ear. "I should have told you ... I should have ..."

I wrapped my hand up and around the back of his head. "Beau ..."

"No, I need to speak now. I need to tell you everything."

"Okay."

He carried me to the bed. After setting me down on the end, he kneeled before me. I lifted the strap of my satchel off over my head and set the bag on the floor by my feet, never taking my gaze off Beau's anguished face. His head was bowed, eyes staring blankly somewhere around the level of my knees. He was visibly overwhelmed by everything he thought he had to say.

I ran my fingertips across his temple, then along the edge of his ear. "Bright in here," I murmured.

Beau immediately stood, crossed back to the door, and flicked off the yellow overhead light. A dimmer wash of light filtered in from the bathroom, fading into deep shadows by the door. This softened the edges of the room, dulling the garish orange and beige bedcover, smoothing the worn tan carpet, and hiding the chipped edges of the fake wood dresser.

Beau kneeled before me a second time, leaning forward to grip my hips, then pressed his face into my belly. He remained silent, though. I was afraid he'd explode if he didn't manage to express himself soon.

"I know I …" He started to speak, then corrected himself midthought. "That first time in the Brave. The night we met. I just … I'm good at that. At sex. But I know you hadn't been with many people before me. That it was sudden for you."

"I asked you to come back with me, Beau. I couldn't believe you'd come with me."

Beau laughed harshly. "And now you know that I'm a whore."

I gripped his shoulders, struggling to ignore the pain that shot through my chest at his choice of words. I needed to say something … to help … to try … but I'd never been tied to someone so tightly that I took their pain as my own, and the feeling overwhelmed me.

"It sullies everything between us," Beau cried.

I pressed my hands to his face, holding him so tightly that my knuckles ached. "No," I whispered fiercely. "Never."

"Listen … listen to me."

"I hear you, Beau."

"I took money from women for sex, even after I left Southaven," he said. "I never asked for it. At first it was just … arranged. Then —"

"Then they wanted to give it to you," I said. "A gift. Just let that be gifts."

"And before?"

"Did you ever harm anyone, Beau? Did you ever physically assault anyone … other than defending yourself from Cy?"

"Not even then," he whispered. "I might have killed him if I'd hit back."

"So you did what you needed to survive. If I'd been you … if I'd had to do what you did, what you were forced —"

"Not forced."

"Coerced, then. As a minor, by people you trusted …"

Beau nodded, though I knew he was simply acknowledging my words. Not agreeing with them.

"Would you love me any less?" I whispered.

"No." The word was ripped from him. As he fought with his emotions, his grip on my hips became harsh for a second, then relaxed.

"I was …" I stumbled over my thoughts, correcting them as I spoke. "The only reason I didn't do more shit was because … no one wanted me. Not until you."

Beau growled, starting to negate my words. But I pressed my hand lightly across his mouth so I could finish.

"Our lives began that night in the Brave." I gazed down at his perfect face in the dim light. Though I didn't have to see it to know it better than my own.

"You'd do that for me?" Beau whispered.

"You did that for me. Why should I love you any less?"

I pressed the lightest of kisses to his lips. I wasn't sure he wanted physical intimacy, given the tenor of our conversation. But I didn't know how to express everything I felt verbally.

Beau flicked his tongue against my lips. I opened my mouth to deepen the kiss, pressing my tongue against his.

"It's different with you," he whispered as he broke off. Pressing his forehead against mine to speak, then kissing me again. "You know that, right? It's not about … proving or taking. It's just this." He ran his hands up my arms, wrists to shoulders, then slipped them down again to flick his thumbs against my erect nipples. Electricity followed in the wake of his touch. His magic stirred up my magic, moving through and around it.

"I know." I darted my tongue into his mouth and wrapped my legs around him as best I could. "I see you. Sometimes all I can see is you."

Briefly removing his mouth from mine, Beau slipped his hands up underneath my tank top and pulled it off over my head. I did the same with his T-shirt as he flicked my bra open. He got my sneakers off with two quick tugs at my heels.

I lay back on the bed to shimmy out of my jeans. Beau stood to divest himself of the remainder of his clothing.

"I don't like this bedspread. It's scratchy," I pouted teasingly.

Beau laughed, sounding more like himself than he had all day. I grinned back at him as he towered over me completely, epically naked.

He picked me up, threw me over his shoulder, ripped the cover off the bed, and then tossed me back down. Bouncing on the springy mattress, I couldn't help but laugh.

"Much, much better," I said.

Beau leaned down over me, planting his hands on either side of my shoulders. Then, not touching me anywhere else, he sucked on my nipples one at a time. The pressure was intense. Almost painful. Needy.

"Salty," he said, appreciatively smacking his lips.

"We could shower," I murmured, though I didn't even remotely want to move an inch away from the bed.

Beau slipped his hand between my legs to make sure I was ready for him. "We'll do that next," he said, lowering his body over mine and sliding into me.

I wrapped myself around him — arms, legs, and heart. Our playfulness dissolved into a pure need to touch and taste and feel. To just be in this moment. Together.

The sun was rising by the time we curled up in bed, freshly showered and with the intention of sleeping. I opted for opening windows over turning on the air conditioning, but it was still too hot to cuddle. We lay spooned without touching, my back to Beau's front.

I'd been drifting for a while when I realized I hadn't said everything I wanted to say. Everything that needed to be said before dawn.

"We might not be able to stop it, Beau."

"I know," he murmured sleepily.

I almost didn't continue. He needed to sleep, to heal his mind along with replenishing his magic.

"The vision of you ... in the parking lot ..."

"Which you stopped."

"Or I put on hold."

"Blackwell isn't going to kill me."

"Chi Wen said I was only successful in thwarting that vision because Blackwell didn't intend to kill you. It wasn't your destiny to die in that parking lot."

"Cy might be an asshole, but he doesn't want to kill Ettie."

"Exactly. It's an accident. I'm not sure we can stop an accident."

"Of course we can. That's what makes things accidents. Their changeability."

I didn't want to argue Beau out of having hope. I didn't want to be that person to him.

"Have you seen different?" Beau asked. "In this newer vision?"

"No, just ..." I said. "Things are piling up ... maybe I just haven't had enough time to really study the sketches."

"But Blackwell has." Beau's sleepy tone sharpened slightly. He tolerated the sorcerer because he respected my choices, but he didn't like him. Certainly not anywhere near as far as he could throw him.

I rolled over onto my back to stare at the cross-hatched pattern of the ceiling. The motel room was slowly brightening. Sunlight was attempting to penetrate the room through gaps in the curtains. Not that it mattered. I was already carving into the pocket of peace we'd created just by voicing my concerns.

"Blackwell thinks the visions are about the drugs. Because Ettie isn't magical, but the drugs are. I think the connection for us is Ettie. Ettie's death."

"To draw us here."

"If you believe that's how the magic works … if you believe that I'm supposed to function as some sort of hand of fate." I still wasn't a fan of the idea of destiny. I liked to think I carved my own path, made my own choices. So the idea that I might not be a hundred percent in control of everything chafed me, though I still had to acknowledge the possibility.

"A conduit, maybe," Beau said, willing to entertain at least part of my hypothesis. "But you chose to come."

I swiveled my head to look at Beau. His eyes were closed, which meant I could stare at him as long as I wanted without feeling weird about it. He reached across, grabbing my far hip to tug me closer.

"We'll get all sweaty," I said.

"That's what the shower is for."

"Oh, yeah? That's what the shower is for? Could have fooled me."

Beau laughed huskily. The arm he'd slung across me grew heavier with sleep. "There'll be more time for words," he murmured.

I let him sleep, thinking I was too wired, too full of questions and concerns to do so myself. But I was wrong. I drifted, then slept without dreaming.

CHAPTER ELEVEN

"CAN'T YOU LET THEM SLEEP LONGER?" Kandy's voice floated in through our open window.

I groaned, rolling away from the sound and wishing it had been a cool breeze instead. I fell instantly back to sleep.

What felt like only seconds later, someone was rapping briefly and lightly on our door. The noise was just loud enough to cut through the regular city sounds that I'd had no trouble sleeping through.

I cracked open a single blurry eye. Beau was already crossing to answer the door. He stuck his head out and engaged in a brief murmured conversation. I was surprised that he was both awake and fully clothed. I needed at least three more days of sleep.

Beau shut the door quietly, as if he thought I might still be sleeping, then turned back to find me watching him from the bed. He'd thrown a sheet over me sometime in the night or maybe before he'd answered the door.

"Who was that?" I yawned as I stretched, then regretted the stretching because it woke me up far too fast.

"The marshal. They got a ping off Cy's cellphone. They need a couple more to triangulate. He just wanted us up and moving." Beau hovered at the base of the bed, staring down at me. His face was etched with worry.

"What time is it?"

"About ten."

I groaned. "That's not even four hours' sleep."

"You could stay here." Beau shoved his hands in the pockets of his jeans, still looking at me steadily but not smiling. He was wearing an emerald green T-shirt I didn't recognize, but which did wonderful, intoxicating things to his dark aquamarine eyes.

"What's wrong, Beau?"

"What isn't wrong?"

"I … I thought …" I sat up, wrapping myself in the bed sheet and pulling my knees to my chest.

"Ah, geez. I'm just being … I just can't shake all this shit out of my head, you know?"

I smiled, but didn't voice a single one of the wiseass comments rattling around in my head. It was definitely not the time to make light of the last twenty-four hours.

Beau laughed, seemingly despite himself. Then he sobered quickly. "I love you like crazy. I don't want you to get hurt."

I nodded. "I can say the same. And I know crazy."

"If you stay here, then …"

"Then I'll be bored?"

"And safe."

"Maybe." I wasn't sure anyone could guarantee anyone else's safety like that anymore. Not in a world full of capricious magic. "I know you don't want me near your family."

"I don't even want you in the same state."

I snorted. "Right. But I get it. I get them, at least on the surface. They can only hurt me by hurting you, because I'm not invested. They're just people to me, not family."

Beau scrubbed his hand across his head, then turned to paw through a couple of plastic bags on the dresser. "Kandy went shopping."

"She picked that T-shirt for you?"

"Yeah." He smoothed his hand across his chest and belly. "Do you like it?"

"I think you already know the answer to that."

Beau offered me a blazing grin.

I fake-scowled at him. "Are there at least tooth-brushes and toothpaste in there?"

"Yep, in the bathroom."

I slipped off the bed to head into the bathroom, noting that the room was embarrassingly trashed from our late evening. I'd have to tidy before we left.

"Is that weird?" I asked from the bathroom door. "Kandy shopping for us?"

"Nah." Beau was still sorting through the bags. "Pack behavior. She's ranked higher than me. Obviously, since I have no official position within the pack. So she's supposed to feed us, clothe us."

Beau had left an ice-white toothbrush for me, taking a pea-green one for himself. I squeezed a generous dollop of toothpaste on it, then wandered over to the doorway so I could see him while brushing my teeth.

He held up two tank tops, one light gray and one charcoal. I pointed to the charcoal one. He tossed it on the bed and returned the other to a bag. He lifted a black sports bra out of the second bag with a sneer.

I laughed, choking on toothpaste. I owned only two bras, but mine were much more about eye candy than support. I could easily go without.

Beau tossed the sports bra next to the tank top, then added underwear and socks to the clothing pile.

I returned to the bathroom sink to spit and rinse.

"You could stay," Beau said again from the doorway. He'd appeared there silently.

I crossed to him, pressing my face against his chest. "I know. But I'm not going to leave you alone with them. Plus … in the newest version of the vision …"

Beau grunted. "I know."

"You looked at the sketches?"

"I know I'm in the room. Ettie, Cy, and me."

"Yeah." I cranked my neck to look up at him. He cupped my head and brushed his thumb against my cheek. "Plus, if I'm there … as well as Blackwell, Kandy, and Henry, then it has to be different. Somehow. Right?"

"Or you're lying dead in the next room."

I nodded, swallowing the fear that was suddenly threatening to take my voice along with my resolve. "Yeah, that could be."

"We don't know how the visions work yet," Beau said. "Maybe you can see beyond your own death."

"I got it the first time." I tried smiling, but the expression felt false so I let it drop.

I deliberately stepped away from Beau instead, letting the sheet drop to pool around my feet. "Did Henry give you a timeline?"

"They're still triangulating."

"So I have time to shower?"

"Yeah." Beau was out of his clothing before I'd even managed to climb into the tub.

He reached over me to knock the shower head so it was directed against the back wall, warming the tile there for a second before he lifted and pressed me against it. "I can be quick," he murmured.

"But efficient, right?" My teasing tone once again dissolved in the wave of desire that the feel of Beau's skin against mine always triggered.

I gasped as he rubbed against me. Then all I could do was hold on to him ... be with him ... taste and touch him.

My Beau.

We didn't have to go far through Southaven to find the triangulated point that indicated the last stationary location Cy had used his cellphone. At least, that was how Henry explained it. However, the newly constructed industrial-looking area we found ourselves in didn't yield any other immediate clues.

The neighborhood was oddly quiet. The area was situated at the edge of the city, but I would have expected more people to be around by late morning. A couple of the streets were blocked off for paving crews, though the equipment was currently unmanned. From one end of the development to the other, warehouse-type buildings were in different stages of construction. Some appeared completed but empty, while others had walls but no windows.

"It's lunchtime," I said.

"Are you hungry?" Beau asked. He'd barely spoken since we left the motel, simply loading our clothing-filled plastic bags into the trunk before he climbed into the back seat with me.

"No, I mean, that's why it's so quiet around here. The construction crews must be off for lunch."

The marshal was texting with someone from the front seat. Blackwell was driving. Kandy was following us in her SUV.

"Looks like the wolf will get her wish," Henry muttered.

"What wish is that?" I asked, because fulfilling Kandy's wishes really didn't sound like a good idea.

"A hunt," Beau said tersely before Henry could reply.

"Or we could just check out the buildings where the pavement's new. Like over there." Where I pointed over Blackwell's shoulder, the asphalt surrounding the buildings was so pristinely black it looked as if it had been laid yesterday. "If this is where Ettie … falls …"

I'd corrected myself midthought, subbing 'falls' for 'dies,' but Beau still flinched. I barreled on, knowing we just had to get through the next few hours and then … well, then we'd know what pain the immediate future held. "We should be looking for a grayish-blue building with a second floor."

Blackwell turned the sedan in the direction I'd indicated.

Beau straightened in his seat. "You think this is where the vision takes place? That this is then? I mean, now?"

"I don't know, Beau. I saw the new asphalt when we first circled past. It … feels right. Like everything is coming to a head. Doesn't it?"

Beau didn't answer.

"Most of these buildings are empty. Or in the process of being occupied," Henry said as he scanned the neighborhood. "Woodworker there. Other custom furniture places. Tile and marble supply place. New and pricey."

"Cy's gotten Byron's attention," Beau said darkly. "So he's taking enough of a market share to alert the local drug lord. High rent probably isn't a concern. Occupying a space in an area still under construction means fewer nosy neighbors."

"Or your drug-dealer friend flags any new product that gets talked about or requested," Henry said. "And Cy was just in the area, peddling his wares."

"He's not my friend." Beau's voice was low and deadly.

The marshal raised his hands in mock surrender, then went back to texting. Blackwell continued to drive slowly down the street.

Beau reached across and took my hand. He brushed his thumb across the butterfly tattoo on my left wrist, sending sweet shivers up my arm.

"Ettie dies today," he said, heavy with unreleased emotion. It wasn't a question.

Threading my fingers through his, I squeezed his hand as hard as I could, trying to give him all the strength I had. It wasn't much, but I hoped it was enough.

"Is you being here going to be a problem, shifter?" Henry asked without looking up from his phone. The question was posed calmly and without judgement. "I was against bringing you both. The werewolf pulled pack rank. But it's shady. The Adepts we're hunting aren't pack."

"One Adept," Beau corrected.

"Two members of the West Coast North American Pack were assaulted," I said. "That's pack business."

Blackwell pulled the sedan up in front of a building with blue siding, parking in one of four newly painted spots. The warehouse didn't appear to be occupied. Or at least it bore no signage near the main front door or the lower-level windows.

"And you?" Henry said to me. "What jurisdiction are you going to cite?"

I saw Blackwell watching me in the rearview mirror as I answered. "I'm here at the behest of magic, sorcerer."

"So you've seen what's going to happen?"

"I have."

"And you've seen me?"

I hesitated. I hadn't seen the marshal. I hadn't seen anyone but Beau and Cy in the lab with Ettie.

Henry snorted. "But you've brought us along, so I'd hazard a guess that it's all going to change now."

"That's the plan," I said, putting on my brave face again.

Henry opened his door. "You're just as blind as the rest of us." He exited the sedan before I could respond. Which was fine, because I didn't have a response.

Blackwell smirked at me in the mirror, but whether he was condemning my ignorance or Henry's, I didn't know.

Beau climbed out of the vehicle and I followed. Kandy drove past in her behemoth SUV, circling the block in the opposite direction once more.

We waited in silence for the werewolf to return. The late morning was cooler than yesterday had been. Either that or I was getting more accustomed to the heat.

A couple of cars drove by a couple of blocks away, but I didn't see anyone in the immediate vicinity.

"Cy drives an old Mustang," I said.

"Yeah, local police have eyes out for it, and him," Henry said. "But I doubt he's stupid enough to be driving it now."

Beau snorted but didn't add anything to the discussion.

Henry tucked his phone away in his suit pocket, lightly touching his badge and the handcuffs clipped to his belt as he scanned the area. I'd seen Blackwell make the same subconscious gesture with his amulet. And Jade did the same with her wedding-ring necklace and the invisible knife she wore sheathed on her hip. I wondered if I checked my diamond necklace like that without realizing it ... finding stability, or comfort, or confidence in its magic.

Kandy was back. She parked her SUV one spot away from the sedan.

"A car dealership is having a grand opening one block east of here," she said as she got out. "Everything else within a two-block radius looks empty or under construction." Then to Beau, she clarified, "So if we have to track, it's human noses only."

"Magic should be easy enough to pick up around here. It'll be completely out of place," Henry said.

"Stopping Cy should be our first priority," I said. "If he's the one who kills Ettie, then holding him should thwart the vision."

"Well, that's a whack of information no one bothered to fill me in on," the marshal drawled.

Blackwell snorted. "Please, you've already put that all together."

"Yeah, but no one was kind enough to actually give me any details. Thwarting a vision, hey? That will look good on the resume."

Kandy ignored the marshal. "Beau and Rochelle, you circle. One block at a time, widening the arc as you go. Beau can find Ettie by scent. Or that Byron shit. I'm not ruling him out in all of this yet. The marshal and I will look for the asshole."

"Asshole?" Henry asked mildly. He was obviously amused at Kandy calling the shots.

"Cy Harris," Kandy spat. "He is the one with the outstanding warrant, right?"

"Not exactly, but finding him will do." Grinning, Henry touched the brim of his cowboy hat in Kandy's direction.

"And me, wolf?" Blackwell asked. He was wearing a perfectly pressed dark navy suit today. I wondered if he'd teleported home to Scotland to get it.

"I was hoping you'd just fuck off."

"No luck with that," Henry said with a laugh. Then he smirked at us when Kandy glowered at him.

Blackwell simply scanned the building before us instead of responding.

Kandy spun on her heel and grabbed Cy's wifebeater out of the back of the SUV. Then she clicked the lock button on her keychain and cut over to the entrance of the blue building.

"I guess that's my cue," Henry said with a lazy grin. He touched the brim of his cowboy hat in my direction, then sauntered off after Kandy. She was already turning the corner to cut between the blue warehouse and the darker blue building next to it.

Each building on the block was fronted by a single span of parking spots situated just off the road. There were easily twelve brand-new warehouses of varying sizes in a three-block radius around us, not including the car dealership Kandy had mentioned.

It was a weirdly empty, freshly painted wasteland. Even in the middle of the day, bright sunlight and all, it felt as if anything could happen here and not be seen or heard.

It would make a perfectly benign place to set up shop for any sort of business that needed extra workspace and didn't rely on public transport or walk-in traffic to drive sales.

Like a drug lab.

Creepy with a side of creepiness.

I shuddered. Beau pressed his hand to my back, but then let it drop away.

"This one?" Blackwell asked, indicating the blue building before us.

"No. I didn't see it from the front, but it's the wrong color."

"I didn't think so," the sorcerer said smugly. Then he started walking toward the next street corner. "Wrong siding. And height."

"You didn't tell Kandy it wasn't this building," Beau said under his breath as we tagged after Blackwell.

"They won't go far," I said. "I just thought it might be better to find Ettie ourselves. And to get her out of here, hopefully in one piece. In the vision Cy enters the room after you do, right? Maybe Henry and Kandy can catch him before he even gets in the building."

Still, despite the evidence presented in the vision, I was hoping it was Cy we found first. I was hoping it was him who'd taken the blood from Beau and Kandy. Or even that Byron had done it. Because I was really sure that even if we thwarted the vision, Ettie wouldn't survive Kandy's wrath.

The instant we stepped between the two buildings on the opposite corner, I knew we were in the right place. As I neared the exact spot underneath the middle bank of windows on the second floor above us, I couldn't hide the shudder that ran through me.

"This is it?" Beau's tone was tense and stressed.

I nodded. "What time is it?"

Blackwell glanced at his phone, then looked overhead. "Twelve thirty."

"We don't have much time," I said. "If it's happening today."

"How do you know?" Beau asked.

"The shadows," Blackwell answered for me. "No shadows at the edges of the building in the sketches."

I nodded.

Beau glanced around our feet. About two inches of shadow edged the concrete foundation of the building to our left.

Blackwell continued onward through the newly paved breezeway between the buildings. We hadn't seen another person yet. Beau lifted his gaze to the window above us.

"Can you tell if she's up there yet?" I asked, just to say something.

Beau shook his head. Hunching his shoulders, he trailed after the sorcerer.

I pressed my hand against my chest, grinding the thick chain of my necklace into my upper ribcage painfully. I welcomed the sensation. I thought my heart might stop beating because it was aching so harshly. The ache increased with every step Beau took toward the final confrontation I'd seen between Ettie and Cy.

I'd seen Beau's sister die over and over again. Her head hitting right where I stood. Her blood slowly seeping across the asphalt. If I didn't stop it, Beau would be here to witness Ettie's death. And he already felt like he'd failed her once.

I inhaled, then tried to exhale all my doubts. I had to see this through.

Beau paused with his back to me. I always forgot his hearing was so sharp.

"Maybe we should just leave," he whispered, still not looking at me. "Maybe our being here causes it."

"We try to stop it," I said, firming up my own resolve. "If we end up causing it ... well ... then that was what was meant to happen."

But even as I said it, I couldn't wrap my head around that notion. I'd come this far and suddenly I wasn't sure which way to step. I was just blundering around ... what had Chi Wen said? 'Trust the magic. Move where

it wills, where it leads, but don't try to alter the path.'
Was I blatantly disregarding that wisdom? Was I ignoring it because I thought I could alter the future? Or was
I simply observing what I knew was about to unfold in
some form beyond my control?

"I just hate this shit," Beau said, echoing my un-
voiced thoughts. "I hate believing in anything more than
you and me. And what I can taste, touch, and feel."

I didn't answer. I didn't have any answer. I wished we
were back on the beach, toasting marshmallows in the
bonfire that Gary and Beau had built. Or before that.
Before Chi Wen had surfaced at the laundromat. Before
he'd unlocked the visions and pushed me back on the
path of … everything I couldn't qualify and couldn't
control. Fate? Destiny? The inevitable? The will of some
divine providence?

Of course, the far seer didn't practice what he
preached. But then, he was one of the nine most powerful beings in the world.

And I wasn't.

I didn't know … anything.

Beau turned back to me. His bright green shapeshifter magic danced in his eyes, then faded into his
normal dark aquamarine gaze. He smiled sadly.

"We're here," I said, knowing he was about to say
the same. "We see it through."

He reached back for me.

I stepped toward him, closing the gap between us
until I could thread my fingers through his.

This I knew.

This connection was real.

I knew Beau. I knew I'd go anywhere with him. Even
if we were heading to witness his sister's death. Even if
nothing we did could change the inevitable.

CHAPTER TWELVE

ETTIE WAS STANDING AT A STEEL COUNTER that ran the length of a freshly painted cloud-white concrete wall. Sunshine streamed in from a bank of industrial aluminum-clad windows situated over the counter. A laundry-sized sink and a shelving unit sat in one corner. The shelves were laden with the printed boxes of diffusers and e-cigarettes that I'd seen in the vision. Larger unopened cardboard boxes were piled on the polished concrete floor in all of the three remaining corners. The room was laid out strikingly similar to the lab at the university, though there was only a single worktable in the center of the space and no second door through which to escape.

It also happened to be the room in which Ettie was going to die.

Beau's sister was clothed in the white sundress with the blue forget-me-nots that I'd seen her wearing in the vision. The dress I'd told her to burn. I wondered if I hadn't said anything whether she would be wearing it. Then, I pushed the thought away as too complex to contemplate in this moment. Her face was covered with a gas mask. It was an odd combination.

Beau and I stood side by side, silently peering through the half-open door. We watched as Ettie slowly and carefully poured some sort of red-tinted liquid from a beaker into a large round-bottomed glass flask suspended over an open flame. The Bunsen burner and flask were hooked up to other tubing and equipment that I had no reference point for. But I got the gist.

Cooking, it was called.

Yeah, Ettie was the chef.

Blackwell was somewhere in the empty rooms behind us, maybe even still on the first floor. Beau had made a beeline through the building and up the stairs the moment we entered. He hadn't bothered to look around. The sorcerer was more cautious.

Everything carefully piled throughout Ettie's lab was new. Based on the diagrams and the pictures on the exterior of the boxes, at least six different types of diffusers and dozens of different types of electronic cigarettes occupied the shelving unit on her right. Price tags were still stuck to three folding chairs propped next to the shelf. A fourth chair was opened up next to a large box that someone had been using as a table. It held a gas mask, empty soda cans, and a ragged-paged porn magazine.

I tried to not gag over the idea of Cy paging through porn while watching Ettie cook.

Several dozen carefully labeled baggies holding red crystalline powder were lined up beside a scale on the counter next to the shelving unit. Though the bags were plumper, the powder appeared to be a duplicate of the drugs Beau had found in Ada's living room. I hadn't seen those in the vision, or in the sketches. I seriously hoped that meant we were early, that the vision was due to happen tomorrow or the next day.

Beau tilted his chin up, opening his mouth to scent the air like a cat would. "That's my blood," he said. "And Kandy's."

Ettie froze, carefully clamping the neck of the flask she was heating before lifting it away from the flame.

Turning just her head, she looked over at us. She didn't put the flask down.

A wooden test-tube rack occupied the center of the counter space to the right of Ettie's arm. Six of the rack's dozen slots were occupied with glass tubes full of what looked like blood. Six other test tubes lay on the counter next to the sink, each tinted with residual streaks of red. Ettie was a tidy cook. She was obviously planning to clean up, maybe even reuse the test tubes.

What if getting Beau's and Kandy's blood had been the plan all along? Maybe that was why Byron had used Tasers to kidnap them, not guns.

Had Ettie texted the drug dealer when she'd first seen us in the corridor at Coulter Hall?

No.

That didn't line up with how scared she was that night, and with how she'd fought back.

Except, there was a diffuser in the vault ... placed there to keep Beau and Kandy under control ... and Ettie was standing before us, surrounded by diffusers and drugs ...

My mind was running wild with terrible scenarios of blame and betrayal. I was squeezing Beau's hand so hard I was hurting myself. But it was either that or throw myself across the room and gouge Ettie's eyes out with my tactical pen. Beau probably wouldn't be a fan of me murdering his sister with a gift he'd given me for self-defense.

Though that would be a hell of a way to thwart the vision.

I eased my grip off Beau's hand. He hadn't flinched or taken his gaze off Ettie, who was also still staring at us. And by us, I meant her brother.

Ettie said something, her voice muffled enough by the gas mask that I couldn't distinguish her words.

Beau snorted.

"What did she say?" I asked. Yes, exactly as if we were watching a movie and I'd missed an important line. This moment, this situation, already blurred the lines of reality all over the place for me. I was missing too much. I didn't need to miss more because of my lack of supernatural hearing.

"This is sensitive, Beau," he said, mimicking Ettie's prim tone perfectly.

Ettie went back to her cooking activities. Apparently, we weren't much of a threat.

Beau cursed under his breath, pushing the door all the way open as he scanned the room.

"Get back, please," he said to me, watching as I took two big steps back into the empty room behind us. "Pull your tank top up over your mouth."

I frowned at him, but I did as he asked.

He reached over to the pile of boxes to the left. He smacked the top one off the stack, exactly like a kitten would bat a stuffed mouse. Except Beau was no house cat.

The box flew across the room, arcing over the table and smashing against the far concrete wall. It exploded in a burst of glass and crushed cardboard.

Ettie screamed, dropping the flask she'd been holding. It hit the steel counter but didn't break. It did, however, knock over the Bunsen burner. She scrambled madly for the open flame, knocking her other cooking equipment flying off the counter.

She managed to right the burner and snuff the flame before it set anything on fire. She ripped off her gas mask and whirled to face Beau. "How dare you muscle in here and try to destroy what I've built!"

"You're in big shit, Ettie." Beau held out his hands to her, calm and placating.

"Right," she scoffed, glaring over Beau's shoulder at me. Her murky brown eyes were clear, not red rimmed like I'd seen them in the vision. "I'm going to die."

Beau pointed to the counter behind her. "That blood you took —"

"You owe me, Beau."

"Fine. But the werewolf is an enforcer for the West Coast North American Pack."

Ettie faltered at that news, then she jutted her chin out defiantly. "An enforcer? Perfect, then. The crimson wolf will be more potent for it. And forget Mom's measly contribution now that I've got your blood."

"You have no idea what you're saying."

The pain in Beau's voice pinched my heart as I stepped past him into the lab. "Listen, I get we don't know each other, but we need to leave. Now. Even a change of location might help."

"Tell you what," Ettie said, turning back to the counter. "You give me a blood sample. I do my thing with it. I'll test it myself. If it's worth anything, I'll listen."

"What the fuck is wrong with you!" Beau roared.

I clamped my hands over my ears.

Just like in the lab at the university, several more glass beakers, flasks, and cylinders broke on the counter behind Ettie. Beau's sister didn't even flinch. In fact, she crossed her arms and leaned back against the counter.

"Who are you to judge me?" she said coolly. "What have you done that makes you so holy?" She glanced at me with a sneer. "Being her ... what? Bodyguard? That makes you saintly?"

"Nothing, Ettie." Beau's shoulders sagged. His exhaustion was more emotional than physical now. "There are people coming. Adepts who aren't going to be happy with this." He swept his arm to include the entire lab. "The drugs you're cooking are killing users. Other Adepts."

Ettie sneered. "Bullshit."

"Are you partnered with Byron? Or was Cy the one who pushed you into this?"

"No one pushed me, Beau. I'm not as weak as you think I am, not as worthless. Not a dud."

"Ettie —"

"No! You want to know the key to all of this? The reason no one can take it away from me? It's me. The recipe? My blood is the bonding agent."

"What do you mean?"

"I figured it out. How it was that you inherited mom's shapeshifting when your dad was just some shitty spell-caster. Why I didn't at least get Cy's abilities. Because my magic is in my blood. I did my thesis on it. How do you think I got the scholarship?"

Beau placed his hands on his head as if to stop himself from hearing the epic hole Ettie was digging for herself. "Jesus, no."

Ettie waved him off. "I didn't talk about Adepts or magic. I'm not an idiot. But I did the genetic and chemical research. I'm not just cooking crystal meth for Cy anymore. This is my art. My great creation."

"You so are an idiot." Beau turned to look at me, completely aghast.

"Fuck you, loser. And what are you good at? What are you worth? Just the money you can make on your back —"

"That's enough!" I shouted.

Both Beau and Ettie flinched.

"This isn't about sibling rivalry," I said, shoving myself into their conversation. "This is about your dad coming in here, bleeding out of every orifice because he's so jacked on this crap you're so proud to be making. This is about him killing you trying to get to Beau."

"That's never going to happen. Cy would never hurt me."

I kept talking, pitching my voice louder than Ettie's to override her stupidity. "In about a minute, a massively powerful sorcerer is going to come in here, take one look at this ... the blood, the crystal drugs ... and freak out. Because you're taking magic and giving it to humans. You are, right? You can't have enough Adept clientele to make the rent on this place. I know you're selling to Sara. She told me about it."

Ettie clamped her mouth shut, refusing to answer me.

"And you've made some sort of deal with Byron, right? Who also happens to be human. Or Cy made a deal. That's why there was a diffuser in the vault. And it's the only way you're here cooking with Beau's and Kandy's blood."

Ettie crossed her arms and looked away from me. Beau sighed heavily.

"Finally," I continued, "like Beau said, Adepts have died. Members of the Gulf Coast North American Pack and others. We haven't called the pack in, because they'll kill you."

"Even if that's true, who says I can't use magic to cook drugs?" Ettie sneered. "It's not like I'm forcing people to use. I'm simply offering a service. A chance to be stronger, faster, calmer ... happy. Look at mom. I've practically cured her."

"Shapeshifting isn't a disease ..." Beau said.

"The Adept say you can't." I interrupted him, ignoring Ettie's slanted justification. "The pack, the witches, the sorcerers, the dragons, all of them. You're lucky it's us standing here. We can dismantle the lab before —"

"Never. Going. To. Happen." Ettie ground the words through her teeth. She stepped back to the shelving unit, then inexplicably pulled a diffuser out of a box and plugged it in.

"She doesn't get it," Beau murmured. "She's not going to get it in time."

"I get it, Beau," Ettie said. Her tone was casual and easy. "I just don't see how it has anything to do with me." She dropped some sort of chalk-like pink cube in the diffuser. "Silver nitrate, in case you were interested. But the rest of the recipe is my secret."

"One you'll take to the grave," I said, pulling out my phone to text Kandy our location. I'd been holding off, but I had no choice now.

"I really don't like you," Ettie said as she dropped another cube in another diffuser. She placed the second diffuser on the counter, leaving the first one to begin misting on the shelf.

"That's okay," I said mildly. "Few people do. It's the truth saying. No one likes that."

"I don't mind it," Beau said conversationally as he took another step into the room. "It's refreshing. No games."

"Well, no games intentionally," I said. "My eyes, too. My eyes freak people out."

"You like that," Beau said.

"Well, yeah. But only lately."

"Time to go?"

"Yeah." I sighed. "Time to go."

"I'll just get Ettie, then?"

I nodded.

In two quick steps, Beau was beside Ettie and throwing her over his shoulder.

Unfortunately, she'd grown up with a shapeshifter, so his speed didn't surprise her as much as I would have hoped.

She cupped her palm over his nose and mouth. He ripped her hand away from his face quickly, but not before he'd breathed in some of whatever crimson drug she'd been secretly holding.

Beau stumbled back, knocking into the table in the center of the room and dropping Ettie. She scrambled away from him, staying low. He pawed at his face, trying to clear his mouth and nose of the drug.

He stared at Ettie ... so utterly betrayed.

"It's okay," she cooed. "I gave you a bit of Cy's painkiller. You'll like it. Who doesn't want to feel invulnerable?"

Beau stumbled back again, groping to find a hand-hold on the table but knocking it over instead. He staggered to the side until he was touching the wall, pressing his hand against the painted concrete to hold himself upright.

I'd seen him in almost that exact position in the vision. Though the room was still too tidy, so more chaos was to come before Ettie died.

"Almost time," I whispered.

Ettie straightened from her protective crouch, looking at me. "Now you," she said as she searched the counter, then found a needle and syringe. "If you are who you say you are ... well, I'll be able to come up with a whole new line. Crimson sight, maybe. If it works, university test scores are going to skyrocket."

Beau shook his head, trying to clear it.

I kept my eyes on him and Ettie as she crossed toward me.

"Stand still, little oracle," Ettie cooed.

I punched her in the gut. 'Go for the soft parts,' Beau had always said.

Ettie bent over with a whoosh of air.

"Yeah, I'm not that kind of girl," I said. I slapped her across the face as she tried to jab me with the needle. It was a weak move on her part, allowing me to grab her wrist and twist it until she dropped the syringe.

I crushed the needle underneath my sneaker, then kicked it away.

"You think you're an Adept, eh?" I asked. I'd never been as angry as I was right now. Had never hated anyone so much in my life. "Let's test that theory."

I grabbed Ettie by the ears, getting two fistfuls of hair in the process. Then I slammed her brain with my oracle magic.

She screamed.

Then she screamed some more.

And I saw ... nothing. A vast, gray, meaningless nothing.

Something hard and cool pressed against the back of my neck. "Let her go, skank," Cy said from behind me. "Or Ettie will be collecting your blood as it pumps out of your brain."

I let go of Ettie. She stumbled away from me, wide-eyed and fearful. Finally.

Beau straightened up from the far wall.

"Brains don't bleed like that, actually." I slowly raised my hands.

Ignoring me, Cy circled around, dragging the gun he held against my head as he did so. He was dressed in his go-to white wifebeater, though this one had been recently washed. And he was amped, even more so than he'd been the other day. His attention was on Beau, though, rather than me. He held a stun gun in his other hand.

"Give me some of the werewolf shit," Cy said to Ettie. "And the stuff you made with Beau's blood, not your mother's."

"I … I …" Ettie was looking at her dad as if she was shocked to see him with a gun to someone's head. Or maybe she was simply still overwhelmed by whatever my magic had done to her mind. "I haven't processed Beau's —"

"Then get to it," Cy said. His arm jerked. He jabbed the muzzle of the gun against my temple hard enough that I hissed in pain.

Beau started to growl.

Ettie backed away to the counter. "Dad —"

"Ettie," Cy interrupted. "There's a sorcerer in the building. I got him …"

My stomach bottomed out.

"But I can't just kill him right off. There's another one with that cunt werewolf. I called Byron for backup —"

"What?" Ettie screeched.

"We can't contain this on our own now," Cy said.

"We already made a deal with him for product distribution. He's already squeezing us —"

"We need enforcement now."

"But Dad —"

"Give me the shit." Cy shoved his Taser into the waistband of his jeans and jabbed his empty hand impatiently in Ettie's direction. His gun shook against my temple as he did so.

Ettie picked up a single bag of what I assumed was crimson wolf.

"And the other."

Ettie hesitated. But then she crossed to the shelving unit to open a box on the middle shelf. Beau took a step closer to her.

"Stay where you are, you little bastard." Cy grabbed my arm and gave me a shake. "I might have made a deal with the sorcerer for the slit's life, but I'll kill her just to spite you."

I locked gazes with Beau. The idea that Blackwell had negotiated some sort of deal with Cy didn't surprise me in the least. Cy had probably incapacitated the sorcerer with his stun gun, then locked him up somewhere. Even so, nothing would hold Blackwell at bay for long. I was also completely sure that the sorcerer didn't keep deals with idiots.

Ettie grabbed a second baggie from the cardboard box, then crossed back to Cy with it and the first bag. "A deal with a sorcerer now? We're already too exposed and —"

"Just take her blood," Cy snapped. "Keep Beau here under the influence of the silver peace shit. I'll hand her over to the sorcerer and he'll walk away."

Beau snorted. He still looked dazed, though not as much as before.

"One vial isn't going to be enough," Ettie said. "If we're trying to create a product line —"

"One is all you goddamn get," Cy snarled. "If you hadn't dealt Byron in and taken blood from the werewolf, they might have all walked away."

"They're here to save me, actually," Ettie said. "From you."

Cy didn't respond. I couldn't see his face. But I could see Beau, whose eyes narrowed at whatever he was picking up from his stepdad.

Ettie looked dejected for a moment. Then she shook it off, turning to grab another syringe from the counter.

"Mind tricks," Cy said to her back.

"Okay." She didn't look at her father.

A hole blew through the interior wall opposite the windows. Magic and concrete exploded everywhere. Heedless of the gun to my head, I dropped to the floor, seeing Beau do the same across from me.

Ettie was slammed forward against the steel counter.

Cy attempted to stand against the onslaught, but his gun was knocked from his hand by debris.

Then two sorcerers and a werewolf burst into the room. Kandy darted across the lab toward Ettie. Blackwell and the marshal came for Cy, who dove on the ground in an attempt to retrieve his gun.

Correction. Blackwell came for me.

The marshal flicked his magical handcuffs at Cy. The cuffs streaked through the air, coiling around Cy's wrists and yanking him to the ground. But not before Cy got his hands on his gun and trained the weapon on Henry.

Beau straightened. Concrete dust crumbled off him as he yelled a warning to Kandy. "Watch out."

Too late.

Ettie, who'd been slumped over the counter from the blast, pivoted as Kandy reached her. She grabbed a massive fistful of baggies in a single swipe, maybe a half-dozen or more. Then she smashed them all into the green-haired werewolf's face.

Kandy grabbed Ettie by the neck, lifting her off her feet and shaking her. Somehow, even while being throttled, Ettie managed to pop some of the baggies open with the force of her attack.

"Put her down," Cy yelled. He was still lying on the ground with his gun pointed at the marshal.

Then he shot Kandy in the back without further warning.

Henry kicked the weapon out of Cy's still-cuffed hands. A split second too late.

Kandy arched back, dropping Ettie and stumbling away from the counter. Powdered red crystal coated her eyes, nose, and mouth. Even her neck and shoulders were dusted in crimson wolf — a drug made from her own magic and somehow bound with Ettie's blood.

It was a massive overdose. Plus, the werewolf had just been shot in the back.

"No. No. No!" Beau held his arms out wide, as if to catch Kandy if she fell, though he was too far away to do so.

Ettie fell to her knees, coughing and holding her throat.

A monster ripped through Kandy's skin. Literally.

I screamed, completely involuntarily. Even in my visions, I'd never seen anything so disturbingly horrific as the furred and clawed monster that emerged from Kandy's body.

Blackwell shoved me behind him, yelling, "Marshal," as he did so.

The monster, which I belatedly realized was some sort of uber-terrifying version of Kandy's half-form, threw its head back and howled. Its long, disjointed snout scraped against the concrete ceiling, which was easily nine feet high. Its jaws were filled with jagged five-inch teeth.

The howl froze us all in place, like prey. It took every other sound with it, deafening everyone in the room.

Beau recovered first. He dashed forward, wrapping his arms around Kandy. He appeared to be attempting to talk her down. I wasn't sure, because I still couldn't hear anything.

Kandy tossed him off her like he weighed nothing. He tumbled back through the destroyed concrete wall and out of my sight. Then she went for Ettie, who threw her arms over her head and screamed.

Before Kandy could chomp Ettie's head off with her massive, misaligned jaws, something snapped around her maw — the marshal's handcuffs. But they had somehow widened to encompass the thickness of Kandy's elongated snout.

She stumbled back, pawing at her face. She was gouging herself with her own claws, rivers of blood flowing down her jaw and throat.

"Stop her! Stop her!" someone was screaming.

Me.

I was the one screaming.

My hearing was back. Everything was still seriously muffled, but I could hear.

Still blocking me from advancing, Blackwell was murmuring something under his breath. Pools of darkness were forming in his hands.

The marshal circled Kandy. She utterly dwarfed him and everything else in the room, yet he was still attempting to get close to her.

Beau rose out of the rubble of the concrete wall behind the deranged werewolf. He had transformed into his own version of half-beast, half-human. He was about a foot and a half shorter than Kandy's beast-form, and covered in short orange fur. His face was a hideous mix of beast and human, though his double fangs were longer than Kandy's canines, and his jaw aligned properly.

Golden magic swirled around the bracelets Kandy still wore, which had grown to accommodate her new size. Then she snapped the marshal's cuffs.

Henry looked absolutely dumbfounded. By his reaction, I surmised that his handcuffs were supposed to be unbreakable.

Dropping the cuffs at her feet, Kandy lowered her head in Henry's direction. Her wolf ears pressed flat against her skull. Her fur held not even a hint of green.

"Her eyes are bleeding," I called out. "Like Cy's in my vision."

"Henry," Blackwell said warningly.

"Just tell me when." Henry was still facing Kandy, holding his hands to the side in a nonthreatening gesture.

"Now."

Henry sidestepped. Kandy swiveled her massive head to follow his movement.

Blackwell threw his spell. Blue-black orbs of magic flew across the room, hitting the uber-werewolf, then spiraling around her like thick ropes. She screamed in pain, the sound of which was slightly more human than before but still terrifying.

Again, heedless of how her five-inch claws tore into her, she shredded the magic like it was a cozy down blanket and she was wielding a wickedly sharp box cutter.

"It's the cuffs," I shouted. "Her cuffs are dragon magic."

"Beau, Henry," Blackwell barked. "We're going to have to let the drug in her system burn off. Back out slowly. We'll contain her in the building."

Blackwell pivoted, grabbing my arm and hauling me out of the lab and through the doors into the empty room beyond.

"We can't just leave," I cried.

Kandy howled again.

I dug in my heels, looking back over my shoulder.

In the lab, Beau was grappling with Kandy again, drawing her attention away from the marshal as Henry darted forward to retrieve his fallen handcuffs.

"No!" I screamed.

Kandy threw Beau off her. Then at the exact moment the marshal's side was exposed to her, she latched onto his torso and chomped down.

Cy had crawled over to Ettie and was attempting to drag her out of the lab while everyone was distracted by Kandy.

The rest of us stared in horror as the uber-werewolf lifted Henry in her jaws and shook him like a rat. Like she was a terrier trying to snap his neck.

Beau roared.

Every piece of glass in the lab that wasn't already broken exploded.

I clapped my hands over my ears. Cy and Ettie stumbled, falling to the ground just behind us. Even Blackwell covered his ears and hunched against the challenge of an alpha predator.

Kandy froze.

Then she dropped Henry at her feet.

The uber-werewolf slowly pivoted to face off with Beau. She snapped her teeth in his direction, her snarls punctuated by bubbling blood at the edges of her jaw. She deliberately widened her stance, one massive clawed foot at a time. Then she spread her heavily muscled arms, ready to accept Beau's challenge.

"We're going to have to kill her," Blackwell said.

He stepped forward.

I grabbed his arm. "What? No!"

He shook me off. "It's Beau or her," he snarled at me. "You pick, then."

I stared at him in utter disbelief. "No," I said again, looking over his shoulder to watch Beau and Kandy as they circled each other. The lab was barely large enough for them to stay just out of striking range. "She's here to save him."

"He's too young," the sorcerer said. "Inexperienced. Struggling to hold his form. She's going to rip him apart."

Kandy lunged, driving into Beau. Her scythe-like claws caught in his ribs.

Something cracked. Beau screamed.

I shouted to Blackwell, "Do it! Oh God, do it."

The sorcerer pivoted away from me, already calling up his magic.

Then Cy jabbed him in the side of the neck with his stun gun.

Blackwell's eyes rolled back in his head. His jaw stretched into a scream he couldn't vocalize. He unleashed a half-formed spell against Cy, but then went down.

Cy followed him to the floor, hitting the sorcerer with the stun gun a second time even as Blackwell's dark blue magic snaked around Cy's body, attempting to subdue him.

That left Ettie and I as the only ones watching through the open door into the lab while Kandy beat the life out of Beau.

Jumbo handcuffs appeared around Kandy's furry ankles, attempting to snap into place. The marshal had apparently managed to fix them enough to trip the werewolf, though they still appeared to be broken.

Kandy stumbled, dropping Beau. He had reverted to his human form at some point.

I couldn't tell if he was still alive or not as he hit the concrete floor. He didn't move.

Kandy went down on her knees, turning her bleeding, blazing green eyes on the marshal. Henry had managed to prop himself up against the fallen table in order to throw his cuffs at her one last time.

Still on her knees, Kandy swiped at the sorcerer, but he flattened himself on the ground and she caught the edge of the table instead. The table spun, crashing against the counter and flipping back to slide to a stop in the center of the room.

As Henry tried to scramble away from her, Kandy opened her massive, toothy jaw to rip his head off.

Then instead of decapitating the marshal, the werewolf faltered. Her eyes rolled back in her head. She transformed into her human visage as she collapsed, slumping across Henry's legs as he, too, fell to the ground.

"About time," Ettie said. She marched back into the lab.

"What, are you crazy?" I shouted after her.

Then Cy hit me with the stun gun. Apparently, he'd managed to shake off enough of Blackwell's spell to move.

I lost control of my mind and body. I fell on one knee.

Cy grunted, shook the stun gun, and jabbed it against my chest again.

Nothing happened.

The gun must have misfired.

I couldn't move, couldn't think, couldn't even call up my magic.

But I could see. I could see Beau.

He was so far away. Across the room, through the door, and crumpled against the far wall. Crumpled in the broken concrete and glass ... there ... without me.

I didn't want him to die. I didn't want him to die alone.

I forced my shaking left arm to obey me.

I reached inside my satchel.

I sprang up onto my feet.

Cy hit me with the stun gun again.

It worked this time, shooting electricity into every limb and scrambling my brain. But not before I jabbed my tactical pen into the side of Cy's neck with every last ounce of strength I could muster.

Then I fell.

CHAPTER THIRTEEN

I BECAME AWARE OF SOUNDS FIRST ... glass crunching underneath footfalls ... murmured voices. I tried to open my eyes, only to realize they were already open but hadn't come into focus yet.

I heard something electric buzz. Then a pained grunt.

I tried to turn my head. My neck muscles obeyed me, but only for about an inch. It was enough to see Ettie, who had her back to me and was currently standing over Blackwell with Cy's stun gun. Evidently, she had just stunned the sorcerer again.

More glass crunched, then someone muttered.

"Dad," Ettie said. "Get those handcuff things. Dad. Are you even listening?"

"We're going to have to kill them all," Cy said from beyond my sight line, somewhere below my feet. He sounded as if he was struggling to get up off the ground. Hopefully from my tactical pen strike. Maybe some blood loss would be good for the asshole. Cleansing.

"That doesn't make any sense," Ettie said. "What makes sense is to contain them until Byron gets here with his men. Lock them all up, quell their magic with the silver peace, and harvest their blood continually. We have more than enough space even if we lease out the first floor. And we'll be obscenely rich."

Wow. That didn't sound at all insane. Or sociopathic, specifically.

Cy stepped into my line of sight to stare down at Ettie, who appeared to be digging around in Blackwell's suit pockets but not finding anything. He lifted one of the crimson baggies to his face and snorted directly out of it. He still had the pen sticking out of his neck.

Ettie grimaced. "Jesus, Dad."

Cy started trembling. Maybe even seizing. The whites of his eyes flickered through his stubby, red-rimmed eye-lashes in a pained grimace that might actually have been ecstatic. He was enjoying the jolt.

Ettie shook her head. She moved on to checking Blackwell's pants pockets but still found nothing.

I should ask Blackwell to magic up my satchel like his suit pockets. I was guessing Ettie was going to search me next, and I really, really didn't want her touching my sketchbook. Though we'd have to make it out of here alive if that was going to matter. And 'magic up' wasn't the correct term. My brain was still as scrambled as my limbs.

The far seer had indicated we'd survive. But he also might not have bothered mentioning the 'possible im-prisonment and slowly being drained of our magic' part of that so-called survival.

"Ettie," Cy gasped as he got himself under control again. "Ettie."

"What?" she snapped.

My eyesight cleared further. My hands were tingling with increasing amounts of pain. Ettie's eyes were red-rimmed like they'd been in the vision. She must have gotten a snootful when she'd hit Kandy with all the newly cooked crimson wolf.

That would explain her jerky movements. And even her bravado. Though that might just have been utter stupidity.

"We can't contain this," Cy said. "Too many Adepts involved —"

"Dad, this is just a bonus," Ettie interrupted. "Think of how many strains we could produce now. I don't know what sorcerer blood will be good for, but —"

"No, Ettie!"

She reeled back from Cy's vehemence, more shocked and pissed off than angry.

"They'll hunt us," he said. "They're probably hunting us now."

"Who?" Ettie sneered. "Over these nobodies?"

"The pack ... the sorcerers ... the witches." Cy took another snort of the crimson baggie. It was almost empty. He rubbed the inside of the bag around on his gums, then dropped it on the ground.

"That's enough for now —" Ettie started to chastise her father.

He backhanded her across the face.

She fell sideways, down on one hand and pressing her cheek with the other. She met my gaze. Anger and mortification flooded her face.

"Go collect what you have," Cy continued, as if he hadn't just assaulted his daughter. Maybe he considered that a love tap. "I'll finish these five off, soon as I get me more strength. Then we'll torch the place."

He pulled the second baggie out of his pocket.

"You're going to die now, Ettie," I said.

The statement came out as more of a threat than the warning I'd intended. But then, I didn't have total control of my mind or mouth yet.

"What are you going to do, Rochelle?" Ettie taunted as she picked herself up off the ground and brushed off her white sundress. A fierce crimson blemish — the result of Cy's slap — stained her left cheek. "You have no offensive power … I've already seen what you had to show me. Nothing."

"I see you," I whispered.

"So what?" she spat. "I don't give a shit about what you see. Hell, I'll harvest your blood and surround myself with seers. See if I give a shit about the future ever again."

"I don't see a future for you at all," I said. "I never did. I just thought I could stop it. I thought I could save you from fate. But magic wants what it wills."

"Oh, yeah?" She laughed. "Time for me to die? And who's the instrument of my death now?" She straightened, flicking her hand to encompass the devastation in the room and all the fallen would-be heroes. "You?" She snorted. "I've got everything here under control."

She walked away from me, crossing back into her destroyed lab and closing the door behind her with a flick of her foot.

Why close the door? I scrunched my eyes, desperately trying to remember what was about to happen, desperately trying to regain control of my limbs.

Blood. Ettie wanted more blood. She wasn't going to follow her father's directives.

I looked up at Cy. "You need to stop," I said as I watched him take the final snort from the second bag of crimson tiger. Or maybe he was finishing off with the crimson wolf.

He didn't heed me. Maybe he couldn't even hear me. He was already bleeding out of his ears. He turned to look down at Blackwell, then grunted. My pen was still sticking out of his neck. He reached up for it, as if he couldn't remember what it was or how it got there.

"No, don't," I said.

Again he ignored me, yanking the pen out of his neck and dropping it to the ground. Blood started bubbling out of the wound.

Ettie was talking to someone in the other room, drawing both my and Cy's attention. I could hear her intonation but not the words.

I remembered the vision.

Beau. She was talking to Beau.

He was still alive.

Hope flooded through my limbs. Maybe if I could move, maybe if I could get between Ettie and Beau ...

I rolled over, ignoring how Cy was vibrating and foaming blood at the mouth beside me. I made it to my stomach. Then to my hands and knees.

I started crawling.

I looked up as Cy stepped past me and Blackwell, who was still prone to my right.

Then Ettie's father inadvertently ripped the door off its hinges while trying to open it.

The room blurred around me, then came into sharp focus as I realized I was now moving through the first stage of Ettie's final moments.

Through the door, she was standing in the middle of the lab, looking down at Beau with a syringe in her hand. She turned to frown at her father, who was barreling into the room in a stumbling, demented rage.

Cy's eyes, nose, and ears were bleeding from the overdose he was currently riding. Blood was pumping out of the wound at his neck.

He grabbed the table that had fallen to its side during Kandy's rampage, tossing it away so nothing was standing between him and Ettie.

No, not him and Ettie.

Him and Beau.

As in the vision, Cy didn't know Ettie was in the lab. Perhaps he thought he was just following through with his plan of killing everyone and burning the evidence.

His daughter shrieked in indignation. She still couldn't see it, still couldn't understand that he didn't see her, didn't know her at all.

He took two steps closer, slowing down as the drugs melted his brain further. But the strength of a weretiger and a werewolf still raged through his limbs.

I kept crawling forward. But I was so, so slow.

Beau sat up.

Cy, snarling, honed in on his good-for-nothing stepson. Blood bubbled across his lips, splattering to the ground.

"Dad ..." Ettie said.

"Step left, Ettie," I cried as I crawled through glass and concrete and blood covering the floor between me and Beau. "One step left, Ettie." I was on my knees already. I might as well beg.

In a final rally of rage, Cy charged the last few steps across the lab, tossing Ettie aside instead of going around her.

She flew sideways over the counter that held the remnants of her 'great creation,' crashing through the window and falling two floors to the sun-warmed asphalt below.

The fall didn't matter, though. Ettie was dead before she hit the ground. She was dead before her body had cleared the window. The back of her skull didn't leave any impression on the concrete window frame that her head hit as she smashed through the glass.

Beau slid his back up the wall, standing to meet Cy's attack. The last bit of Cy's brain dissolved as he lunged forward. He fell, arms still outstretched to strangle Beau. He didn't move again.

Beau stumbled to the broken window, passing through the final echoes of the vision as he leaned across the counter to look down at Ettie lying dead on the breezeway.

I made it to my feet. Hearing Blackwell do the same behind me, I turned to catch the sorcerer's gaze.

He scanned the lab around me, nodded, then brushed his fingers over his amulet underneath his shirt. He disappeared.

I followed Beau to the window, not fully in control of my limbs yet. I wrapped my arms around his shoulders and pressed my face against him, seeing echoes of the fulfilled vision as it repeated on the back of my eyelids.

Then I looked out the window.

Below us, Blackwell was bending over Ettie, who was sprawled across the sun-softened, newly paved asphalt between the buildings. The sorcerer looked up at us in the window. He shook his head.

Beau let out a strangled cry, as if he'd been waiting for this confirmation of Ettie's death. He turned away from the window, sagging against the counter.

"Rochelle." He shuddered, pressing his hand over his eyes. "Is that it? Is that all you see?"

"I see you, Beau. I still see you."

His shoulders shook. Sobbing silently, he sank into a crouch next to the counter. I wrapped my hand around the back of his neck. He pulled me to him and pressed his face hard — too hard — against my belly. Heat boiled off him. He was sick, fighting the effects of the drugs.

Blackwell appeared in the room. His white dress shirt wasn't so pristinely clean and pressed now. His neck was badly blistered from the stun gun. He cast a grim gaze around the destroyed lab, taking in Cy, Kandy, and the marshal on the floor.

"Damn," he said. For a moment, I thought he might be concerned about Kandy and Henry. Then he added, "I've got the girl's body cloaked for now, but we're going to need witches to clean up this mess. Which will put me in debt to the Convocation."

"Make it my debt," I said.

"Our debt." Beau lifted his face away from my belly to speak.

Blackwell eyed us. Then, nodding, he pulled out his phone as he spun back toward the door. "Stay away from the werewolf until you know she's okay. And Rochelle? If you insist on calling attention to yourself in this manner, it will be more difficult to protect you."

"Protect me from who?" I called after him.

Blackwell didn't answer as he walked away.

Beau pulled away from me. After a series of deep but shaky breaths, he managed to cross over to Kandy. He was too weak to continue standing, so he sat down hard next to the wounded werewolf. Then he pulled her awkwardly into his lap.

"Rochelle," he said. "Check the marshal."

I hadn't realized I was clinging to the counter for support. It took me a second to force my hands to let go of the edge.

Beau's eyes glowed green as he rocked Kandy in his arms.

"Beau," I said as I stumbled around Cy's body to kneel by the bloody marshal. "You'll hurt her. What if … anything is broken?"

"It's not," he said. "We're pack. Kandy, and I, and you are a pack. I say it's so. I claim it to be."

I wasn't sure what Beau was talking about, but the marshal needed my attention more than I needed to unravel whatever magic he was trying to access.

Henry was badly wounded. He was clawed and cut and covered in his own blood. His skin was hot, as if he was also burning off the drugs, except I didn't think he'd been exposed to any. I stood up and started looking for something to staunch the massive bite wound at his belly. I found his cowboy hat first, though, putting it on my own head so I wouldn't lose it.

"We're pack. We're pack," Beau murmured over and over again as he rocked Kandy. "My strength is your strength. We are pack."

I found some kind of absorbent cleaning cloths under the counter. As I crossed back to press them to Henry's belly, a tiny breeze brushed by me ... some touch of magic transferring between Kandy and Beau.

The werewolf groaned, opening her blazing green eyes. Then she violently pushed away from Beau to throw up all over his feet and the marshal's shoulder. She pressed up onto all fours. Her mousy brown hair fell over her strained face. She threw up again.

Beau rubbed his hand on her back as Kandy continued to purge the drugs from her system. The handcuffs were still tangled around her ankles, though not locked. He tugged them away with his other hand.

"Damn," the werewolf growled. She spat out another mouthful of bile. Then she lifted her glowing green eyes to look at me. I froze under her fierce gaze and looked away. But instead of ripping out my heart, she dropped her chin to look at the sorcerer dying on the floor before her.

"I bit him," she said.

"You did."

"Ah, fuck." She crawled forward, brushing my hands away to lift the towels from Henry's belly. Then she swore. And swore again.

Unsteady, she gathered the marshal in her arms, dropping him twice before she managed to lift him fully off the floor. She tried to stand while carrying him and fell again.

Beau gained his feet, reaching for Henry.

"No!" Kandy snarled. "He's mine. My responsibility." She struggled to stand again. Then, carrying the dying sorcerer, she slowly walked out of the lab.

I looked at Beau. An utter dread of what was to come, what I couldn't see coming, settled deep into my belly. Now Beau would leave. Just like everyone left me. Because of my magic ... because I could see, but not accurately, or ... or ...

Beau was staring down at Cy's body. "Let's get the Brave and just leave. Leave and never, never come back." He didn't look up from the bloody corpse of his stepfather.

"I didn't stop it, Beau. I'm not sure ... maybe I could have ... but ... I ... I wasn't strong enough. Or smart enough."

He looked at me then. His eyes were blazing green, as Kandy's had been. His cheeks were streaked with tears. "We all make choices. Including Ettie. Then there's everything else we can't hope to control." He reached for me. "You and me. Beyond luck, you said."

Aware that I'd underestimated him again — that I'd maybe even underestimated myself — I twined my fingers through his.

"I would give anything to just leave this to Blackwell and the witches and run away with you," he whispered.

"But ..." I sighed. "But ... your mother."

He nodded.

Someone had to tell Ada that her husband and child were dead. In the grand scheme of doing things the proper way, I was fairly certain that responsibility fell to Beau and me.

Not that I had any burning desire to be proper, just … human? Humane?

If that was even possible in this case.

Ada wasn't going to take the news well. Maybe it would be even worse for her coming from Beau. For some reason, that made my heart heavier.

Running away was a good, perfectly selfish plan. One that I could really talk myself into if I tried hard enough, especially with Beau limping beside me and putting so much weight on my shoulder that I was having a hard time walking in a straight line. Get the Brave and screw off, leaving everything to Blackwell to sort out. Hide away and let Beau heal, physically and mentally.

Except Kandy had apparently collapsed halfway down the gray-painted concrete stairs that led to the first floor. Henry was still in her arms. She didn't look like she'd be getting back up on her own. At least not doing so and text messaging at the same time, as she appeared to be attempting to do.

Her clothing was all but shredded, but my phone had survived. Nice.

"Stop staring," she snarled as she caught sight of us hovering on the stairs above her. "Rochelle, get your ass down here. Take my keys and pull the SUV around. Beau, go back upstairs and collect everything resembling drugs or blood before Blackwell gets his hands on it."

"He's calling in witches," I said lamely.

Kandy snorted. "Burn it if you don't want to touch it."

Beau nodded. His face and shoulders were once again tight with tension. Apparently, we weren't getting away from here so easily. He brushed his fingers against my palm, then turned back the way we'd come.

"He's injured," I snapped at Kandy as I jogged down a few steps, then climbed over Henry's legs to grab the keys she was holding up to me.

"We all are," she snapped back. "Deal with it. If witches are coming, we need to get Henry out of here. He won't survive their scrub session."

I wasn't exactly sure what she meant, other than the idea that the witches would rather dispose of Henry than heal him, which didn't seem right. But maybe I was missing some vital piece of information. Kandy wasn't exactly in a chatty mood, though, so I kept my mouth shut.

I walked down the remainder of the stairs, then turned back to look up at her. Kandy looked like a completely different person without her green hair. But as I gazed up at her as she stared down at Henry, I wondered if it was more than just the hair.

"He's going to be okay, right?"

Kandy didn't take her eyes off the marshal, whose upper body was slung across her lap while his lower limbs sprawled across the stairs below. "Maybe," she said through gritted teeth. "If the bite heals quickly. Then ... if his magic is strong enough ... and adaptable. Go, Rochelle."

I turned, stumbling out of the warehouse and backtracking to where we'd parked the vehicles. Feeling suddenly exposed to the world in the blistering sunshine, I kept an eye out for any curious onlookers. Hopefully, my dark clothing would hide most of the blood it had probably picked up. Any injuries I'd sustained probably hadn't had time to bruise yet.

I didn't see anyone. Apparently, we were damn lucky that the commercial neighborhood was in the final stages of construction.

Blackwell's sedan was gone from the parking lot, but I doubted the sorcerer was just going to disappear. Not until the witches showed up at least.

I climbed into Kandy's SUV, barely needing to adjust the seat to reach the pedals. The werewolf was tinier than she appeared. Attitude added inches, apparently. Then I drove the block and a half back to the warehouse.

Beau and Kandy were waiting just inside the steel-and-glass front entrance. A discreetly sized, printed metal sign hung to the right of the door. *Harris Industries*. The sign was so new that Cy or Ettie hadn't even removed the protective plastic when they'd hung it up. Maybe they'd been planning on doing a grand-opening ceremony or something.

And now they were dead.

Remnants of the now-realized vision floated to the forefront of my mind. I shoved the images away to focus on Beau's face through the SUV windshield.

Harris Industries had brought this all on themselves. Cy and Ettie had been responsible for deaths and ... Kandy's possibly lethal psychotic break ... and ... I ... I still couldn't shake the memory of their lifeless bodies ...

I parked sideways so that I blocked the door with the massive SUV, though I still didn't see anyone else in the immediate area.

Beau and Kandy lifted Henry into the back seat, then Kandy crawled in after him.

I climbed out of the driver's side and crossed around the vehicle to pass the keys to Beau. As I did so, I was hit with a sick desire to peer around the corner of the building to see if Ettie's body was still lying on the asphalt. I ignored the impulse and climbed into the passenger seat.

"Where to?" Beau asked as he adjusted the driver's seat all the way back to accommodate his long legs.

Kandy didn't answer.

"We can't go to a hospital, right?" I cranked around to look at Kandy and the marshal, who was once again slung across the werewolf's lap.

Henry's face was ashen. He looked younger and more vulnerable without his cowboy hat, which I was still wearing. He looked as if he really needed a hospital. As if he needed an ambulance, actually.

Kandy's phone pinged. She fished it out of her back pocket, glanced at the screen, then answered the text.

My butterfly tattoo stirred on my left wrist. I pressed my right hand over it. Then, following an impulse, I looked out my side window.

Blackwell was watching us from the door of the warehouse. He met my gaze, then lifted his own phone and nodded toward the back of the SUV.

He wanted to be updated about the marshal.

I nodded, but I wasn't fooled. Henry was a useful tool, not a friend of Blackwell's. Just like the rest of us.

"Your mother's place," Kandy said.

"What?" Beau asked.

"You heard me."

"I thought … the pack … in New Orleans. Doesn't he need —"

"He needs an Alpha. He has you and me for pack."

"But —"

"Desmond is coming."

Beau fell silent, gripping the steering wheel as if he was thinking of refusing.

"Drive." Kandy's voice was pitched low and edged with steel.

The steering wheel creaked beneath the pressure of Beau's grip. All the muscles in his arms flexed, his flesh rippling.

"Beau ..." I whispered.

He started the engine, pulling away from the warehouse to circle back to the highway.

"This isn't going to be pretty," he muttered.

"It never is," Kandy said. "The aftermath is always a bitch. Your mother needs to hear the news from us."

"We were already heading that way," I said snidely. I wasn't going to be schooled by a werewolf.

"Fine. Go, then," Kandy said. "That's our responsibility whether we want it or not. And so is Henry."

Beau didn't offer any further protest, but the hair on his arms had taken on an orange sheen. I reached over and stroked my fingers playfully over this thin pelt. Beau removed his left hand from the wheel and touched the back of my hand lightly. The orange sheen faded as he relaxed.

"What did you mean when you said Henry will only survive if his magic is strong and adaptable?" I asked Kandy.

Beau glanced up at the rearview mirror. "You think he'll change? From a single bite?"

"I can barely remember it," Kandy said. "But I was in some sort of crazy, amped-up version of my half-form. Right?"

"Yeah," I said.

"So it depends on what the drug does when an Adept takes it," Kandy continued. "Does it actually create some sort of magical boost? Or just the illusion of it?"

"No way Cy was suddenly that strong just because he thought he was," Beau said.

"Then Henry is doomed. He might have been anyway, because it was … me who bit him."

"And you're an enforcer. So you're … extra special?" I asked. "Blackwell said he's surprised you didn't take the beta position instead of Audrey."

"Not all of us are as power hungry as that evil asshole," Kandy said. "I can't believe I just left him there, untouched. Did you get every last crystal of that shit, Beau?"

Beau nodded. "Blood's soaked into the floor in places. I didn't know concrete was absorbent."

"The witches will take care of that."

Henry groaned in pain.

"Hey, hey," Kandy said, almost cooing. I wouldn't have thought the werewolf capable of being so soft and soothing. "It's going to be okay, marshal."

"My handcuffs?" he asked, so weak he couldn't even open his eyes.

"Fucking sorcerers and their fucking toys," Kandy snarled, looking up at Beau questioningly. Well, the soothing cooing was certainly short-lived.

"I got them," Beau said.

Kandy growled, then pulled a bottle of water out of the back cupholder. She chugged the bulk of it, then tried to make Henry take a sip. He wasn't particularly helpful about swallowing, which triggered more rumbling growls from the back seat.

Funnily enough, I found hard-edged Kandy more reassuring than the mousy-haired caregiver she was channeling now for brief moments. Hard-edged Kandy meant everyone was going to survive, even if she had to hurt them to guarantee their safety. That logic was okay by me.

CHAPTER FOURTEEN

"Why is the Brave parked in front of Ada's house?" I asked, seriously pissed off as I swiveled around to glare at Kandy in the back seat of the SUV.

She bared her teeth in my direction but kept her attention on Henry in her lap. "The proper response is 'thank you,' oracle."

I glared right back at her. I really wasn't a fan of someone hot-wiring my home.

Lara hopped out of the Brave as Beau pulled into his mother's driveway and parked. The brunette werewolf was swathed in purple silk, looking just as lovely as she had in Portland eighteen months ago. Just laying eyes on her made me seethe with jealousy. It was a stupid, utterly instinctive reaction.

"Lara?" I cried. "You let Lara drive?"

Beau snickered.

"She totally has a thing for you, Beau," I said, instantly feeling utterly stupid over my petulant tone. "I don't like people touching my stuff."

Beau reached over, brushing his fingers against my forearm.

"Sorcerer dying here!" Kandy snarled.

We scrambled out of our respective doors.

It was midafternoon. The baking sun was still high in the sky as Lara practically skipped across the dead lawn toward us and snatched the cowboy hat off my head.

Grinning madly, she slammed the hat on her own head and struck a pose, pursing her plump, purple lips in Beau's direction.

He shook his head at her.

"Lara!" Kandy snarled from the back seat of the SUV.

Laughing, Lara spun around so that her purple skirt flared prettily. Then she climbed in the back seat of the SUV with Kandy and Henry.

"See?" I said to Beau.

He smiled weakly at me, but his attention was on the house. Specifically, he was looking at Ada hovering in the front doorway. He lifted his hand to wave at his mother, but she turned away and crossed through into the living room.

Beau's hand dropped back to his side.

Ada crossed by the front window, picking up what appeared to be an electronic cigarette.

Beau turned to look behind us.

Ada crossed back to the window. She was now vaping what I seriously doubted was nicotine.

A car door closing drew my attention back to the street.

Desmond, the Lord and Alpha of the West Coast North American Pack, was striding toward us from an SUV identical to Kandy's. He'd parked on the other side of the street.

My stomach bottomed out. I hadn't met anyone who scared me quite as much as the pack leader. Not even Jade Godfrey. Mostly because the dowser didn't have the magical hold or pull over Beau that Desmond did.

The alpha was casually dressed in jeans and a tan T-shirt that barely managed to stretch over his massive shoulders. But there was nothing casual about the stony expression on his chiseled, broad face, or how his green shifter magic always appeared to whirl within his topaz-brown eyes.

Yeah, Desmond scared me enough that I instantly dropped my gaze to his feet and shuffled sideways to place the SUV between us.

Beau nodded to the alpha, not meeting his gaze.

"Your mother appears to be waiting for you, fledgling," Desmond said. His tone was completely unyielding.

"Yes." Unwillingly, Beau turned his body toward the house.

Desmond opened the door of the SUV, leaning in to talk to Kandy.

"The Brave would be better," Lara said from inside.

Ignoring my knee-jerk reaction to get involved in the conversation, I jogged to catch up to Beau.

"Damn shifters think everything belongs to them," I muttered as I folded my hand into Beau's larger, warm embrace.

"They see you and me as pack, so the Brave is ours to share."

"If it helps Henry, I'm okay with it."

"Me too."

We stopped at the base of the front steps. Ada had retreated from the living room window as we'd approached the house.

Beau took a deep breath, squeezing my hand.

"Can I come with you?" I asked.

"Please."

We walked into the drugged-up tiger's den together.

"So you've come back." Ada spoke from her vantage point by the window as we entered the living room. She must have moved back to watch the shapeshifters in her yard as we crossed through the entranceway. "And you brought friends." Though the 'friends' was definitely sarcastic, Ada didn't sound particularly stoned.

The living room had been tidied, though the wall where the coffee table had hit was still dented and the recliner was missing. Someone had cleaned up after Beau's tantrum, finishing off what Kandy had started. The diffuser on the mantel was just barely misting. Ada hadn't bothered to add more silver peace. Or she'd burned through her supply of shifter suppressant. If so, there wasn't any more to be had, not with Ettie dead.

My heart pinched uncomfortably. I didn't want to feel sorry for this woman. I already knew she was a horrible mother. Sure, she was obviously haunted by her own shit. But still, Beau didn't deserve to be treated like garbage.

"Yes." Beau shoved his hands in his pockets and moved to stand beside his mother at the window. She didn't look at him. "Ettie's dead, Mom."

"You already said that." Ada's tone was flat and emotionless.

"No … I said that we were here to warn her."

"Cy hasn't come home yet. It's been a few days now, I think."

"He was here yesterday. I'm sure you noticed him beating me on the front lawn."

Ada didn't answer. Beau squeezed his eyes shut and rubbed his forehead, probably pissed at himself for mentioning the physical abuse.

"He was always good to you, Beau," Ada said. "Put a roof over our heads. And you mouthed off. I knew you were bad news the moment I laid eyes on you. Just like your father."

A pained moan involuntarily ripped out of my chest before I could stop it. Beau half turned to me, raising his hand to hold me off.

I had a difficult time swallowing the venomous retort lodged in my throat, but I nodded stiffly to Beau.

"Ettie and Cy are both dead, Mom."

Beau's tone was so soft and caring. The woman didn't deserve him. She'd torn him apart. She'd let him be abused his entire childhood, then had pimped him out when it became apparent he was worth good money.

And I only had to take one look at her to know she'd deny any knowledge of abuse or of coerced sex-trade work. Hell, Beau would free her from the responsibility of that himself. He would suggest he'd been a willing participant in it all, right up until he hadn't been anymore. He would say that sometimes he threw the first punch at Cy.

Beau lightly touched Ada's shoulder, trying to comfort her. His capacity to care was staggering.

I had to look away. I was already crying, attempting to be silent as my nose filled with snot and I had to breathe through my mouth. Still, I wasn't going to leave Beau. If he could handle being here, so could I. I'd promised to stay by his side. Forever.

"Mom?" he asked gently.

"I heard you."

"I'm not sure about their bodies. The witches —"

Ada shrieked. The sound was startling and ear-splitting. She turned against Beau, flinging herself at him and raking his chest with clawed fingers.

He grunted but held his ground, attempting to wrap his arms around her. After what felt like hours of struggle, he managed to lock her in a hug.

Ada allowed herself to be pinned to Beau's chest, but she held her arms tucked tightly into her body, her hands protectively curled over her heart.

She banged her forehead on Beau's collarbone — three times, hard. Then she turned her head to the side. The streaks of blood on her face weren't her own. She'd gouged Beau's chest.

It was everything I could do to not pluck her eyes out for hurting him, over and over and over again.

She's Beau's mom. She's Beau's mom. I chanted the three words in my head, repeating them until they meant even less to me than the sentiment did. Still, the mantra kept me in check.

Beau relaxed his grip on his mother, rubbing her back. Ada opened her eyes, met my gaze, and sneered.

She twisted away from Beau's arms and stalked over to the couch. Hunching there, she reached for a beat-up metal cashbox sitting on the coffee table that I didn't remember seeing last time. Flipping the lid open, she retrieved a baggie of what I assumed was crimson bliss and started filling her electronic cigarette.

"That's it?" Beau asked.

I couldn't stand the pain in his voice much longer. I was going to tear down this house and set it on fire —

"What else do you want?" Ada asked. "You were always so needy, so jealous. Well, you have your way now, don't you? You have me all to yourself."

"You think you're some prize?" I blurted. Though through the tears and the snot, it didn't sound quite as fierce as I was going for.

"It's okay, Rochelle," Beau said.

I shook my head. None of this was okay. Nothing had been okay since we'd set foot on this property. And it had nothing to do with my vision.

"You can't rescue someone who doesn't want to be rescued," I said, repeating what Beau had said to me a few days after we met. At the time, I'd thought he was part of a massive delusion. Now, I wished I'd remembered his wisdom back in Oregon.

"I know," he whispered.

Ada leaned back on the couch and eyed me while she vaped. "You going to show me my future?" she asked. "Like you showed Cy?"

So she suddenly did remember seeing Cy yesterday? Or was pretending her husband hadn't been home with Beau just some game?

"I've seen enough of your future, lady."

Ada snorted a laugh. "You think Cy and Ettie would be dead if you hadn't come here to save them? And showed him what you did?" She lazily lifted her hand until she was pointing her index finger at my heart. "I blame you."

"Unfair —" Beau started to interject, but I cut him off.

"I'll take it. I don't know if what I showed Cy would have made any difference to the outcome … except to maybe make him think twice about his own actions. But I was there. I, at least, made some attempt to stop them while you sat here feeling sorry for yourself. Letting them kill innocent people with their drugs."

"You know nothing about it."

"I know I don't have a mother. I know that in that moment … in that brief drift between being awake and being asleep … every night for eighteen years, I wondered …" My voice broke despite my resolve. "I wondered who she was, and if she would have loved me. I wondered how life would have been different if she'd lived. And now, I see you. And I thank god, or magic, or whatever it was that made me an orphan, that made me think that I was delusional, crazy, for years ..." I was yelling now. "I thank all of it that I didn't have to grow up with you as a mother. With your destructive self-hatred attempting to corrode my self, my soul. I also thank whatever made me that Beau made it out. That he walked away as intact as he is."

I couldn't see through my tears anymore, so I turned my blurred gaze away from Ada and dug around in my satchel for Kleenex.

"That was quite a speech," Ada said.

"It was," Desmond said.

He was behind me suddenly, in the archway that led through to the front door. Crossing over to me, he pressed a wad of tissue into my hands.

I gladly took the offering and shuffled over to Beau while blowing my nose. Beau borrowed a sheet of Kleenex to wipe his eyes as well, then tucked me firmly next to him. Despite the early evening heat, I was happy to be pressed against his warm body.

Desmond paused in the middle of the living room to stare down at Ada on the couch. The alpha filled the room even more than Beau did, though he was four or five inches shorter. Again, I took it that this was an attitude thing. Or maybe some sort of magical presence.

Ada didn't meet Desmond's gaze, but she still managed to mouth off around her electronic cigarette. "How dare you enter my home without permission?"

"What are you going to do about it?" Desmond's tone was smooth and unaffected, yet so terribly threatening. All the hair on the back of my neck stood up as he continued. "You can't even raise your head to me, let alone a hand or claw."

Ada lifted her head defiantly, but she ended up focusing her gaze somewhere around Desmond's right shoulder.

He tilted his head to smell the air.

Oddly, Ada flinched.

"I know you," he said.

Ada shook her head.

"Your scent is weak, sickly. But I know it …" Desmond turned to look back at Beau, then took a step to lean in and smell him. "Beau … Jamison," he said, thinking out loud.

Beau nodded.

"Tigers are very rare. It's not completely unheard of for a shifter to inherit a rare or dormant gene from a parent, of course. Or for a cat to show up in a wolf family. When we didn't recognize your last name, Audrey and I assumed you were such an anomaly and that you didn't know your parentage. You allowed us to think so, offering no clarification other than that you wished to be unaffiliated with any pack. If we'd happened upon you under any other circumstances, without the oracle in tow and Blackwell at your heels, we would not have been so … accommodating."

Desmond paused, waiting for further clarification. But Beau remained silent.

The alpha returned his attention to Ada, who was burrowing deeper into the couch and frantically sucking on her adult pacifier. "But your mother is a tiger as well."

"Yes." Beau squeezed his eyes shut as if waiting for some sort of terrible yet unavoidable doom to befall.

"Adelaide Llewellyn," Desmond said.

Ada flinched again.

Beau went stock-still.

"I don't know you." Ada, suddenly defiant again, locked her gaze to Desmond's. He took a step toward her. She scrambled forward to grab the metal box from the coffee table.

Desmond frowned, glancing back at Beau and me. "She's an addict?"

Beau didn't answer, so I did. "Yes."

"What drug could counter a tiger's metabolism? This crimson bliss that Kandy texted about?"

Beau sighed and rubbed his face. "Yeah. Before it was just ... a lot of whatever she could find. And now this ... new thing, this silver nitrate thing that Ettie developed combined with the crimson drug, which may be some crystal meth derivative. Or at least that's what Ettie started out cooking."

Desmond grunted. "Kandy's been keeping me up to speed. Thank you, by the way, for helping her ... stay contained."

Beau looked at the floor. "I got her into this mess. And I couldn't stop her from ... Henry."

"If there is blame to be meted out, it doesn't fall on your shoulders. Kandy takes her counsel from ... higher powers."

"The far seer," I murmured.

Desmond nodded. "And even then, I understand it was more of a suggestion."

"I'm not sure guardians simply suggest anything," I said.

"Powerful allies, guardians and dragons," Desmond said. "But dangerous to play with." He rested his stony gaze on me for a moment, then looked to Beau. "And with Henry, well ... not many Adepts could have stood against Kandy at all." Pride edged the alpha's words, but then his tone turned cooler. "What I don't understand is why you didn't go to Francois years ago? Living here in

Mississippi, he's your pack leader. When you came to me in Portland, you claimed no affiliation."

"I have none."

"By choice, or because of your mother?"

Beau shook his head but didn't answer. He was still trying to protect his mother.

Desmond turned to look back at Ada. "Adelaide Llewellyn. Living like this, raising your son outside of the pack ... you don't recognize me?"

Beau's mother shook her head vehemently, but even I could tell she was lying. Desmond stepped toward her, then went down on one knee beside the coffee table to reach out his hand. "It's Desmond, your ... second cousin. I was probably ten when we last saw each other. And you were what? Twenty? At Mount Whitney. For your father's birthday pack run. Don't you —"

"No, no, no!" Ada screamed, scrambling away from Desmond as she clutched the metal box to her chest.

"I won't hurt you," Desmond said. "You shouldn't be like this. How ... why have you been living like this?"

Ada crawled off the couch and scuttled over to Beau. She had the gall to cling to his leg and sob wildly.

Beau reached down for her. She clawed at his hands, drawing more blood.

"Enough!" Desmond's alpha magic whipped around the living room, raising every hair on my body. "You've hurt the boy enough, Adelaide Llewellyn."

Ada stiffened, then let go of Beau's leg. She lifted her red-rimmed gaze to Desmond, who loomed over her as a mountain looms over a mouse.

"You're like all of them," she mumbled. "You just want to take. Take everything I have. Now you've taken Ettie and Cy ... and you want Beau. I can see you want my beautiful boy."

"Mom," Beau said. "You're mixing everything up."

Desmond stepped closer to Ada, his shoulder almost touching Beau's chest. "You are sly for a tiger, Adelaide Llewellyn. It doesn't become you."

"What do you know about it!" she screamed. Her changeability was intense ... and awful.

"What do you mean by 'take everything I have'?" Desmond asked. "Are you claiming you were abused? By whom? Why run when there are laws in place to protect you?"

"He wanted me to marry," Ada mumbled.

"A wolf?"

"Of course not."

"Well, what was your objection?"

Ada struggled to find the words to construct her accusation. Or maybe she was trying to formulate a lie? Except who tried to lie to a shapeshifter?

"Mom," Beau said. "This ... Desmond is ... he'd shield you if you asked for help."

"I don't want it," Ada screamed. "None of it. The magic, the change, the responsibility."

Desmond snorted. He turned away to retrieve, then paw through, the metal box Ada had dropped in her bid for Beau's sympathy.

"But ... you said they beat you," Beau said. "Raped you. Caged you."

"Who?" Desmond asked.

Ada crawled over to where her electronic cigarette had fallen to the floor. She puffed on it, but it was empty. She eyed the cashbox, which was now irretrievable in Desmond's hands.

"If I say it was no one, that there wasn't any abuse, any rape, will you give me my medicine?"

"Was it no one?" Desmond's tone was soft again, but laced with steel.

"They wanted to," Ada spat. "They wanted … sex. In animal form. That's criminal."

"They?" Desmond asked.

"My father … demanded the bloodline be kept pure. That I was bound to breed with whomever he decreed."

"I hear the same from my father every time we talk," Desmond said. "Though perhaps with less … ritualistic fervor. If I'm understanding your objection. But he can't force me to comply. And neither could your father. The Assembly relishes enforcing their rules and restrictions."

Ada didn't answer.

"Did they beat you? Rape you?"

Ada glanced at Beau, then looked away from us all. "No."

"What?" Beau cried.

Desmond flipped the lid closed on the metal box and tucked it underneath his arm.

"You promised," Ada cried.

"Oh, I'll get you medicine," Desmond said.

"I'm not going nowhere."

The alpha turned away, crossing back toward the front door. Lara had appeared there at some point. He gave her the metal box and she passed him a cellphone.

"My entire life …" Beau whispered. "You lied."

"So what?" Ada spat. "What do you care? You think being under his thumb would be better? Then go."

"Whose thumb?" I asked.

"David," Desmond replied, though his attention was on the text or email he was writing. "David John Llewellyn. Beau's grandfather. He died about ten years ago."

"Good for him," Ada said. She began pulling the cushions off the couch, presumably looking for any trace of her drugs lost there.

"My entire life …" Beau repeated.

"You are so goddamn stupid. Pretty but so stupid. You think someone like my father would have accepted you?"

"David would have been pleased to have a strong, capable tiger in the family," Desmond interjected. "I'll have your uncle get in touch with you, Beau."

"No," Beau said.

Desmond glanced up from his phone.

Beau shook his head, just once. He was angry, and sad, and … overwhelmed.

"When you're ready, then."

"Sure, throw money at the boy. He's good at turning tricks."

Ada's nasty words were barely out of her mouth before Beau had grabbed her by the neck and heaved her off the couch.

Then, in a blink, Beau was on the ground at my feet and Desmond was between Ada and her enraged son.

"She's not worth it, Beau," Lara whispered from her vantage point in the entranceway.

Beau's shoulders were heaving.

I couldn't tell if he was sobbing or laughing. I was afraid to touch him, then felt stupid. He was my Beau. I knew him. Ada wasn't going to destroy that with words.

"We make our own family," I said as I knelt down before Beau and pressed my hands to his cheeks. "We've made our own family."

He pressed his hands over mine, met my gaze, and swallowed hard. Then he nodded.

"Me or Francois, Ada," Desmond said. "You pick."

"I'll never follow a Llewellyn again," Ada snarled. Her focus was firmly fixed on Beau.

"Good. Francois is already on his way. Beau and Rochelle will be coming with me."

"Over my dead body," Ada said.

"That can be arranged," Lara said with a vicious smile from the doorway.

Desmond snorted at his pretty-in-purple enforcer.

"What?" she asked innocently.

"We give blood a chance."

"One more chance, then."

Desmond laughed. "As many chances as they need. I should check on Henry. Beau?"

Beau nodded, rising to his feet. He tucked me against him and we walked awkwardly to the front door, barely fitting through the archway side by side.

Lara stepped back as we approached, but she reached out to touch Beau's shoulder as we passed. He paused.

Inexplicably, she touched my cheek lightly as well.

"Pack," she murmured. Then she spun away, skipping out the door and down the stairs ahead of us.

I looked up at Beau. He looked down at me and pressed a kiss to my forehead.

"Do you want to say goodbye?" I whispered.

"Nah," he said. "Been there, done that."

We left Desmond in the living room with Ada. As we were crossing the front lawn to the Brave, another SUV pulled up to block the driveway.

A dark-haired, slim man in a cream linen suit stepped out of the vehicle. Lara skipped over to greet him with a pretty curtsy. Her giggle was a welcome contrast to the grim mood that still weighed down the muggy afternoon.

"Wolf," Beau said, falling easily into our established routine of identifying and explaining magic to me.

"What is it with shapeshifters and gas-guzzling cars?" I asked.

Beau lowered his voice. "You know what they say about big cars ..."

"Big egos?"

He laughed.

Lara twined her arm through the newcomer's. Two more burly men stepped from the SUV, following behind Lara and her companion as she led him up the lawn toward the house.

Beau stepped off to the side of the front path as they approached.

"This is Beau and Rochelle," Lara said as they passed but didn't stop.

"Together?" the man asked. His Southern accent contained a blur of French. "A witch and a shifter?"

"Well, you know," Lara said. "They're young." She turned back and winked at us.

The two bodyguard types eyed us, both of them a similar height to Beau. Then they followed Lara and their boss into Ada's house.

"Francois?" I asked Beau, who hadn't turned back to watch as the werewolves invaded his mother's living room. "And did Lara just lie about me being a witch?"

"She omitted the truth. To an alpha. For us." He sounded epically weary. "Let's go home."

I grabbed his hand and started pretending to drag him toward the Brave.

He laughed at my silliness.

"We're only steps away," I said.

Beau swept me up in his arms. "Let's keep it that way." Then he carried me to the RV.

The drive west was slower than we'd come east. Mostly because Henry was healing in the back bed of the Brave. Kandy drove her SUV alongside, and tucked into bed with Henry every night. Supposedly, close proximity was important because she and Henry shared magic, but the werewolf wasn't much of a long-term sort of caregiver. Desmond and Lara had flown back the same day they'd arrived in Southaven.

Desmond had vouched for Beau and his mother with Francois. He'd guaranteed that they'd had nothing to do with Cy and Ettie's drug business. Apparently, the alpha had flown in from Portland at Kandy's behest just to save all of us from the Gulf Coast North American Pack's chopping block, possibly perjuring himself for Ada's sake. Or maybe that was for Beau's sake. As soon as Kandy had figured out Cy's complicity, she'd alerted Desmond.

They'd kept me out of it altogether, which was cool. But it also reminded me of Blackwell's prediction that the pack would protect me, but only by locking me in a gilded cage.

Granted, that was said when he was attempting to convince me to go away with him. And the sorcerer didn't like other Adepts much. But then, neither did I. Apparently, that made us well suited for each other. Possibly unfortunately for me. Though, again, I really didn't pick up the evil vibe everyone else did from Blackwell.

Maybe I was willfully blind. Maybe the sorcerer had lived in my head for so long that he was a part of me somehow.

Anyway.

So now we owed the pack and the sorcerer even more than we had before, but Beau didn't seem weighed down by that obligation.

He also didn't ask about Ada. Not about what had happened after we'd hidden out in the Brave, nor where she was now. So I didn't either.

We played cards and ate. Henry was quiet most of the time, and really sleepy. Kandy and Beau downloaded and compared weather apps. They were concerned about the phases of the moon.

Kandy stained the bathroom sink with her green hair dye, and then had a yelling match with Beau about it somewhere in the middle of Arkansas. We were dry-docked, so they took off into the wilderness to sort out the argument.

The marshal and I hunkered down while they were running, enjoying a cooler evening beside a small fire.

I'd almost drifted off to sleep when Henry spoke.

"I've been thinking about the tattoo you promised me," he said.

"Promised?"

He laughed, then flinched as he pressed a hand to his waist.

"I thought it was healed?" I asked. "I thought when Desmond came …"

"I'm not a werewolf," Henry said. "I might never be … functional that way. So the pack magic helped, but it couldn't do all the work. Thankfully, sorcerers don't take too long to heal themselves."

"So? The tattoo? Let me guess. Handcuffs?"

Henry shifted his gaze from the dying fire to look directly at me. His lips were crooked with a smile that didn't quite reach his dark-shaded, cobalt-blue eyes underneath his cowboy hat. "If that's what you see. If that's what you draw when you think of me."

"You think the tattoos are magic. I don't —"

Henry reached out, hovering his fingers over the skeleton key tattoo on my forearm but not touching me. "I think you're just coming into your magic, oracle. I think you can help me … if the wolf arises with the full moon."

"You want me to … you think a tattoo can suppress your … wolf?"

"I was damn lucky the bite didn't kill me. But the bitten rarely fully turn. If they do turn and can control themselves, they only turn with the moon cycle and only partway. Half-human, half-beast."

"Werewolf."

"Exactly. Like the myths. But I have you. And you owe me a favor."

"Do I?" I asked, already knowing that I did.

Henry finally rested his fingers along the tattoo of the key on my forearm. I could feel the burble of his sorcerer magic against my skin, but only barely. "You will think of me, oracle. You will think on a way I can harness my wolf, every day. Fold its power into my sorcerer power. Its strength, agility, and senses. Then you will draw."

"I can't do what you're asking," I murmured.

Henry withdrew his hand. "Maybe not today. But you will, Rochelle Hawthorne."

I narrowed my eyes at him. I'd introduced myself to him with my legal last name — Saintpaul, not Hawthorne.

"Yeah." He laughed. "I worked that out for myself. Next time you see Blackwell, you might want to ask him about your mother."

"Why?"

"Rumors."

"About her death?"

Henry nodded.

"And my father?"

"A sorcerer, judging by the magic I can feel from the tattoos. No idea who he was, though."

Silence fell between us. I wasn't surprised that Blackwell was possibly hiding some kind of connection to my mother. How else would he have known about me? If I asked him, he'd probably just say he'd been waiting for the question.

"A tattoo of handcuffs," I said. "To harness the wolf."

"Yes." Henry's voice was heavy with sleep.

"I'll think about it."

"And help me to bed?"

"And help you to bed."

I stood, brushing sandy dirt off my jeans, then took the hand Henry offered me. I had no idea if I could do as he asked, but I had to admit I was intrigued by the idea. "A werewolf-bitten sorcerer could be pretty powerful," I mused.

"If the power can be controlled," Henry said as he shuffled toward the Brave, leaning heavily on my shoulder.

"That would be more than a favor owed."

Henry grinned. "Yeah, I'm damn sure you're going to need a federal marshal checking up on you, Rochelle Hawthorne Saintpaul. Often."

"Not by choice."

"It never is."

Henry opened the door to the Brave. By transferring a bunch of weight off my right shoulder and onto the interior door handle, he managed to lift his foot to the first stair. He was okay using the backs of the front seats and the kitchen counters to stabilize himself the rest of the way, but I followed just in case.

Beau would be back to snuff out the fire, but I thought it might be a nice change to sleep outside tonight ... in our sleeping bags underneath the stars ... in the middle of the world ... yet separate.

Maybe that was exactly where we belonged.

Acknowledgements

With thanks to:

My story & line editor

Scott Fitzgerald Gray

My proofreader

Pauline Nolet

My beta readers

Terry Daigle, Angela Flannery, Gael Fleming, Desi Hartzel, and Heather Lewis.

For their continual encouragement, feedback, & general advice

Carol Anne Newsome — for the tactical pen

Billy Kring — for tactical pen info/advice

Al Hesselbart and Nick Russell — for the RV information

Heather Doidge-Sidhu — for endless triple checking

The Retreat

For their Art

Irene Langholm & Elizabeth Mackey

MEGHAN CIANA DOIDGE is an award-winning writer based out of Salt Spring Island, British Columbia, Canada. She has a penchant for bloody love stories, superheroes, and the supernatural. She also has a thing for chocolate, potatoes, and sock yarn.

Novels

After The Virus
Spirit Binder
Time Walker
Cupcakes, Trinkets, and Other Deadly Magic (Dowser 1)
Trinkets, Treasures, and Other Bloody Magic (Dowser 2)
Treasures, Demons, and Other Black Magic (Dowser 3)
I See Me (Oracle 1)
Shadow, Maps, and Other Ancient Magic (Dowser 4)
Maps, Artifacts, and Other Arcane Magic (Dowser 5)
I See You (Oracle 2)

Novellas/Shorts

Love Lies Bleeding
The Graveyard Kiss

For recipes, giveaways, news, and glimpses of upcoming stories, please connect with Meghan on her:

Personal blog, www.madebymeghan.ca
Twitter, @mcdoidge
And/or Facebook, Meghan Ciana Doidge
Email, info@madebymeghan.ca

Please also consider leaving an honest review at your point of sale outlet.

Time to stock up on chocolate.

You're going to need it.

AVAILABLE NOW
-Amazon-iBooks-Kobo-B&N-
-Smashwords-

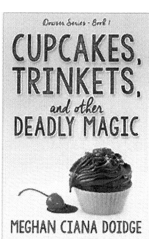

Dowser Series - Book 1

CUPCAKES, TRINKETS, and other DEADLY MAGIC

MEGHAN CIANA DOIDGE

Dowser Series - Book 2

TRINKETS, TREASURES, and other BLOODY MAGIC

MEGHAN CIANA DOIDGE

Dowser Series - Book 3

TREASURES, DEMONS, and other BLACK MAGIC

MEGHAN CIANA DOIDGE

Manufactured by Amazon.ca
Bolton, ON

17157156R00171